Coolibah Creek

About the Author

Kelsey Neilson has lived in outback Queensland all her life. She draws inspiration for her writing from her deep connection to the land and her interactions with its extraordinary custodians. She is passionate about advocating for the keepers of the bush – the resilient, determined, dedicated people who make the outback their home and their heritage. She lives on a cattle property with her husband and has two adult sons.

KELSEY NEILSON

Coolibah Creek

ARENA
ALLEN&UNWIN

First published in 2015

Copyright © Kelsey Neilson 2015

All rights reserved. No part of this book may be reproduced or transmitted in
any form or by any means, electronic or mechanical, including photocopying,
recording or by any information storage and retrieval system, without prior
permission in writing from the publisher. The Australian *Copyright Act 1968*
(the Act) allows a maximum of one chapter or 10 per cent of this book, whichever
is the greater, to be photocopied by any educational institution for its educational
purposes provided that the educational institution (or body that administers it) has
given a remuneration notice to the Copyright Agency (Australia) under the Act.

Allen & Unwin
83 Alexander Street
Crows Nest NSW 2065
Australia
Phone: (61 2) 8425 0100
Email: info@allenandunwin.com
Web: www.allenandunwin.com

Cataloguing-in-Publication details are available
from the National Library of Australia
www.trove.nla.gov.au

ISBN 978 1 74331 446 3

Cover design by Julia Eim
Set in 12.5/17 pt Sabon by Midland Typesetters, Australia
Printed and bound in Australia by Griffin Press

10 9 8 7 6 5 4 3 2 1

The paper in this book is FSC® certified.
FSC® promotes environmentally responsible,
socially beneficial and economically viable
management of the world's forests.

For my sister
Kristen

Chapter 1

Rebecca loved working in her garden, which she'd pretty much created from scratch. She especially enjoyed it on days like these. The morning was unseasonably cool, with a pleasant southerly whispering through the tall gums around the Coolibah Creek homestead yard. A melodious tinkling from the wind chimes on the verandah answered the butcherbirds' beautiful song. Busy willie-wagtails hopped across the lawn, waggling their tail feathers and chattering incessantly as they fed on tiny insects.

Escaping the drudgery of the kitchen early, after the men's lunches had been packed and they'd left for the day to fix a windmill in the back paddock, Rebecca paused to savour her garden and breathe in the morning air. She often spoke to the birds that were permanent residents in her yard. She shared the excitement of their nesting each year and watched how they adapted to life according to the season.

There were hundreds of different animals living in her garden, which she'd lovingly created in the harsh surroundings of western Queensland. Her oasis was bursting with greens of every shade, exploding with a myriad of colours, filled with intoxicating fragrances and buzzing with the noises of energetic creatures moving about. She turned on the tap, and a sprinkler sputtered and spat before spraying life-giving bore water across the thirsty lawn. Rebecca was grateful every day for the underground artesian water supply they had at the homestead and she looked out to the stoic windmill that was dutifully turning and pumping on the morning breeze. The good wind meant that the tank would be full and Bec would have an abundance of water for her garden.

In her garden paradise, Bec could take leave from the horrors of the drought and the pain it imposed on the land and on her heart. Outside the homestead fence lay the hot, dusty redness of the everlasting plains. It had been another very dry year at Coolibah Creek and she scanned the horizon, not in hope but from habit. She saw again the cloudless sky and parched red earth of the plains meeting in a straight line as far as the eye could see.

It was hard work looking after all the flower beds, trimming shrubs and trees, keeping everything weeded and mulched and mowing the thick lawn but she enjoyed the physical exertion, and the rewards, though hard won, were worth it.

She'd been looking forward to a day without the continual interruptions of the men turning up, always hungry,

Coolibah Creek

constantly unable to find anything without directions, from phone numbers to windmill parts, even their own hat sometimes. A fleeting smile crossed her face as she conceded to herself that she quite enjoyed their little dependencies and she would miss the men terribly if they were gone for more than the day.

Bec knelt on the plush carpet of lawn and began to pull soft weeds from the loose brown soil. Without looking, she tossed them into the yellow plastic bucket beside her. Bounce, her four-month-old Jack Russell, was darting about through the shrubs exuberantly, high on all the fascinating aromas, seeking out the swift 'shaky paw' lizards, which she flushed from their hiding places and chased as fast as her little legs would carry her. Every few minutes she would circle back to Bec for acknowledgement of how clever she was, before scampering away on another quest.

Jess, the more mature blue heeler, lay just behind Rebecca, flat out on her side, enjoying the warmth of the sun on her old bones and ignoring Bounce's repeated attempts to make her play.

Bec's thoughts turned to daydreaming about having her own children playing on the lawn someday, when she was suddenly brought back to earth by shrill barking from Bounce. She looked over to see the terrier furiously digging beside a weathered house stump.

'Oh, Bounce, one day you'll get a shock and catch one of those lizards. Come here!' she called.

Bounce jumped in the air and did an about face, looking at Bec, her pretty white face covered in dirt.

'Come on, Bounce. Come here, girl,' said Bec. Bounce looked back at the hole she'd dug, gave one more defiant yip and scurried back to Bec's side, sneezing and snuffling and rubbing her face on the lawn, causing Bec to laugh out loud. Bounce was a constant source of entertainment and amusement.

Her attention returning to her garden, Bec worked on in the heat and was just thinking how good an icy orange juice would be when she heard a loud crash come from somewhere inside the house. Startled, she got up and strode towards the house, wondering what on earth was going on as Bounce yipped and ran about her wildly.

Kicking off her shoes on the verandah, Bec went inside, stopping in her tracks at the door to the kitchen where two heavy canisters from the top of the microwave lay on the floor. Puzzled, she picked up the tins and placed them back in their positions, wondering how on earth they'd fallen down.

Shrugging, Bec headed back outside to pack up her gardening tools and turn off the sprinklers. Bounce met her at the bottom of the stairs, head cocked sideways with a quizzical expression on her face.

The wind had swung around to the north. It was now hot and promising to get much hotter before the day's end. Having returned all the gardening paraphernalia to its proper place, Bec retreated again into the cool of the house. In the kitchen she frowned as she saw that Andy had left his cap and sunglasses on top of the fridge next to the potted plant and two vases of dried flowers. Rolling her eyes, she snatched the cap and glasses as she passed, put them on the bench and flicked the switch on the kettle. Grabbing a tumbler from the cabinet, she took out a bottle of orange juice and then rummaged in the freezer for some ice.

As she did so, from the corner of her eye she saw a flicker of movement. She looked up and gasped as she saw, less than a metre from her face, the black eyes of a snake. Frozen in fear, her heart thumping in panic, her reflexes kicked in and she slammed back into the doorjamb. Adrenalin coursed through her as, transfixed and breathless, she pressed herself against the wall, staring into the eyes of the massive snake now waving its head menacingly at her.

Glancing to the right for a fraction of a second she looked at the two-way radio on the far wall, which suddenly seemed miles away. To get to it she would have to move slightly closer to the snake. Still holding its stare, she inched sideways. The snake reacted immediately, its body twisting into a tighter coil as it raised its head higher. Bec edged incrementally along the wall and around the sink, each tiny movement agonising.

After what seemed forever, she finally made her way into a position that would allow her to retreat. Then, with an involuntary scream she leapt backwards.

The snake ducked down momentarily before moving into an even more threatening pose, flattening the back of its neck defiantly.

Bec grabbed blindly for the radio mike with trembling hands, keeping her eyes on the snake. Finding the mike, in a thin, shrill voice, she called, 'Andy! Andy! You on channel, Andy?'

When no reply came, she called again, this time louder and with more urgency. 'Andy! Andy! Andyyy! You on channel, Andy!'

'Yeah, love. What's the matter?' he replied, his voice full of concern.

'There's a great big brown snake on top of the fridge!' Bec gasped.

'Where? In the men's quarters?' asked Andy.

'No. No. In *our* kitchen!' she screamed. 'Right here!'

'Get the gun, Bec. Shoot it,' said Andy firmly.

'What about the house?' cried Bec.

'Don't worry about the bloody house,' came Andy's reply. 'Go now. Get the 410 and shoot it. I'm on my way.'

Rebecca dropped the mike and started inching along the bench again towards her escape route past the fridge, where the snake continued to stare at her. Careful not to make any sudden movement, she forced herself towards it despite every instinct screaming at her to go back. She was almost past the end of the bench when the snake launched itself at her with incredible speed and ferocity. She reeled away screaming, falling on the floor and hitting her head on the metal leg of a kitchen chair, then frantically clambering away from the snake, too afraid to look back.

Scrambling to her feet, she stumbled towards the front door, all the while feeling like she was moving in slow motion. She threw the door open and flung herself outside. Hand shaking violently, she rolled up her sleeve, looking for a bite. Air rushed from her in relief as she saw the skin was unbroken. She choked back a sob of relief and made her way towards the shed on unsteady legs.

Armed with the loaded shotgun, she gingerly entered the house. Just as she did so, Bounce made a sudden dash inside, caught up in all the excitement. Both hands on the gun, Bec pushed the pup outside with her foot and slowly closed the door behind her.

Creeping towards the kitchen, Bec's senses were on full alert, gun raised and ready. Though she'd killed snakes before she'd never expected to encounter a deadly king brown *inside* her house. Gun pointing down, she finally reached the doorway of the kitchen and peered through it, wide-eyed.

Incredibly, the snake was still on top of the fridge, a loop of its body hanging over the side. Steadying herself, she slowly raised the gun to her shoulder and took aim. Then, holding her breath like she'd been taught as a kid, she squeezed the trigger.

There was an instant explosion of noise and blood and she watched in revulsion as the snake curled and writhed around trying to bite the gaping wound in its belly. Blood spurted from the snake's body, splashing onto the walls and running red streaks down the side of the fridge as it continued to thrash about. Repeatedly it struck at the wound, the clear, yellow venom running down its scales. Suddenly two transparent egg-like sacs squeezed from its torn belly and dropped onto the top of the microwave with an awful 'Plop! Plop!' The force of the fall from the fridge burst the sacs and, to Bec's horror, two wriggling baby snakes swam about in the blood-streaked mucus.

Bile rose in her throat and the gun began to slide from her limp hand, the barrel clattering onto the floor. The sound jolted her alert and she snatched at the shotgun and got a better grip on the weapon.

Tearing her eyes away and clutching the gun to her chest, Bec ran out the front door, slamming it behind her. Tears ran down her face as she headed towards the sanctuary of the shed. Just before she reached it, Andy appeared. She fell into his embrace and sobbed uncontrollably against his chest, shaking with shock.

'Where is it? What happened?' said Andy.

'I shot it but it's still alive!' she cried. 'There's blood everywhere!'

'It's okay, it's okay. I'll deal with it now,' said Andy, taking the gun from her, retrieving a shovel from the shed, and striding towards the house.

Chapter 2

Even all these years after marrying Andy Roberts, Bec still found him incredibly attractive. Not quite six feet in height, his athletic build made him look taller than he was, with a broad chest and wide shoulders that ran away to narrow hips. His sun-bleached sandy hair was wavy and just long enough to rest on the collars of the faded blue work shirts he favoured. He had an easy smile and his dark brown eyes danced when he laughed.

Bec particularly loved Andy's slender hands and long, square-tipped fingers. They were the hands of a working man, leathery and brown, quick and capable, incredibly strong and yet amazingly gentle. She had a lot of respect for the way those skilful hands controlled his horse. 'Soft hands' was the perfect expression for the way he rode. She thrilled to their tender touch on her skin when they made love.

Bec felt the warmth of love spread through her chest as she ran her hand across Andy's shoulders. He sat slumped backwards on a kitchen chair, elbows propped on the backrest. She shared his anguish but held back the tears that threatened to come.

The gut-churning tension of the storm-watching season was getting to them both. They were in the worst run of dry years in the history of Coolibah Creek and yet again the weather had promised much and delivered little. The cattle were weak, though some of the cows were still delivering their calves onto barren earth. It was hard to say which was worse: a searing hot day when the mercury soared to forty-five degrees with blue skies or a stinking humid day, when storm clouds built, promised and teased, then either melted away or burst, releasing their moisture over a narrow strip, usually outside the boundary fence. Sometimes the evening breeze would carry the sweet smell of rain and Rebecca would breathe it in as if she were a perishing animal.

'Tomorrow's another day, Andy,' she whispered.

'Yep. One day closer to rain,' replied Andy with all the false confidence he could muster. Then, changing the subject, he said, 'I want to get a caretaker organised for you.'

'For me! Why?'

'Because you shouldn't be here alone. Look at what happened the other day with the snake,' said Andy, getting up and taking her in his arms.

Bec went to speak but Andy interrupted her. 'No. I'd never forgive myself if something happened to you while I was away. Sam's just been retired by one of the big company places. He's a real good man, a gentleman and the most honest bloke I know. I want to offer him a job as a, you know, caretaker/gardener.'

'*Gardener!*' said Bec, stepping away from him. 'Hang on. That's *my* garden. I've worked my guts out getting it going and *nobody* is taking it over!'

'Whoa, whoa, whoa!' said Andy, laughing. 'Sam won't be interested in your flowers and pot plants. He'll want to grow a big veggie garden for us, like old Charlie had here years ago. Plus, he'll look after the chooks and we might break in some new milkers as well.'

'Oh, so this "gardener" is not entirely for me then?' Bec teased.

'Well, maybe I'll get a twist out of him too, but the main thing is you won't be here by yourself.'

'Oh alright. If you insist,' she said, prepared to do anything to help Andy gain some peace of mind.

'Good. I'll ring him and get him to come on the mail truck and we can pick him up on Friday,' said Andy. 'I've organised a ringer to arrive that day too. He's only a kid but he's supposed to be pretty handy with a horse.'

Bec nodded and gave him a long hug. Clearly Andy had been planning this thing with Sam for a while, but if he could help them both out there was no use complaining.

When Friday came it fell on Bec to make the trip into town to pick up Sam and the ringer because Andy and George, his Aboriginal offsider, were out fixing yet another problem with the windmill.

Bec quite enjoyed the three-hour drive on rough dirt roads to Telford, the little one-pub town where they bought all their stores and supplies. As she drove, she watched the soft pastels of dawn turn to burnished gold and red as the sun rose over the rolling plains of Coolibah Creek. Despite the drought, Bec loved the far horizons, the open spaces and big skies of their country. It was in her soul and she couldn't bear to be away from it for long.

After they fell in love it had taken Bec a while to work out the difference between Andy and herself with regard to the land. If anything, he had an even deeper connection with it having grown up on Coolibah. He was in tune and at one with nature. In the good years he'd swum with his Aboriginal mates in the muddy creeks for hours, laughing and splashing, diving in the mud for mussels, porpoising around, trying to sneak up on wood ducks and water goannas. Free and unshackled by neighbours or rules, they had spent days building elaborate cubby houses in the coolibah trees on the creek, catching lizards and frogs and exploring at their leisure.

Andy had literally grown from the Coolibah Creek earth. The prime beef produced by Coolibah's native pastures and the organic homegrown vegetables nurtured in Coolibah's red soil and fertilised with the cattle's manure sustained his growth, supplemented by fresh milk from the cows and creamy hand-churned butter. He'd spent nearly all his life drinking rainwater from the tanks when there was any and bore water from the mill when he had to.

During the dry times when he was a kid, Andy had described how he and his friends would run through the bulldust, dragging their toughened bare feet so that powdery clouds of dirt billowed around them, coating their bodies, settling on their faces and stiffening their hair. Once he and

Coolibah Creek

his mates were totally caked with dirt, they would race to the lawn, turn on the sprinkler and canter through it on imaginary horses, rivulets of red water streaking their wiry bodies.

When Andy was five years old he'd joined his older sister, Louise, in being taught by their mother, Joyce, in the corner of the verandah designated as the schoolroom. Joyce had also taught Andy's two great playmates, Clarry and Henry. Each day through their primary school years they spoke on the two-way radio to their teachers in Coombul, a mining town three hundred kilometres away, and worked from the school papers mailed to them weekly from the School of the Air.

Andy had learnt about life and death early, helping his mum save the first litter of pups the old blue bitch, Sally, had when he was seven. Six months later he mourned the death of his pup, Boss, when it died from snakebite. He'd experienced the excitement of seeing a new flush of calves come, bred from expensive stud bulls, and been overcome with sadness when his father had to shoot beloved breeders and valiant old stockhorses during drought years.

Despite his home schooling and then five years of boarding at secondary school, Andy saw his real education as having occurred outside the classroom. He'd grown and revelled in the freedoms of his bush surrounds, where he learnt to ride and break in a horse, crank-start the big, slow-revving Lister pump-jack motors to get water, and ride a motorbike through the steep-banked river channels while dodging logs and hidden washouts.

Andy's father had taught him everything he could about cattle – how to handle them in the paddock and how to anticipate their every move in the yards by the way they moved their heads, eyes and ears – so that by the age of twelve Andy was an accomplished cattleman. It was in his blood. Max, the wise and gentle father of Andy's best mate, Clarry, taught the boys how to plait leather, make hobbles for the horses and track the bush animals and find bush tucker.

We need some sons, Bec thought wistfully as she drove along the dusty gravel road. For three years now she'd been off the pill and, though Andy kept saying, 'Nature will do things when *she's* ready not when *you're* ready,' she knew it had been too long and there must be some sort of problem.

She frowned as she remembered Andy's immoderate reaction when she'd tried to broach the subject one night. After confessing to having had a fertility test, she'd gently suggested the next step towards starting a family might be up to him.

'If you think I'm going to wank into a bottle at some hospital . . . Jeez, Bec. Can't you just let things happen?' he'd shouted before storming out of the bedroom and outside onto the verandah.

Bec had known it would be a sensitive issue but she hadn't been prepared for his reaction. After a few minutes she'd gone out to the verandah and sat in the chair beside him. They'd both stayed silent, staring out into the night, gradually allowing their emotions to settle. Eventually she'd reached out and placed her hand over Andy's.

'You're right,' she said. 'Just can't mess with Mother Nature. Sorry.'

After a while, Andy had said in a quiet voice, 'Having kids is so important to me – something I just expected to happen. It *has* to happen. I need children to hand Coolibah down to when we're old, to take the Roberts' name and to take on Coolibah Creek. Louise isn't interested. I just –'

'Let's give it some more time,' said Bec, interrupting him. 'We're young and healthy and, hey, it's so much fun trying.' She leant over and slipped her hand inside his shirt, caressing his muscular chest. Andy had paused for a moment before reaching out for her and pulling her closer to him, bending his head to kiss her upturned face.

Rebecca was jolted from her daydreaming by an emu running out onto the road in front of her. She veered slightly to the left to avoid braking on the loose gravel. The emu threw its head back and careened away to the right, tripped over a low turkey bush and rolled away in a flurry of legs and feathers and red dust.

You need to pay more attention to where you're going! Bec chastised herself. She turned on the radio to hear a newsreader announcing a bucket of Federal government money for the resumption of private land to protect 'significant' wetlands in the outback. The report cut to an interview with an English environmentalist who recommended 'that all the cattle and sheep should be removed from outback Australia' and said how appalled she was by the devastating levels of degradation the livestock were causing. *Where do they find these extremists for comment*, Bec thought. Nobody was more aware of the need to keep the rivers and wetlands healthy than the people who depended on them. 'We're all hands-on conservationists with skin in the game, not like you and your ill-informed, judgemental . . .' Bec said out loud.

Furious, Bec turned the radio off. The hordes of people attacking graziers sanctimoniously as the drought raged on made her so angry. Every night there was footage on the telly of some barren paddock with dying sheep or cattle accompanied by a biased commentary that implied the state of the land was caused by grazing. It was simply not true. Andy's family had been grazing on Coolibah Creek for over a century and the land had fundamentally remained in pristine condition – the recent push to have the Lake Eyre Basin listed as World Heritage was proof that the resource was in such an unaltered and healthy state as to be worthy of the nomination. The land used the extended dry periods to rest from pasture production. The seasons controlled grazing with absolute authority.

Sighing, she connected her iPod to the sound system and chased the angry thoughts from her mind by singing along loudly for the final hour's drive into town.

Chapter 3

Andy and George arrived at the bore bracing themselves for the unpleasant job ahead of them. Despite the rails and guards, a cow had become wedged, upside down, in the trough. When Andy had last checked four days ago there weren't many cattle watering there and the tank had been overflowing and everything was fine.

As Andy and George got out of the Toyota they had to endure the hopeless looks of the emaciated cattle standing under the stunted gidgee trees. Over fifteen hundred kilometres from cropping areas, huge freight bills ruled out the option of feeding hay to the cattle. The drought was so widespread now there was no agistment available – and Andy couldn't buy grass at any price. The cattle market had crashed under the weight of numbers and, with his cattle in such a weakened state, sending them on a long trip to the saleyards wouldn't be good for them. The breeder cattle he'd kept were taking their chances at survival. A bullet was the only other option, and Andy reckoned the cattle would rather be given the option of trying to survive than be shot.

As they neared the trough the stench hit them with force, burning their nostrils and coating the back of their throats and tongues.

'Aggh. She's been here a while, hey boss?' said George.

'Yeah, George. Poor old bugger. She's battled on so long. Now this. She must have been pushed and just toppled in she was so weak.' Andy thought how cruelly ironic it was to see a cow drown in the middle of a roaring drought.

Four stiffened black legs rose from the trough like burnt tree stumps. The rotting carcass was bloated and swollen and jammed in tightly. The crows had been picking at the hide and the water was crimson with putrid blood. A hot wind rippled the water's surface and the decaying skin flapped around in the murk. Wounds on the legs were packed with masses of boiling yellow maggots.

Andy knew they'd have to pull the carcass out with the ute and just hoped it would hold together. George fetched a chain from the vehicle and they encircled the legs with it, hooked it up to the ute and reversed away. As the chain took up the strain, the legs bent over but the body didn't move. It was stuck fast and Andy didn't relish the task of bucketing the cow's remains out of the trough. He carefully released and then pulled again on the chain with the ute, hoping to break the suction between the carcass and the trough. After a few tries it shifted and came free, flopping out onto the ground.

Andy dragged the carcass well away from the watering point. He and George then unscrewed the bung from the trough and released the stinking, soupy water before cleaning the trough thoroughly with brooms and shovels. With the stench permeating their clothes, skin and hair, they climbed the narrow ladder of the big iron tank and plunged in – clothes, boots and all – to wash away the smell. When they clambered out, the burning wind dried their clothes quickly and the searing temperature tightened the skin on their cheeks and lips as it drew the moisture from them.

'Better keep going, George. We'll boil the billy at the next bore, hey?' said Andy as they walked back to the car.

George and Andy rattled along the fence line, which danced in the heatwaves in front of them before disappearing into a floating mirage in the distance. The road was rough and dusty and they bounced along in silence, each with their own thoughts. Andy wondered how Bec was travelling. The road to Telford had been cut up badly by the constant stream of road trains, hauling three double-decker trailers of cattle at a time out of the shire. Wheel ruts half a metre deep carved up the track and ground it into treacherous bulldust. Along other stretches the gravel had risen to the surface making the steeply cambered road slippery. The slightest lapse of concentration could end up in a four-wheel drift or the vehicle fishtailing from side to side. He reassured himself that Bec was a good driver.

Andy reflected on how much he missed her, even when they were parted for only a short time. She'd been his rock as they'd battled through this endless dry. He hadn't noticed how heavily he was leaning on her until she'd gone to visit her mother for a week and he'd felt himself teetering on the edge of an abyss without her. His emotions had been amplified lately as he drew on all his inner strength to fight the impact of this relentless ravaging drought. A lump caught in his throat as Bec's beautiful smile flashed through his mind.

She had her father's dead straight black hair and hazel eyes, and her fair skin was sprinkled with freckles. She was feminine and curvy and she sure wore her blue jeans well. Andy loved her for the fire in her belly and, in contrast, for the softness that came to her eyes when they found an orphan calf or shared a glorious sunset together. The simple touch of her hand could heal him. She made love in the same way she did everything else, with uninhibited passion and total abandonment, evoking a sense in him that no one else had ever done.

*

After Bec arrived in Telford she and Frank Cooper, the store owner, started loading the back of her station wagon with cooler bags and cartons of fresh vegetables, milk and tinned food.

'I wonder when this weather's gonna break, Beccy,' said Frank.

'I wish I knew, Frank. I hope it's sooner rather than later, though,' Bec replied as she swung a fifteen kilogram bag of sugar into the car.

'It's deathly quiet here in town. Getting a bit tough on the old bank balance really,' said Frank. Bec knew he was carrying large accounts in the red for many of the property owners. 'No stock camps working cattle, no shearers about, even the road contractors for the council have moved closer to the coast looking for work. No terrorists –' Frank's slang for tourists, '– either at the moment. Bit too hot for 'em yet I think, eh mate.'

'Yeah, it might be just a touch too warm. It was forty-five at home the other day,' said Bec.

'Here's the mail truck,' said Frank, as he hoisted in a drum of flour to complete the load.

Bec looked up to see the old red Dodge truck approaching, a mountainous assortment of freight piled high in its tray. With a squeal of brakes, it came to a halt in front of the store and the driver, Bob, climbed out of the cabin, his threadbare work shirt drenched with sweat. His passengers, Sam the gardener and the young ringer, stepped out of the truck too, Sam's tufts of snow white hair luminous in the summer sun.

After mumbling a greeting to Frank and Bec, Bob shuffled to the back of the truck as the young Aboriginal man sprang up onto the load and retrieved his swag, a canvas duffel bag and a huge blue suitcase. Quite small in stature, he had to use both hands in order to lug the suitcase to the edge of the truck.

'Hey, watcha got in here, Sam? Strike a light, he's heavy this one, eh,' he said.

Rebecca smiled up at the younger man and, leaving the back of the car open, walked over to the old gentleman, who looked dapper in a white shirt. 'Hello. You must be Sam,' she said. 'I'm Bec Roberts from Coolibah Creek.'

Holding her palm loosely in his, Sam dipped his head and replied formally, 'Pleased to meet you, Mrs Roberts.'

Bec looked up into the wide smile of the man on the truck and reached up to shake his hand too.

'G'day, Missus,' he said.

'G'day. How are you battling with that port?' asked Bec.

'Aww, I got him now, Missus,' he said, heaving it over the side, where Bec and Sam eased it to the ground.

Jumping nimbly down from the truck, the ringer said, 'My name's Nudding, Missus.'

'Sorry?' said Bec. 'I missed that.'

'Nudding, Missus. You know, like zero Nudding.'

'Oh right,' said Bec. 'What's your real name, though?'

'Oh well,' said Nudding, looking sheepish. 'My real name's Herbert but I don't like that name.'

'Okay. Nudding it is,' said Bec.

Turning to Sam who was dragging his heavy port towards her car, she called out, 'What *have* you got in that port, Sam? Looks like it's full of lead!'

'It's just a few torch batteries, Mrs Roberts. Andy said I might be milkin' and I only ever milk before daylight, don't like flies, so I thought I might need a few batteries for me torch.'

Bec and Nudding joined forces with Sam to slide the suitcase on to the top of the tinned food and then Nudding shoved his swag and duffel bag in before Bec closed the door.

'Well, that's definitely loaded,' said Bec, clapping the dust from her hands. 'Let's grab a drink and some lunch before we go.'

Bec introduced Sam and Nudding to Frank and they bought some pies and Cokes at the counter.

'Come out the back. Too many flies outside in that heat,' said Frank, who was renowned for loving a chat and had a smoko area at the rear of the shop closed in with shade cloth. Frank talked and drank coffee while sharing the local gossip with them.

Coolibah Creek

'Well, Frank,' said Bec, after she'd drained the last of her Coke. 'We better hit the road. Plenty to do at home.'

'Yeah righto, Beccy. See you next time. See you, fellas,' he said then trudged back into the store's cool interior.

※

There wasn't much conversation during the trip home. The old bushman and the young ringer seemed a little shy of her. Sam sat in the front dozing while Nudding rode in the back, fidgeting and nervous for a while until he too succumbed to the car's air-conditioning and drifted off to sleep.

After a couple of hours' travel, they were roused from their slumber when Bec braked as they came to the Lennodvale boundary gate. Sam went to open his door but Nudding said, 'I'll get 'im, Sam.'

Scalding heat rushed into the car as Nudding opened the door and got out to open the gate. Suddenly he let out a frenzied squeal.

'HEEYYYY! WAASSATT!' he yelled and leapt backwards, throwing his hands in the air and bumping into the rear of the car.

Bec and Sam got out to see what all the kafuffle was about. Nudding was swiping at a huge grasshopper with his hat. Eventually he knocked it to the ground and with lightning speed jumped on it with both boots. His eyes were like saucers and his breathing was laboured as he walked around shaking his head and holding his chest.

'Ho! Missus! That mongrel nearly give me a heart attack! Crikey he's a big one, eh? He bit me hard too, that mongrel,' said Nudding, shaking one of his hands. 'I just hate insects!'

23

Bec stifled her smile as she dusted down the boy's back. 'There you go, Nudding. Just grab that water bottle out of the back and we'll have a drink.'

She was reaching into the front of the car for the mugs when a vehicle, coming from the opposite direction, pulled up and showered them in red dust.

Just like you, you inconsiderate old bastard, thought Bec as she recognised Doug O'Donnell's battered car. She slammed the wagon door shut, knowing it was too late and the cabin would now be filled with fine dust.

'Well if it isn't Mrs Roberts,' called Doug O'Donnell, leaning out the driver's window and leering at her with his watery, red-rimmed eyes. 'You're loaded up. Stocking up for the wet season, are you?' he said sarcastically, ignoring Rebecca's passengers. His wife, Maggie, was seated in the front with him and she smiled apologetically at Bec.

Bec loathed Doug O'Donnell, whom she regarded as a loud and obnoxious know-it-all. He and Maggie were Bec and Andy's closest neighbours, with the house they lived in on their property, Lennodvale, only fifty kilometres from Coolibah Creek's homestead.

Fifteen years younger than Doug, and in her late thirties, Maggie was a lovely Irish woman. Unlike other Irish people Bec had met over the years, she was extremely quiet and withdrawn. Rarely seen without a wide-brimmed straw hat to protect her milky white skin, she had a bright red birthmark covering half her left cheek. She was completely devoted to her two teenage boys – Sean, fourteen, and Daniel, thirteen – who were away at boarding school for most of the year.

Rebecca always felt sorry for Maggie. Doug kept her downtrodden and never seemed to show her even the slightest kindness, let alone love or affection. Even from a distance the smell of rum on Doug's breath was powerful. He had no respect for the law or rules of the road. But despite his drinking and his neglect of Maggie, Bec had to admit Doug was a good father to his sons. He was hard but fair, and he'd brought up his boys to be capable beyond their years.

Doug shouted that he and Maggie were off to collect the boys from boarding school for the Christmas holidays. 'No rain this year. You can count on that,' he added in his usual negative way. 'We should just give up hope of a season this year.'

'Have a good trip then. I'll bet you can't wait to see the boys, hey Maggie?' said Bec and, waving goodbye, she poured water for the three of them. Nudding had cautiously opened the gate again for the O'Donnells. 'See you after the big wet, ha, ha, ha,' Doug yelled as he roared through the gate, throwing up dust in his wake.

Chapter 4

Bec pulled up beside the men's quarters – an old, three-room timber building with a gauzed-in verandah and a shower, toilet and laundry area out the back. Tail wagging furiously, Bounce scampered about Bec's feet as she stepped out of the car, and old Jess barked loudly at Nudding and Sam until Bec bent down to pat her head and said, 'It's okay, Jess. This is Sam and Nudding.'

'She won't bite,' she assured Nudding, who was looking a little nervous.

Nudding opened up the back of the car and took down Sam's port and lugged it into the quarters. Sam grabbed a swag and followed him in.

The poddy calves in the wooden milking yard behind the quarters spotted Bec and began their hungry chorus, bawling loudly. She had twelve at the moment, all orphans of the drought.

'Oh poor babies. You're alright. It's not even your feed time yet,' Bec cooed, the sound of her voice strengthening their bellows to be fed. Once the men had unloaded their gear, Bec drove the car back towards the homestead and pulled up outside the small gauzed-in building where the station-killed meat was processed. Andy was looking very pleased with himself.

'Hello, baby,' he beamed. 'How was your trip?'

'Yeah, good. No problems,' said Bec. 'The road's cutting up pretty bad. What've you been up to?'

Andy opened the door, inviting Bec inside.

'Ta-da!' he said, throwing his arms wide in a mock gesture of showmanship. There, hanging on two stainless steel hooks was the freshly killed carcass of a huge goat.

'Where on earth did you get that?' she asked incredulously. They'd been living on chicken, sausages and 'town' meat for months because there'd been nothing fat enough to kill on the property. Accustomed to living on fresh meat, they were all heartily sick of the 'town' fare.

'George and I were checking the boundary fence in the channels when we came across him. Remember the time we caught those two young billies and I knocked their nuts out? This is one of 'em,' he said triumphantly.

The carcass was massive for a goat. Hanging by its hocks from the rail, it almost touched the cement floor.

'He was standing up on his hind legs with his front legs way up in the top of a mimosa bush eating the seed pods. We were just poking along and we were downwind of him so we got the jump on him a bit. I tell you what, he could motor! I had the quad bike flat out through the scrub for a good while before I eventually bent him back towards George,' said Andy, a grin on his face. 'George pulled on to him on the red four-wheeler and back-legged him. Rolled him alright, but in the cloud of dust he made when he pulled up, he couldn't see ol' Billy. Next thing the goat charged and hit the back of the bike. George was standing up, looking around and when the goat hit he lost his balance and plopped back down on the seat, gunning the bike at the same time. It shot forward and George did a full backwards somersault off the back.

'George didn't know which way was up for a while, on his hands and knees with a cranky goat stomping its feet into the dirt and angling his head to charge,' said Andy, laughing so much that he was struggling to keep telling the story. 'He was stranded, eyeballing the goat in a Mexican standoff. I had to roar up from behind on my bike, grab the goat and tip him over, otherwise George was going to cop it for sure. But it was hard to hold him.'

'Yeah, yeah, but what happened then, hey boss?' said George, returning from the shed with a wood saw, and looking at Bec. 'That ol' goat kicked the hell out of your husband. He a big strong bloke that goat and he's got no tail, like a bullock.' Now George started to laugh. 'Yeah, he bucked around, spinning and kicking with the boss here hanging on. He drug him about there a good while till I got hold of that bugger by the horns.'

Eventually, covered in dirt and burrs, they had wrestled the goat to a standstill and Andy had killed it with an incision into the spinal cord at the base of the goat's skull.

Sam and Nudding had finished unpacking their gear and ventured over to the butcher shop. Bec introduced everyone. Andy and Sam shook hands and then Andy said, 'I hear you're a good ringer, Nudding.' The young man hung his head and hid his eyes under his hat, embarrassed by the compliment, but his handshake was strong.

'Got a bit of fresh meat there, Andy?' said Sam, and Andy launched into the retelling of the yarn about 'how the goat was got'. Bec was sure it would soon be a favourite.

She drove the car back to the house and went inside to change into some old clothes while Nudding and George unloaded the boxes and groceries. Bec took Sam over to show him the poddies, which hadn't let up on their bawling to be fed, then they fed the chooks and the dogs while Andy butchered the goat. The carcass was incredibly fat considering the state of the pastures available and they were all looking forward to sampling it.

'Don't worry about tea, Bec,' called Andy. 'George is cooking the ribs in the camp oven at the quarters.'

Great! thought Bec. The curried ribs George made in the camp oven were a specialty, and any night Bec could get out of cooking was a welcome relief for her.

***

As the sun set in another rusty cloudless sky, the day cooled dramatically. Bec had enjoyed a cool shower and now, as she combed her freshly washed hair, she wondered what Andy was up to. He hadn't come back to the house yet and it was almost dark.

Just as Bec was heading out to see how George was going with the rib bones, the front door swung back and there stood Andy, wearing jeans and the white shirt she had given him for his birthday. His tanned skin was glowing and his dark eyes were filled with love as he offered a bunch of freshly cut blossoms from the garden. 'Happy anniversary, darling,' he said softly.

Bec had completely forgotten about their anniversary and she just stood there, surprised, accepting the flowers and feeling a little guilty as Andy gave her a hug. Her eyes brimmed with happy tears and she hugged him back. 'Happy anniversary,' she managed to get out as she drew away from his embrace, a smile on her face.

'Come on,' said Andy. 'I'm going to take you to dinner.'

'Can't wait,' she replied. 'I love George's curried rib bones.'

'Sorry, love, this is going to be a private dinner party. Come on, let's go,' he said as he grabbed her hand and marched her out to the ute, still carrying her flowers.

'So where are we going?' asked Bec as they drove off into the twilight.

'You'll see,' he said, reaching across to touch her cheek.

The road followed the line of the creek south of the homestead where silhouetted coolibahs stretched up begging arms to the orange sky. After a while, Andy turned off the road onto a long disused track that Bec knew led to their special place on the creek, which was normally a picturesque waterhole lined with silver gums and coolibahs. One tree in particular was an ancient landmark. The enormous bauhinia, or bean tree, spread out five thick trunks from its base, its black boughs reaching up, rising on a gentle angle into an umbrella of millions of tiny dark green leaves.

It had been heartbreaking for Bec and Andy to see their special place ravaged by the drought so they'd stopped going there, but now Bec smiled as she saw a soft red glow radiating from under the monumental tree. As they drew nearer she was enchanted to see a little square table draped with her best white tablecloth, and on it a single candle glowing warmly inside a glass lantern. Red gidgee coals broken into uneven squares glowed under a barbecue plate and the smell of wood smoke rose on the evening air.

Andy didn't speak as he got out of the car and came around to open Bec's door. 'Madam. Please be seated. Your meal will be served presently,' he said with a plummy English accent as he took her hand to help her from the car.

'Thank you, kind sir,' said Bec, impressed by all the planning he must have put in to the dinner.

Andy pulled a chair out from the table for Bec and then grabbed an esky from the ute and produced two chilled glasses and a bottle of wine.

'Something smells good already,' said Bec, noticing the tantalising aroma of roasting potatoes.

'If madam will excuse me momentarily, I need to attend to the sleeping arrangements,' said Andy, springing up into the back of the ute and unrolling his swag before coming back to the fire, plucking the potatoes from the coals and placing them in the camp oven. Then, with an exaggerated flourish he uncorked the wine and poured it into the chilled glasses.

His voice was deep and sincere, his face suddenly serious, as he touched his glass to hers and said, 'To my beautiful wife, who has given me the best years of my life.'

Bec smiled and looked deeply into his eyes. 'To my wonderful husband, who has made me the happiest woman in the world,' she replied huskily, leaning forward over the table to kiss his lips.

The beckoning signals of Andy's desire sent shots of pleasure throughout Bec's body and their kiss became intensely passionate as the magic of the moment seized them both. Andy released her, stood up, came around the table, swept her up in his arms and carried her to the back of the ute where he gently set her down on an unrolled swag. They didn't speak as he got up on the ute to join her. There was no need for words.

Kneeling, facing each other, eyes locked, they undressed. The night had fallen over them like a cloak – black, velvet and sprinkled with millions of stars. Firelight silhouetted the muscular outline of Andy's shoulders and dark hair sprung from his bare chest to a line across his hard stomach and loins. She reached out to touch him, almost reverently, as he propped himself on one elbow, savouring the moment, his dark eyes drinking in the sensuous lines of her figure, his hand caressing her skin. Wrapped in the cocoon of the night, there were no barren plains, no starving stock, no dry waterholes, just Bec, Andy and their love.

Andy bent his head to kiss her and their desire exploded with an urgency and hunger that consumed them and carried them away.

Afterwards they lay in contented silence, a night breeze cooling their bodies, which were hot and sweaty from their lovemaking. They stared into the darkness and it was as if they could reach up and grab a star, such was the closeness of the sky.

'Well, the entrée was delectable, delicious and dangerously good,' murmured Bec, rolling onto her side and making little circles with her finger in the hairs on Andy's chest and feathering his shoulder with kisses.

'Mmm, makes you hungry for the main course though, doesn't it?' He brushed the hair from her face and kissed her forehead. 'Come on. Let's eat first.'

Chapter 5

Bec felt overcome with remorse after she slammed the phone down on her mother. Katherine had called again hoping to convince Rebecca to come into Coombul for the annual Rotary Fundraiser Ball. Try as she might, Bec couldn't make her mother understand that at this time, when there was death and devastation all around them and the drought was chipping away at their future every day, they were simply not interested in dressing up and going dancing. Bec had been very short with her during their conversation and knew she'd hurt her mother's feelings. Not just about the ball. She and Katherine were very close – best friends really – but Bec just couldn't cope with her mother's constant pressure for her to have a child. It seemed that she worked the subject into every discussion they had.

For goodness sake, I'm only thirty years old, thought

Bec. *It's as if Mum thinks that having a child would miraculously solve everything.*

Bec knew that her mother lived in a bit of an emotional void due to Bec's father's continual dalliances with other women. *Still, thought Bec, that didn't mean she had to fill that void by pressing her daughter to give her a grandchild to love.*

Damn Dad, damn the bloody drought, damn the bank, damn Louise and her slimy husband . . . thought Bec as she started to cry. Andy's older sibling, Louise, had been ringing and asking for money again. They still owed her money from when the estate was settled after Andy's parents were killed. All of the bills were mounting up. They had no saleable cattle. She flopped back into the chair and sat staring out into the garden as salty tears streamed down her cheeks. *What happened to the carefree days when she and Andy would be at every social function in the district,* she wondered. *When would it all end?*

Bec's father, Stephen Hogan, was a solicitor, Rotary president, federal Member for Telford, husband to Katherine, father of Rebecca and Ben, and a serial womaniser. Everybody knew of his philandering ways, and the town of Coombul was constantly abuzz with gossip about his latest conquest. An exceedingly handsome man, he had a relaxed, confident manner and a ready smile. But it was his charismatic charm that women found so irresistible.

And although her father loved her mother, he seemed to believe it was his right to pursue any woman he fancied with no regard for Katherine's feelings. He was so sure no one would ever tell her directly about his dalliances that he was often reckless. And though her mother adored him,

Katherine merely 'existed' in their marriage now, and Bec knew how much it hurt her every time she found evidence of his infidelities.

It was the night of the Rotary Fundraiser Ball. Katherine hung Stephen's freshly laundered tuxedo in the cupboard. She walked around to the other side of the walk-in robe to put her outfit together. At fifty-one, Katherine Hogan was still a very attractive woman. Always impeccably groomed, as befitted a woman of her standing in the community, she had thick blonde hair and a very pretty face with flawless skin and perfect features. And though she couldn't deny she was jealous of her husband's unseen lovers, deep down she clung to the thought that she still owned his heart. She was the mother of the children he loved, she organised their home and social life and still slept in their king-size bed.

Stephen was a successful businessman and money had never been an issue. Her life was full and busy through the days but empty and sad most nights as she lay in their bed wondering whom he was with. The emptiness had become much worse since her children had grown up, with Rebecca living out at Coolibah Creek and Ben off in London, married to Sarah, a woman he'd met when he was training as a medical intern in England.

But then Stephen would saunter through the door, running his hand through his hair, ruffling it, unknowingly making himself look boyish, dishevelled and even more handsome. He would scoop her into his arms and hold her as if she were the only woman in the world. He had that way about him and there were few occasions when she didn't succumb to his embrace. He still made her feel so beautiful, so special.

She had tried to talk Bec into coming up for the dance but she and Andy were just so emotionally and physically exhausted from struggling with the drought conditions that they wouldn't be able to enjoy themselves anyway. She felt totally helpless not being able to ease their pain. She knew she shouldn't have pushed Bec about a baby, she just felt that a child would bring so much joy into their lives. She sighed and selected a pair of silver shoes to match her gown and flicked through a selection of evening clutches for the right accessory.

She heard Stephen's car in the driveway and delayed going to the shower so that she could speak with him. She walked out to the hallway in her bare feet and towelling robe to meet him.

'Hello, gorgeous,' he said, briefcase in hand, tie askew from where he had loosened it.

'Hello, darling,' Katherine replied, walking into his arms.

Stephen put down the briefcase and pulled her to him. 'Guess what? I'm taking the most beautiful woman in Coombul to a ball tonight,' he murmured, nuzzling her neck.

'I was just going to the shower,' said Katherine, removing his roving hands from under her robe. 'How was your day?'

'Interesting, very interesting. I'll have to give Bec and Andy a call. Are they coming tonight?' he asked.

'No. They're not coming. I did my best but they just don't have any enthusiasm for anything lately. I'm worried about Bec,' said Katherine, frowning.

'Yes, I know,' Stephen replied. 'I'm not sure if the information I found out today is good or bad but a mining company has apparently held a mining tenement over a big chunk of Coolibah for twenty years and they're looking at going into exploration phase on it.'

'Mining for what?' asked Katherine. 'Who are they? Shouldn't they have contacted Andy?'

'The company is called Phosec. Mayor Dawson and I met with one of their directors and his PR guy today. I was surprised when they rolled out the map and saw the tenement was smack bang in the middle of Coolibah,' said Stephen.

'What are they looking for? I didn't know there were any minerals out here.'

'You'd be amazed if you saw the maps of the mining tenements across the Telford region. There's hardly a hectare that doesn't have a claim over it. They said they've known the deposit was there for some time but mining hadn't been feasible in the past. They weren't forthcoming about what's changed to make it feasible now or what they were looking for, which they said is confidential at this stage. Apparently they just wanted to give us the heads up that they'll be around. They have to put a public notice in the papers when and if they start moving any ground.'

He shrugged off his jacket and removed his tie before continuing. 'There's no road or rail infrastructure out here to take out large amounts of ore or coal, so maybe it's gas. They could build a pipeline, though it'd have to be a big supply given the distance from here to anywhere major.'

'What will it mean for Andy and Bec?' Katherine asked.

'I don't know. They said they'd sent landholders a letter of request for a meeting. They'll have to set up a land access agreement and if there's any impact on Coolibah from the company's activities, Andy could probably make a claim for compensation. But it's all very mysterious at the moment. They'll have to get through the hurdle of native title and dealing with traditional owners before anything substantial begins,' Stephen explained.

'Bec will be furious if they want to go anywhere near her precious rivers,' said Katherine, with a worried expression. 'That's if she has the strength to fight them. She seems to have lost her spark these days.'

'Let's worry about how long we can shower before the hot water runs out,' said Stephen, taking Katherine's hand and leading her off to the bathroom.

〜

JRR–001 was the number plate of the red Porsche that pulled into the parking lot outside the hall. Justine Rachel Rand – number one. Her golden bangles jangled as she got out of her car and tossed her auburn hair from her face. Her honey-coloured skin and almond eyes came from her mother's Spanish ancestry.

Justine was the only daughter of Jonathon Rand, a wealthy local businessman. He was accompanying her to the ball. Tall and busty with an athletic appearance gained through hours of gym work and jogging, Justine was smart too and had gained a Bachelor of Science majoring in Environmental Earth Science at the University of California Berkeley.

Justine never missed an opportunity to make an entrance, so she purposely arrived late at functions. She stood at the entrance to the ballroom with her much shorter, balding father whose chest was puffed out with pride as he ushered his beautiful daughter into the room. The pause at the doorway, as if she were waiting to be announced, had worked and now she had the room's attention.

Justine glided forward with natural grace, flashing a broad smile at her father's close friend, Mr Goodman. She wore an emerald silk gown that was little more than a piece of exquisite filmy fabric. Over each shoulder hung a diamante jaguar, the tails of which disappeared over her shoulders. Stretching down towards her amply filled décolletage, the golden jaguars held one front leg under their bodies and thrust the other forward, reaching out and clasping the slippery cloth in outstretched claws before it fell in a cowl across her naked breasts. From behind, the jaguars' diamante tails picked up the sides of the deeply plunging back line. At her throat she wore a one-carat diamond on a delicate gold chain and a number of tiny diamond bracelets on her slender arm. When she moved, the thin fabric caressed her and shone where it touched her body.

Justine loved the reaction she was getting. She smiled and made small talk with Mr Goodman as she scanned the room for a target. Justine was becoming bored with the locals, the young yuppies, the husbands and sportsmen of the town. She'd already had her pick of them, and once she had them she immediately lost all interest.

In the corner of the room, towards the stage, the sight of broad shoulders in a well-cut tuxedo caught her attention. Elegant and tall, the man had his back to her and was speaking to another man. The two finished their conversation and the broad-shouldered man turned towards the room. His thick hair was perfectly cut and groomed and his tanned face broke into a lopsided grin as he acknowledged someone nearby.

Justine took in a sharp little breath. She could feel Stephen Hogan's presence even from this distance. She'd had a crush on him when she was a gawky teenager. He looked a little older, yes, but better. Was that possible? The man had always oozed confidence and charm but now there was something else, some other quality, strong yet intangible.

Justine puzzled over what it was as she strolled over towards the centre of the ballroom and took a glass of champagne from a waiter. She chatted with a group of young people but her attention was on Stephen. Watching him work the room with such style, socialising, smiling, nodding, frowning, giving the right reaction to each individual.

Gradually he made his way around the crowded ballroom, stopping at the group Justine was with. He placed his hand on one of the young men's shoulders and whispered something conspiratorially into his ear. Harry threw back his head as if he were going to burst out with laughter but stifled his reaction to a chuckle. Stephen shook hands all around, making small talk about the last local football game. When he came to Justine he gave Harry a questioning look to prompt him to introduce them.

'Stephen, this is Justine Rand. Justine, this is Mr Hogan,' said Harry.

Stephen's handshake was firm and dry. Justine couldn't help but notice the size and rough texture of his hand despite being held captive by his direct, appreciative and piercing gaze. His grin showed slightly irregular white teeth and creased his eyes and cheeks, emphasising his high cheekbones and strong jawline. The impact was enticing. A shiver ran across Justine's back and she shuffled her feet before she spoke in a calm voice.

'Hello, Mr Hogan,' she said, returning his stare.

'I remember you, Justine. Please call me Stephen,' he replied, smiling.

Justine's hand was still burning from his touch as he moved on to another group. She excused herself and headed for the ladies' room. Inside, she looked at herself in the mirror and took a deep breath.

Whew! What was it about that man?

It was a long time since Justine had felt like an awkward teenager, but that was exactly how he had made her feel. She didn't like losing self-control. With trembling fingers she took the lipstick from her purse and chided herself sternly.

She smoothed the coral colour over her full lips, turned her face from right to left and swivelled around to check her posterior before striding back out to the ballroom. As she walked from the dimly lit hallway into the function room she noticed that the room was quiet and everyone's attention was focused on the stage.

Stephen stood at the microphone, tall and resplendent. 'Ladies and gentlemen,' he began. 'It is my very great pleasure as Member for Telford and president of Coombul Rotary Club to welcome . . .'

Justine felt as though his deep voice was permeating her skin and vibrating inside her. Glancing at the people around her, she saw they were all hanging on his every word. She realised then that the quality Stephen had, which she hadn't been able to define at first, that extra something that so enraptured her, was power over people. It excited her and she didn't resist the feeling, allowing him to get under her skin. A flush of heat coloured her cheeks and she thought about how she could get closer to him. Very close.

Chapter 6

Justine was having coffee with her old friend Brendan Oliver. They were enjoying one of their favourite pastimes, people watching.

'She's so ugly you'd have to tie a chop around her neck so that the dog would play with her!' Justine leant forward, green eyes dancing with mischief.

'Oh no, darling. You couldn't do that. The fat bitch would eat it!' said Brendan.

Justine spluttered in her cup, almost choking on the coffee as she burst into a throaty laugh. 'Oh Bren,' she said, 'I've missed you.'

Justine and Brendan had been friends since primary school. Brendan now owned the local gym and was editor and owner of the *Coombul Courier* newspaper. They were very much alike. Both twenty-four, both beautiful and educated, both spoilt rich brats and both loved men.

'Now, there's something far more pleasing to the eye,' said Brendan, wiggling in his seat and raising one of his arched black eyebrows as Stephen Hogan strode into the café.

'You can keep your eyes off him,' said Justine. 'I have plans for him.'

'Ha!' Brendan scoffed. 'You and a hundred other women in town. Maybe he's ready for a change.'

'Sorry, sweetie, you've got no chance with this one,' Justine purred through her teeth, ogling her prey as he stood at the counter.

Brendan studied her face for a moment before speaking. 'So you've applied for the enviro job with Phosec Mining, I take it?'

Justine had fallen back into the pattern of telling Brendan all her secrets, so he knew she wanted to stick around for a while and make a play for the local member. He'd told her about the position being advertised in the newspaper before it went to print.

'Of course. My interview's tomorrow,' Justine replied absently, still watching Stephen.

'Oh well, good luck with the interview. It's fun to have you back in town,' said Brendan, rising from his seat and fussing over his clothes. 'Better go. I have a couple of stories to pull together before deadline today. Ciao, gorgeous. Phone me afterwards,' he tossed over his shoulder as he walked away.

Justine lingered over her coffee. She smiled at Brendan's brisk little mincing walk. He was so funny. He was about the only person she had any feelings of warmth towards other than her father. Perhaps it was because he was so totally unaffected by her feminine wiles. He was clever, a talented journalist who had higher ambitions.

Still smiling with fondness, she scooped up her keys and stood up. She had an interesting day ahead of her: selecting just the right outfit for her interview, the perfect perfume and shoes, and she had to compile an inventory of the perfect lies she needed to tell to be certain of the correct result.

Browsing through her walk-in wardrobe, she chose a classic suit in mushroom pink crepe, which on anyone else would have probably looked quite bland. It was plain, but beautifully cut. The straight skirt was satin lined and hung softly to just above her knees. The bodice was fitted, not tight, but firm enough to emphasise her cleavage. The jacket cinched her waist when buttoned, highlighting her hourglass shape and calling attention to her willowy grace. Justine chose a matching pair of court shoes to go with her outfit. They were perhaps one shade darker than the suit and had enough heel to show off the bronzed turn of her fine ankles.

The outfit was perfect for the interview.

༄

The clock on the wall showed one minute to ten as Justine approached the reception desk at Phosec Mining's new offices. Justine noticed that the overweight receptionist had beautifully manicured nails. She flashed her most ingratiating smile at the girl, gave her name and took a seat.

Behind closed doors the CEO, Mark Bruckhurst, frowned as he reviewed the people they'd seen already. None of them had been suitable. The work he wished to get done with the selected environmental person was to be the very basis of the platform from which he planned to launch Phosec's Coolibah Creek project. He rose from the big leather chair and stretched before walking down the hall to call in the next applicant. When he opened the door to the foyer he saw a stunning young woman there.

'Miss Rand, would you like to come through, please?' he said, as he held the door open and gestured for her to go before him.

'Good morning, Mr Bruckhurst. Thank you,' said Justine, smiling at him.

When they reached his office, Mark held out his hand. 'Justine, isn't it? Please call me Mark.'

His hand was strong and cool. He was a man who looked after himself, Justine observed: medium height with dark brown hair beginning to grey at his temples. He gestured to the vacant chair and sat down behind the desk with the others. Justine waited until he was seated before she crossed one long tanned leg over the other, sat straight in her chair and relaxed her hands in her lap.

There were three people in the boardroom to conduct the interview. Mark introduced them. All three of them were seated on one side of the vast wooden table. Phosec Chairman Angus Dalgliesh was short and bald. A roll of pink fat squeezed out from above his starched white collar and there was no definition between his head and neck, making Justine giggle inside when she imagined what Brendan would say. His close-set beady eyes undressed Justine as she smiled and said, 'Good morning.'

Toast! she thought, knowing she had Angus's vote already.

Marion Tate, the other director, was a small, thin woman with fine bones. *She looks like a sparrow*, thought Justine. *Damn, I didn't count on a woman being here. That makes things a little more difficult.* To Justine, men and women were two totally different sets of cards to play, which was fine if it was one or the other but not when she was trying to win over both. Her mind raced to find a new angle.

'Good morning,' she said, wondering how she'd find this woman's soft spot. *Everybody has their price.* She shuddered as she remembered her bulky lesbian professor at uni. Justine had paid a huge price for her first class honours in environmental science, but she couldn't come home to Daddy without the very best results.

As the interview progressed, Justine noticed Mr Bruckhurst flick through the files in front of him. She assumed he was comparing her to some of the people they'd already interviewed. He was sharp, and challenged her with probing questions. Dalgliesh was virtually salivating and didn't have his mind on the task at hand. Marion Tate questioned her suitability for all the fieldwork that would be required.

Mrs Tate had the weather-beaten look of an outdoors type, thought Justine as she shaped her answer. 'I was raised on the land at Mireendah, our family acreage and olive grove, Mrs Tate. I'm accustomed to the dust and flies, and the mud, if it ever rains. One of our employees was hopelessly bogged at Coongoola Lake just the other day. Daddy sent me down to get him out. I have been driving four-wheel drives since I was seven.'

Director Tate cocked her head to one side in a birdlike way and regarded her. 'Coongoola Lake?'

'Yes. That's right,' said Justine.

'Oh. The birdlife there must be prolific at present, given that it's the only decent body of water left for hundreds of miles.'

Justine detected the excited edge in the director's voice and asked, 'Are you interested in birds, Mrs Tate?'

'You could say they are my passion, Miss Rand, but I digress. My apologies, Mark. Please, go on.'

Yes! Justine thought triumphantly. She had this job in the bag. Mrs Tate would not be able to resist the warm invitation, which she would extend to her, to visit Coongoola Lake whenever she wished. It was on Daddy's land.

Tate's right. Dalgliesh is right . . .

Justine gave all her attention to Mark Bruckhurst.

'Miss Rand, you do understand there will be a confidentiality condition on your employment as environmental scientist with Phosec for our project in this area until the initial environmental impact studies are done and before we go out to community consultation? Considering your local connection to the community, how will you manage the confidential nature of your work?'

'I would expect, Mr Bruckhurst, that you will not require me to wear a Phosec logo on my clothes or drive a Phosec car at this stage. I'm in the process of establishing a consulting business to service the increasing interest in environmental protection of the arid land wetlands, so I will be operating under my own banner. There will be no problem whatsoever with confidentiality. I can explain, however, that if a new person were to come to town for the position, a lot more questions would be asked. I believe my local status is a distinct advantage in this instance.'

Justine smiled at all three directors encouragingly. 'Outside my credentials as an environmental scientist, as a local I believe I can be of great assistance through to the community consultation phase as I have a good understanding of the demographic of the area and how to communicate effectively with them whatever the message.' She saw Dalgliesh nodding slowly although he was yet to lift his eyes away from her chest to her face.

The interviewers asked numerous questions that Justine was able to field in a relaxed, self-assured way. The meeting concluded and Dalgliesh insisted on showing Justine out, walking just behind her down the long corridor. *Pig*, Justine thought as she felt his little beady eyes on her swaying bottom.

She reached the foyer and turned to dazzle him with her most brilliant smile. 'Thank you, Mr Dalgliesh. I look forward to meeting you again soon.'

'Please call me Angus, Justine,' he coaxed, reaching out to place a sweaty hand on her arm.

Justine knew the job was in the bag, so she turned her mind to how she could quickly go about setting up the consulting business. The idea had come to her on the spur of the moment in the interview so she had better get it happening and fast.

Outside in the sunshine, she paused at the Porsche to phone her father. 'Hello, Daddy. Yes, I know you're busy but I really, really need you to help me with something.'

Daddy always fixed things for his little girl.

Chapter 7

Copious clouds of dust rose and swirled in the heat of the midday sun as the light aircraft landed on the dirt strip at Coolibah Creek. Its two crumpled and pale passengers and the pilot alighted onto the burning red ground.

'It's extremely rough flying today,' said the young pilot, stating the obvious. 'It's the heat.'

Louise and Laurie Connor looked very much out of place in their designer clothes and shoes, trendy hairstyles and sunglasses. Bec was always struck by what an attractive woman Louise was, but she knew she was as cold as the ice-blue colour of her eyes. She had the same thick tawny hair as Andy and a slender willowy body. Her husband's fair skin was perpetually white due to lack of outdoor activities. Laurie's face was flushed in the heat and his small black eyes darted about.

Bec guessed that what had drawn him and Louise together was their innate greed and ambition to rise up the social ladder. When she'd started going out with Andy he'd introduced her to them and she'd disliked them almost immediately even though they had always been pleasant to her to begin with. *Just in case you thought you might be able to use me in some way*, Rebecca thought. She found their whole demeanour off-putting and maintained a deep-seated mistrust of them. Their impromptu visit was entirely unlike them, given the regimented order of their lives and the fact that neither of them liked the bush.

Back at the homestead, Bec smiled graciously as she set down the tray of coffee and biscuits on the table in the dining room. Louise didn't like the verandah, where Andy and Bec had their smoko. There were always flies or bugs, and today it was far too hot for her.

'This is the opportunity of a lifetime for us, Andy,' Louise gushed, placing her perfectly manicured hand on Andy's brown arm. 'I know things are a little bit tough here at the moment, but I really need the money now.' Her voice was soft and pleading and she gazed at Andy with huge blue eyes.

Andy tried to be patient with her. 'Louise, as I explained to you on the phone, we just don't have the money to give to you. We had those cattle on agistment for twelve months – a lot of cattle, Louise, a lot of money – then to get less than a hundred dollars a head for them and all the while feeding lick supplement out to our breeders at Coolibah and paying wages with no income. It's been seven years of drought. There is no money.'

He laid out his latest bank statement on the table. 'Here's our overdraft. Even if it rains tomorrow, it'll be at least three years before we get any decent cash flow. We're only holding mainly empty females and not many of them. We have no steers or sale cattle. It's going to take years for us to recover. We can't access any more money from the bank because we cannot show any cash flow for the foreseeable future, especially as it still hasn't rained.'

Bec knew that Andy was frustrated with Louise because she just couldn't seem to get the message. She'd been raised at Coolibah but hadn't taken any of it in. Andy told her that Louise had always lived in a fantasy world and generally their parents had given her whatever she wanted. They had enough to deal with and Bec could see he was fighting to control his anger as he sat opposite his selfish sister.

'But you still have the substantial asset of the property,' Laurie chimed in with his whispery voice. 'And what about the mining company that's sniffing about, could that be lucrative for you?'

Bec was fuming. Laurie was less than half as smart as he thought he was. He was a wizard with anything electronic or technological but his business sense left a lot to be desired and his people skills were negligible; hence his business limped along and often went backwards. Louise had always been accustomed to just demanding what she wanted and getting it, and splashing money around as if Andy owned a dozen cattle properties not one.

Ignoring Laurie's question about the mining company Andy got angry. 'We've been over this so many times, Louise,' he said, banging the table, causing Laurie to flinch and pick at his collar. Bec was quite sure Louise had never been entirely honest with her husband about the actual state of her family's finances.

'Dad and Mum lost sixty per cent of their savings in the 2008 stock market crash. They bought you that flash property in Toorak with most of what they had left so that I could inherit Coolibah and pay you the balance of your equal share over time. It's all in the will and the contract between us.' Andy's eyes fell to the table as he continued.

'Then when I was old enough to run the joint, they decided to spend their savings and see the world, and then . . .' Andy stopped, still overcome by the sadness of the tragic loss of both his parents in a foreign country.

'So you've come a long way for nothing,' Andy said, looking directly into Laurie's eyes until he looked away.

Louise turned on the waterworks. She was playing her trumps one after another. Bec couldn't stand the performance any longer. She got up from the table and walked out into the garden, breathing deeply through her clenched teeth.

෴

Andy's depression seemed to deepen after they left. Bec knew he felt betrayed by his sister and disappointed to see the manipulating person she'd become.

'Wonder what will happen with the Phosec company. It seems a bit off with all the secrecy around it. Why can't they say what they're looking for?' said Bec, to break the silence.

'Don't know, love. We'll have to play it by ear. No use worrying about it. There's nothing we can do to change it and we have enough on our plate,' Andy replied.

Bec could see a lot of potential problems with a mine smack bang in the middle of their operation. What if the production meant chemical run-off into the rivers? All the company's trucks and equipment would be driving through their paddocks. There would have to be a big camp of workers for sure. Where would they get their water and power? How would they dispose of their sewage? It was a long way to town. But she didn't speak of her concerns. Andy had enough to cope with.

She pushed the issue aside and changed the subject, struggling to put a cheerful tone in her voice as she tried to lift his mood. 'Mum and Dad are coming out this weekend,' she said. 'I'd like to talk to Dad about our idea of accessing the artesian basin. I reckon that it's the way of the future and you and I could put together a really good proposal for a feasibility study at least.'

Andy turned to Bec, a tired expression on his handsome face. It broke her heart to see the shadows of defeat in his eyes. A flicker of interest peeked through the sadness and he replied, 'Yeah. Yeah, there's got to be a better way. We've got to work towards never ever being in this situation again. But it's all about money and, really, who's got any at the moment?'

'I know that, but I think it will do us good to get the thing down on paper and at least have as much as we can worked through for when the time is right,' said Bec. 'We can quiz Dad about where we might be able to apply for government assistance to get something like this going. Surely someone in parliament has some vision and foresight. With water, out here, we could start with a clean slate and build a revolutionary integrated sustainable food production system, using what we know about all the mistakes intensive farming has made in the past. You've never been a victim, Andy, and neither have I. We can't let this drought turn us into victims. I reckon our idea could be the way we can take back control of our future.' Bec tried to reignite Andy's enthusiasm for his idea.

'I suppose that would be good, love. Just seems to be so much to look after at the moment that there's no room for anything new.' Andy rose stiffly from the verandah chair.

'I'm headed out to Rainbow bore and the western side lick run. Might have another poddy by this evening; saw a lonely little fella there yesterday. If he still has no mum, Nudding will catch him and we'll bring him home.' Andy kissed Bec on the cheek and squeezed her arm. Andy and Rebecca were so connected to their land and their livestock, it was heartbreaking to see them suffering.

'Think about our water project while you're driving around the run. It's important. We should get it all down,' said Bec.

'I think there's plenty of time for that; it's a long way off yet I reckon. But yeah, I'll think on it.' Andy plucked his hat from the rack and, jamming it down on his head, walked out into the heat of the afternoon. Jess opened one eye and raised her head from her position under the stairs in the shade but didn't jump up and follow her master.

Andy and Stephen got on well. Stephen's energy and magnetism were impossible to ignore and his positive outlook for the future and firm belief that a change for the better was always just around the corner was infectious. Bec was glad he was coming. She wasn't looking forward to having Doug O'Donnell for dinner on Saturday night, but it would be good to see Maggie. They were firm friends, even though they didn't see each other much, especially since the drought had virtually brought all social events to a halt. They shared a love of all things living: plants and animals.

※

The never-ending sameness of the hot dry days continued and Andy was happy to see Stephen and Katherine had arrived when he came home from his daily run. Was it Saturday? Must be. He often lost track of what day of the week it was. As he got out of the old Toyota he saw the O'Donnells' vehicle coming at breakneck speed down the road. *Oh well, there's bound to be some lively discussion over dinner*, thought Andy.

That night, after a few beers around the barbecue discussing the drought and the likelihood of rain, everyone adjourned to the living room where Andy was keen to get a game of poker going.

'I've been talking with Andy about our idea to get access to the artesian basin. If we had water, and lots of it, there's no limit to the diversification we could get into,' Bec said to Stephen as they carried the dessert through to the living room.

'Ah yeah . . . but you can't make it rain. What are you going to do, grow grapes or what was the latest craze? Emu farming?' Doug slurred and gazed around with belligerent eyes, looking disdainfully tolerant of the dreamers surrounding him.

Maggie blushed in anticipation. She knew that Doug would interject scornfully at some point. He was so set in his ways and thought he knew everything. She absolutely loved Andy and Bec's ideas but she would never dare let on, only to Bec.

'Once established and labelled, our natural grass-fed organic beef will be an entirely different product to the oceans of beef available around the world. The exclusive, natural clean green image of our product will maintain demand as it will be a completely different consumer base,' Andy explained, ignoring Doug's comments.

'What about when this dirty big coalmine cranks up in the middle of Coolibah? That might be a bit of a bummer for your organic clean green image stuff,' Doug went on. Rumours had been flying around the district about the mystery mining lease.

'Nobody knows what they are looking for, Doug. I doubt if it would be coal, or if it is then there must be a lot of it. It's a thousand kilometres to the nearest railhead,' Bec pointed out to Doug and continued on regardless of his reaction.

'We could even have our own organic feedlot running all year round turning off enough prime beef as we possibly can during the dry years to maintain a trickle of product and keep the top shelf products available, even if only in small amounts, until the seasons fall in our favour again,' Bec enthused.

'That could be a bloody long time,' said Doug. 'Been seven years so far this drought. How you gonna keep gettin' the cattle?'

'If we could kill and process here, we could use the effluent and by-products to fertilise areas for pasture or crop growth and being such a dry climate the threat of insect damage is greatly reduced.' Bec was really getting into it and having Doug to bounce off was stoking her fire.

'All the forced sale cattle that currently move off the shire will be eligible to be processed here. Even though the condition on them will not allow them to make the grade for prime, there will be another niche market available to us for lesser cuts at lower prices. Why not make the cheaper cuts available? Everybody would like to eat our product but the prime cuts will be out of some people's price range. Organic mince and sausages would allow a much broader market for sales. Still at least double the return to the grazier than you're getting now, Doug, even in the dry times. Imagine if you could walk your sale cattle to the processing plant. No stress on the cattle, no big freight bills, greatly improved product. When everybody's business becomes much stronger due to the significant increase in income they'll have more options because they'll be more profitable. The country here in Telford Shire will then be able to sustain smaller herd numbers for longer, keeping the supply chain ticking over as the dollar value per head is significantly increased.'

'Fewer cattle over longer periods will have positive results for land condition and pasture response. So it's a win–win situation, if we can only get the water up,' Andy added.

'Well what about when we get a big flood? I remember back in '74 when everyone was under water for months. What about then, hey? What about then?' Doug wouldn't be beaten.

'Doug, in '74 the whole of the state was under water for months, but we survived,' Andy answered.

'Just think of the huge lift in production once the waters recede. It would be doubled, probably tripled,' said Stephen.

'And besides, many products are seasonal, like mangoes and stone fruit. Just because they're not available all year round doesn't mean that they're any less saleable,' Katherine contributed.

Bec interrupted the conversation to ask, 'Who's for coffee?'

'I'll give you a hand,' said Maggie as she followed Bec into the kitchen.

'Sorry, Bec,' said Maggie as she put the kettle on the gas. 'Doug knocks everything. It doesn't matter what it is. If it's new, he's against it.'

'Don't worry about it, Maggie. A healthy debate is a good thing. There're going to be plenty of knockers if we try to get this concept up and running, so it's good practice for us to find the right answers for them.

'Come out to the verandah,' she said, wanting to change the subject and at least talk about something pleasant with Maggie. 'I want to show you my new plants. I'm so proud of them. I didn't think that they'd flower in this weather but they have.' As Bec went to lead Maggie through to the back verandah she suddenly reached out and grabbed Bec's arm. 'There's something I have to tell you, Bec,' said Maggie.

Bec took both her hands. They were trembling

'For goodness sake, Maggie. What is it?' she said looking into her friend's anxious eyes.

'I'm pregnant,' Maggie said.

'Well that's wonderful news!' Bec said. 'I take it you haven't told Doug yet or he'd be boasting.' Bec was sorry immediately that she had vocalised what she was thinking.

Maggie looked troubled and afraid. Bec put her arm around her friend's shoulders and led her out into the garden.

'No. I haven't told him,' Maggie confided. 'I'm not quite seventeen weeks along, so there's still a chance I could miscarry. Not that I'm hoping that will happen, it's just that . . . well I'm older now and the boys are growing up. I suppose I didn't consider that I could possibly have another baby at this stage.' Rebecca was surprised that her friend could be so far along; she wasn't showing but Maggie always wore loose, flowing bohemian type dresses and she was tall.

'Everything will work out. Just think, maybe you'll have a little girl this time. What a blessing.' Bec smiled at Maggie but a sliver of sadness and envy pierced her heart as she longed for her own child.

Chapter 8

Bec and Andy flopped into the squatter's chairs on the verandah. It was almost eight thirty and it seemed the unremitting demon of the drought meant the sun stayed longer in the sky each evening. The men and animals had all been fed and the couple were both exhausted. A creeping feeling of lethargy and defeat was spreading through them a little more each day as the seemingly endless persecution persisted. The temporary lift to their sagging spirits that had come with Stephen and Katherine's visit had evaporated on the hot blast of wind that blew gritty dust into their disconsolate faces. Louise had been on the phone again, needling, pushing, demanding money from Andy. She was relentless. Bec and Andy had had a preliminary meeting with a couple of Phosec Mining representatives.

'It sticks in my neck that those Phosec blokes think if they wear a pair of moleskins, a blue shirt, some RM boots and a hat and ask you about the drought it's going to give them some sort of breakthrough connection. The fools don't know how hard it is to earn your hat where we live, to wear in your boots on your own dirt. Gets up my nose. They could at least treat us with a little respect. We're not idiots,' Bec ranted.

She had an intrinsic mistrust of mining companies. They had heard all the horror stories of the coal seam gas boom in exploration and how the mining companies were running over the top of people. 'What's the point of meeting with us? They didn't tell us anything at all. Just that they needed an access agreement,' Bec went on. 'Luckily we can count on Dad for legal advice.'

'That's for sure,' replied Andy. 'Imagine if we had to cough up for that at the moment. Anyway, they said it'll be a few months yet before they do anything. Seemed to me like they wanted to find out just how desperate we are.' He reached for her hand.

'I just can't believe Louise, though.' His tone was more one of bewilderment rather than ire. 'My own sister, born here. What's wrong with her?'

'You'll have to talk to her. I just can't,' Bec replied. 'She has the legal right, you know.'

Andy ran his hands through his hair and sighed. Rebecca could make out his features in the dim pastel light of the evening. He looked so tired. She thought about how his tiredness was much more than physical. Rest would not heal his exhaustion. The phone call from Louise was a straw that could break the camel's back.

Ships of the desert. That's what we are. A couple of camels, Bec thought.

'This country needs so little water; it gives you so much from so little but we can't even get that little bit of rain.' Andy put his hands behind his head, thrust out his long legs and stared out past the garden to the parched plains beyond. 'If I had a magic wand or ten million dollars I would be drawing up that water. It wouldn't stop the droughts but we'd be able to get through and not go so far out the back door financially that we couldn't get back in the game when it rains.'

'You couldn't irrigate the whole of Coolibah,' said Bec as she handed him his cup of tea. 'Two hundred thousand hectares is a lot of ground.'

'No, I know, but we could at least put in some ponded areas and rotational grazing systems that would keep our breeders alive,' Andy explained.

'You'd have to be careful not to use up the soils too much over time. They're not very nutrient rich and need the rest time that a drought brings to recharge.'

'You're right, Bec. We'd have to be very careful how the whole system was managed, but with the right advice, the right spelling, grazing and mowing back in from the start and some supplementary stuff like algae, there must be a way.'

Bec could see he was struggling to make his tired brain think.

'Yeah, like producing algae for fodder. It's amazing to think that's possible. But algae needs water, and water is what we don't have,' said Bec.

'But there's literally an ocean of beautiful, wonderful clean water under the ground. It's a kilometre down and it would cost millions to bring up and build the infrastructure to make it viable. Oh well, a man can dream,' said Andy, squeezing her hand.

Dreams might be all we are left with, thought Bec. *All our lifetime goals and dreams could be crushed if it doesn't rain soon.* The feeling of powerlessness was overwhelming.

'We would need to know how quickly the aquifer would refill, so that we could put a definite figure on the long-term availability and how much we could use,' said Bec.

'If we had that amount of water the ways in which we could diversify would mean that we could rely on other industries for income, other than grazing, through the dry years: like sandalwood, aquaculture, horticulture. There are endless opportunities but everything needs water and a fair bit of it. If we could unlock that water supply . . .

'Did you see that?' Andy's body became tense as he gripped the arms of the chair and leant forward intently.

'What?' said Bec, looking around.

'Lightning! In the west!' Andy stood up slowly and crept forward to the verandah railing as if he were sleepwalking, his eyes searching the now blackened horizon of the western sky.

Bec was on her feet. She'd seen a glimpse of shadowy clouds in the west at sunset, but she'd so often been disappointed that she'd forgotten about it.

'There!' said Andy, pointing out into the night.

'I saw it!' she said with disbelief. Lightning in the west was the most positive sign they could have for rain at this time of year.

They watched in silence as the flashes of lightning became more frequent, down low on the horizon, popping like flashbulbs in the night sky. As they stood together, almost forgotten images of running creeks and the first precious sprouts of growth pushing triumphantly through the bare earth, proudly wearing their beautiful bright green colours, floated through their troubled minds.

Hours passed and still they watched the storms build and rise up in the sky. They watched with such an aching hunger, willing the storms to come over, yearning for the sound and smell of rain with every fibre of their being. They didn't communicate their mutual feelings, as if talking about a miracle might somehow jinx their chances. Eventually, at midnight, as the furious electrical storms started to dissipate in the distance, Bec asked, 'How far back, do you think?'

'A long way, love. A long way.' Andy sighed. 'Hope somebody got something. Hope they're not just dry storms; not that there's any grass left to burn. Reckon they look to be about Davo's joint.'

Davo owned a rough block of mulga scrub about a hundred and sixty kilometres to the west. A good mate of Andy's father, Davo had been to Vietnam and the rum had him now. He'd never married and he claimed Andy as family. Davo lived like a hermit with his kelpies, cattle dogs and his cockatoo, Charlie. He was tough as nails, a jack-of-all-trades, a master of improvisation and a very good bush cook.

Even in the feeble moonlight, Andy and Bec could see the telltale plumes of white cloud that appeared like opening fans in the sky as the thunderheads 'blew up'. They had released their cargo and their energy and were now showing the first signs of dispersing and melting away.

Andy put his arm across Bec's shoulders and gently

Coolibah Creek

turned her towards the door. 'Let's go to bed. Tomorrow's another day.'

~

The shrill sound of the phone ringing woke them from their sweaty, restless slumber. Andy, instantly awake, fumbled for his torch. Coolibah Creek was too remote to be connected to grid power and in drought times it would be extravagant to use the diesel required to run the generator at night. Stark naked, Andy leapt out of bed, checking the time on the bedside clock on his way out to the phone. It was 4.15.

'Hello,' he said curiously.

'How are you, boy?' Davo's croaky voice came down the line.

Should've known, thought Andy; 4am was Davo's start time.

'Davo,' he said. 'I'm good, mate. Did you get some rain?'

'Naaa. Not much in 'em, hey. Just a couple of gallopin' scuds.'

Andy's heart sank. He really thought they looked like good storms. He was hoping –

'Only four bloody inches!' Davo shouted. 'Hey, rain here, boy! Water everywhere!'

Andy slapped the phone table. 'Four inches! A hundred millimetres,' he said through a wide smile. 'Bullshit, Davo!'

'No, boy. Fair dinkum. Yeeheehaa,' shouted Davo, and Andy could hear Charlie the cockatoo going berserk in the background. He could tell from the slur in Davo's exuberant voice that he had been celebrating through the night.

'Just built up from nothin', hey. Built up and built up, then came across in a line about nine o'clock and just poured. She was a wild one, boy. Shook the old goondi, and me dogs were terrified. Those pups have never seen rain. Mad wind with it. The old chook house got flattened. The chooks are wishing they were ducks this morning,' he said, laughing and setting off the cockatoo again.

'Four inches.' Andy was stunned. 'Good on you, Davo.'

Bec had got out of bed and was now standing at the phone with Andy. They were both naked. 'What is it?' she said sleepily.

'Davo's had four inches!' said Andy.

'What. Four inches! NO! Fair dinkum!' Bec's hands covered her open mouth and she jumped up and down on the spot like an excited child.

'Do you reckon it went far?' Andy asked Davo.

'Well, it came in from the west so, yeah, I reckon I got it all over, but I'll tell you tonight.'

'Righto, Davo. Four inches. Unbelievable. We'll hear from you tonight.'

Andy hung up the phone and grabbed Bec in a bear hug, lifting her off the floor and twirling her around in the darkness.

'I thought they looked good,' he said, still holding her, 'but I wasn't game to hope. It's the first decent fall of rain in the district for two years. The storms have been dry for so long . . .' his voice trailed off.

Suddenly Bec kissed him passionately, clinging to him fiercely; she wrapped her legs around his waist. Andy carried her back to bed, where they made love in the apricot glow of the dawn.

Coolibah Creek

Waking with a fright, Andy sat bolt upright. Sleep had claimed them both like a drug and now the morning sun was glaring accusingly at them through the bedroom window.

'Davo's destocked,' Andy mumbled, running a hand through his hair.

'Bec, Davo's destocked!' he said, shaking her until she sat up in bed, staring at him with startled eyes from under her tangled black fringe.

'What? What are you talking about?'

'Davo's destocked. Why didn't that hit me before? You distracted me, you wicked little vixen,' he said, grabbing her around the waist and pulling her on to his chest. 'Davo's got no cattle at Balmacarra. There's no way he'd have the cash to buy cattle and truck them there. He spent a fortune on lick and feed for his weaners last year before he got rid of them.'

Andy sprang out of bed and rummaged through the dresser drawers for his clothes, which he quickly pulled on as he strode to the bathroom. Bec followed, snatching a satin robe and following him in bare feet.

'Are you saying we could take the cows there?' she asked.

'Exactly,' said Andy.

'But they're too weak. They'd die like flies if you tried to truck them out.'

'We won't truck them out,' Andy said, splashing water over his face and neck. 'We'll walk them out.'

'Walk them? There's no feed,' said Rebecca.

'There's no feed here either, and they're still walking around. They might as well be heading to where there's going to be some feed in a few weeks' time.'

Bec trotted along behind him as he marched towards the kitchen. 'Andy... Stop... It's over a hundred kilometres away, there's no water.' She dived around in front of him putting her hands on his chest to stop him.

Andy's wet hair was slicked back from his forehead, his brown eyes no longer sad and defeated, his big shoulders no longer slumped. 'I'll find a way,' he said with such fierce determination that Bec's hands slid away from his chest and she stared dumbly up at his face.

'You will,' she said. 'We're late. I'd better get brekkie on.'

Andy kissed her on the cheek and strode outside. It was Sunday and he started the generator so that George, Sam and Nudding could do their washing. Over the last couple of weeks they'd been slowly moving the cows north to the paddocks where trees on the river channels had dropped most of their leaves and straws of windblown grass lay in divots and ditches on the banks. The starving stock licked up the brittle fare and continued their quest for survival. Andy loaded the Toyota with one hundred kilo lick blocks and set off round the top half of the run. He drove on autopilot, his thoughts galloping and tumbling as he planned his droving trip to Balmacarra.

By the time he returned to the homestead around midday a solid plan was cemented in his mind and he was agitated and impatient to get the ball rolling. While Bec made fresh tea and a sandwich for him he rang Davo. The fortunate friend had just returned on his four-wheeler and was jubilant as he relayed the news that the rain was indeed widespread, running into creeks and filling the dams.

Andy quickly outlined his proposal. He wanted to walk a thousand cows from Coolibah to Balmacarra. He'd pay

Davo for the agistment by leaving an agreed number of females there when the drought broke and by bringing a team of men over to muster the piker bullocks and scrub bulls that had been avoiding Davo when he mustered for years.

'I like it. I like it,' said Davo. 'But mate, there's no water across that track.'

'I'll handle that problem, Davo. Do we have a deal?' asked Andy.

'I'm in,' said Davo, the excitement in his voice nearly matching Andy's enthusiasm. 'I'll cook and bring me dogs for the trip.'

'I'll be over in a couple of days and we'll sort it out in a bit more detail. Better get on to organising this water and some round bales. Cheers, Davo,' said Andy.

'Yeah righto, Andy. Think I'll go and lay in the creek for a while. See if I can soak that water up through me dry old hide,' teased Davo as he ended the conversation. Davo had been squirreling cash away for decades and he was well placed to purchase some cattle at the right price to restock Balmacarra, but Andy didn't know that. Davo knew that the deal would be a real saviour for his friends.

Bec had been sitting at the table listening to Andy's conversation with Davo. When he hung up, he drew in a deep breath, leant across the table and took her hands in his.

'Here's the plan,' he said. 'We try to get a thousand breeders together, the ones we reckon are strong enough to walk there.'

'But it's not a stock route that way,' said Bec.

'Weona's destocked and Gungalla have no stock in the paddock the road goes through,' said Andy. 'There's been no water there for over twelve months. It's all dams in that country, no bores. The mulga should be untouched through there and it'll help us to get them through that last thirty kilometres. All I need is their permission to go through, and I can't see that being a problem.'

'So what about water?' asked Bec.

Andy reached into his shirt pocket for his battered notebook, and showed her the rough map he'd drawn in it. 'It's forty ks to our western border. We have four bores out that way.'

'Yep,' said Bec. 'Then it's a hundred and twenty ks to Balmacarra.'

'Coley hasn't worked for months,' said Andy of his old schoolmate in Coombul. 'All the road contractors in town are out of work. He's got two 20 000 litre tankers just sitting there. I'll buy a couple of poly troughs and he can cart the water from home. I'll get some liquid supplement to add to the water for the cattle. It will help to keep them going. We'll drive across there tomorrow and mark out the camping spots. I reckon we can take them about four to six kilometres a day, depending on the going. We'll have to rest them every third day and fill them up with hay.'

'Hay!' said Bec. 'You'd need so much. It's so expensive.'

'I know, but they won't make it without it and, remember, we'll be going to free grass and saving our nucleus breeders. Fifty years of breeding, Bec,' said Andy, his voice cracking. 'We'll need four hundred round bales, minimum. With all the trucks sitting down around the country we should be able to organise it and get the hay dropped off across the track at each third-day rest stop. Once we get into the mulga, they'll be right. Gungalla's only had a few head down there early when they fluked a storm last January.

It only put a splash in the dam so they had to shift them off again by March. No, the mulga through there should be enough to get them through to Balmacarra.'

'What about the roos through Weona? They'll enjoy a bit of hay before we can get the cattle there. Electric fence won't stop them.'

'A couple of Davo's dogs will, though,' said Andy. 'I'll set up a running chain for them on the sites and Davo can keep them watered and fed. Besides, there can't be many out there; there's no water around.'

'Would it be easier to bring it in a load at a time and have it dropped off the day before or something?' asked Bec.

'No. I just can't risk it. If something happens and it doesn't arrive, we'll be stranded,' said Andy. The plan was crystal clear in his mind. 'By the time we get to Balmacarra with the cows, the new feed from the rain should be grown out and seeding,' Andy said visualising their arrival.

'Sam will have to look after things here. It'll take us about a month to get across there. You and me, George and Nudding will take the cattle along. Davo can take the truck and set up camp. We'll need to order in some more feed for the horses.'

Chapter 9

Andy spent the rest of the day on the phone ringing neighbours, Coley and others, organising trucks for any hay he could secure. Coley had jumped at the chance to help, saying that his missus would be pleased to get rid of him for a while after such a long time sitting around with no work. Andy virtually had to buy hay before it was cut, demand was so high. He decided not to call his bank manager. The money he had to spend would push him over his limit but he'd deal with the bouncing cheques when the breeders were on good feed. The accounts wouldn't fall due until he got the cattle over there. He had to do that first. Every day counted. The hay alone would cost over twenty thousand before freight. Coley was working for nothing and Andy only needed to supply the diesel, but he still had to pay for the water supplement, the troughs and pipe.

At dinner he outlined the plan to the men, who immediately got caught up in his excitement.

George looked Andy in the eye and said, 'I won't be drawin' any of me wages, boss. Not till it rains, hey.'

'Thanks,' said Andy, touched by his friend's understanding and commitment.

'Don't reckon I'll be goin' in to town till the winter's passed either,' said Sam.

'Thanks, Sam,' said Andy, wishing his sister could show a little of the same compassion.

He got back on the phone chasing hay through into the night until Bec pointed out that it was after nine o'clock and people would soon be in bed. Reluctantly Andy put down the phone.

They went to bed but neither of them slept. They talked and talked about the trip, trying to anticipate problems and find solutions. After they'd been over it a hundred times they lay in thoughtful silence in the blackness of the night and waited for daylight.

The week that followed was filled with frantic activity and everyone felt a new sense of purpose. Bec continued to phone all over the country for hay and ordered and packed the supplies for the trip. Andy called in to see his neighbours to talk about coming through their places, and neither of them had any problems with it. They had heard of Davo's rain and were envious of Andy's reprieve but encouraged to see that rain could indeed fall from the sky.

Andy drove the truck in to Coombul to pick up the water supplement and two six-metre poly troughs. George and Nudding ran the bores, shod the horses and packed the camping gear. Sam greased the hobbles, cared for the poddies and started on his garden.

Once the hay was sourced, Andy and Bec started moving the cows to Stockyard bore, cutting out in each paddock, leaving the weakest and taking the strongest on. In no time they were creeping along behind the last mob that would bring together their herd of close to a thousand cows.

Head down, eyes on the ground, Bec rode her mare behind the skeletal beasts. It was mid-morning, the heat was already savage and it rose from the sunburnt earth to scald her face. The shuffling herd didn't bother to bend their heads to the brittle grey stubble that was all that remained of the pastures. Rebecca was watching the grass stubble passing by under her boot wondering how the cattle survived on it when she drew rein abruptly. Her horse tossed its head and shuffled sideways.

Bec slid from the saddle and stared at a tiny grey-green plant growing in a shallow cleft in the soil. Delicately set in a cluster of scalloped oval leaves was a single purple flower. It had five perfect lilac petals and five bright yellow stamens thrust out from its centre in an amazing show of defiance against its circumstances. Bec squatted on her haunches beside the plant and gently stroked the tiny blossom with one finger. She rose and took the water bottle from her saddle and carefully poured a cup of the lukewarm liquid into the crater around the tiny plant.

She lingered for a moment longer, staring with disbelief at the precious little flower and all it stood for. To her it represented hardiness and determination, resourcefulness and hope. It was an inspirational example of what it would take to beat this drought: a monument to how little moisture was required by this dormant land to produce new life. She drew in a deep breath, straightened her back and pulled back her shoulders. *Thanks little flower*, she thought as she remounted her horse and pushed on along the fence.

The first load of hay arrived and Andy went with the trucks to put it out at his chosen locations along the route. As the trucks kept coming they worked virtually around the clock, but the long, hard hours could not dent their enthusiasm for the task. Katherine arrived from Coombul, determined to give a hand.

'Look, I'll just tend to your garden, feed Sam and do the housework for you while you and Andy get ready to go,' she said to Bec.

It was lovely to have another female about the house. She and her mother had always been close, and they talked and talked as they set about tackling the jobs at hand. Despite their still desperate situation, the atmosphere at Coolibah was charged with energy now that they all could focus on doing something instead of languishing in the hopelessness.

A few days before the Coolibah mob was due to leave, Maggie surprised Bec with a visit. They had been speaking a lot on the phone of late as Maggie's pregnancy progressed and the inevitable delivery date neared.

'Hello, Maggie,' called Bec as she walked out to meet Maggie, who was struggling to get a huge box out of the back of her station wagon. 'Let me get that,' Bec added, taking the box out of Maggie's hands.

'I've brought you some things for your big trip,' said Maggie, smiling.

'Come on in, Maggie. Mum's here and the men are all away. I'll put the kettle on. I'm guessing you've brought something that'll go well with a coffee,' said Bec.

'Maggie!' called Katherine, holding her arms out. 'How are you, darling?'

Maggie accepted Katherine's hug and kiss on the cheek with a little blush and a smile. 'I'm fine, thanks, Katherine, but it's been so hot and dry, not good for my skin at all.'

'Look, Mum,' said Bec. 'Maggie has brought a whole box of goodies for our trip. You make the coffee and we'll unpack the surprise.'

Maggie was obviously excited about the gifts she had brought and she became animated as she brought each item out one by one. 'There's six cakes of my homemade lavender soap and some little bags of potpourri for your duffel bag. You'll need some feminine pleasures on the droving trip.' Maggie handed the carefully wrapped packages to Bec.

'I've crocheted you a couple of good strong hand towels as well. You'll need something a bit sturdier when you're cooking over an open fire.' Maggie piled the beautifully crafted items on the table. 'Here's a bottle of our favourite face cream,' she said with a smile.

'Oh no, Maggie,' Bec protested. 'You keep that. We haven't been able to get it for ages.'

'No, no. I got two the other day when I went in for the scan. You take it.' She pressed the squat bottle into Bec's hand and cupped her own over it. 'And a tin of Anzac bickies and two of my fruitcakes. They'll last and they'll travel well,' Maggie said.

Tears pricked Bec's eyes as she embraced her friend. 'I don't think they'll last long, Maggie. They'll all be eaten once the boys discover them. Thank you, you're so thoughtful.'

'That's okay. It's the least I can do,' said Maggie.

'Coffee's made,' said Katherine, bringing the steaming cups to the table.

'One more thing, Bec,' Maggie grinned as she took the last dish out of the box with a flourish. 'Caramel and coffee cheesecake!'

'Oh yum. My favourite. You're really spoiling me now.' Bec took three plates out of the cupboard and brought a knife to slice the delicacy.

Later that afternoon as she waved goodbye to Maggie, Bec felt an unexpected shiver of foreboding as she watched her friend drive away. She didn't like to be leaving her at this time. Maggie had no one else to turn to.

Inside the house Katherine was clearing the table.

'Mum,' said Bec. 'Can you give Maggie a ring every couple of days? She's often on her own and . . . she's got nobody out there other than the ringer, Lance, when the boys are away at school. Doug treats her worse than a dog and he doesn't seem to care or understand that she's in a pretty delicate situation with this pregnancy; she's not a teenager anymore.'

'I know. He is truly disgusting, that man. Ooh, he gives me the creeps!' said Katherine, shuddering. 'I'll make sure to stay in touch with Maggie. Try not to worry, Bec.'

Bec sat unmoving in the kitchen chair.

'You okay?' asked Katherine, putting an arm around Bec's shoulders.

'I'm not sure, Mum. I've formed a really deep connection with Maggie and her baby. Perhaps it's because Andy and I are so desperate to have a baby of our own. I think I'm getting a little bit silly about it,' said Bec.

'Bec, you're not being silly. You have a natural connection to all babies. Look at the pen full of poddies you have, and how much you love puppies, birds. You just love babies, so you're naturally going to be very connected to your best friend's baby. Just allow yourself to enjoy the pregnancy with Maggie. You'll need to pay attention because your own baby will be along all in good time.'

Bec smiled at her mother, not quite believing her comforting words but thankful for them all the same. 'Well, it's no good sitting around here brooding, better get out and feed the poddies and I've still got packing to do for the move,' she said, getting up and striding out of the room.

'I'll get tea on,' Katherine called after her.

Chapter 10

After feeding out the first load of hay to the assembled breeder cattle the afternoon before, Andy, Bec, Nudding, George and Davo set off with the mob for Balmacarra at four o'clock the next morning.

The cows were easy to pick up from the bore. They hadn't left a skerrick of hay on the ground and they had hung around waiting for another miracle. The summer moon was full and sunk behind the shadowy ridges in the west as if beckoning to them to come that way. Its kindly glow was all too soon replaced by the fierce, sullen glare of the sun that burned into their backs like a pursuant foe.

The temperature was well into the forties by the time they reached their first stop, Black Tank bore. There was a little paddock around the tank and a trough so Andy put the horses in there and everyone except Davo drove back to the homestead.

Davo stretched out under a gidgee tree, put his battered hat over his face and slept. His four best dogs, Hopscotch, Tiptoes, Bundy and Boozer, circled the mob. Not that they needed holding. After waiting their turn to drink, the cattle sank to the powdery dust and rested too.

Each day they drove the cattle on to the next water on Coolibah Creek where there were holding paddocks. The drovers returned to the homestead to sleep each night until the fourth night, when Davo took the camp truck loaded with swags and assorted camping gear, bags of feed for the horses, a generator and a freezer, fuel and water tanks and other essentials to Rainbow bore, the last water on Coolibah Creek. Despite the heat and the dismal landscape the travellers' spirits were high. Davo's cheerful personality and sense of humour enhanced the mood of the crew.

The first major test for the droving trip came when the mob reached the first dry camp through the boundary at Weona. There was no water and Andy and Bec had to test their watering system.

Coley and Andy had fashioned brackets along the side of the tankers to carry the troughs. The troughs were relatively light and easily unloaded. Like silver anacondas, big flexi hoses snaked out from the rear of the tankers and locked to the trough inlets. Andy drove steel pickets into the ground at the four corners of each trough and in the middle, and then twisted ten-gauge wire between them to hold the troughs in place. Once the troughs were positioned, filled with water and medicated with liquid supplement, Bec and Nudding cut out about seventy head from the lead of the herd. Davo set his dogs up on an imaginary line and they held the remainder of the mob back while Nudding and Bec took the leaders forward to the water.

The dogs spaced themselves evenly across the face of the waiting mob. Alert and fast, they scanned the line and ran at any transgressor that broke away and put it back in the herd. Nudding and Bec held the cattle on the watering trough making sure they all went in to drink before moving them past the tankers to where Andy blocked them up and held them. It took a couple of hours to water the cattle this way but everything worked perfectly. After they'd finished watering they moved the mob on about half a kilometre to where Davo had set up camp earlier and rolled out some hay. The hungry cattle devoured the hay, finally sinking to the dusty earth at sundown. The cows were too exhausted to bring up a cud to chew and they turned their heads back to their bony shoulders and slept.

That evening, the cheery mood of the drovers had not been quelled by the excruciating heat of the day and they sat in the glow of the fire and enjoyed Davo's corned beef, complete with white onion sauce and four vegetables. The old-timer's stories were captivating as they sipped billy tea in the welcome coolness of the night air. They yarned about droughts, dogs and horses, droving days of old and floods. Davo told of the time they swam fifteen hundred steers across the flooded Diamantina River channels. There were five kilometres of channels to cross.

'Yeah, we were covered in 'em. Big orange centipedes, long as your hand and thick as your finger.' Davo shivered as he relived the yarn. 'They were all over the horse's neck, all across the rump, thousands of 'em, hitching a ride and getting out of the water. They don't bite, you know,' Davo explained to his audience who were riveted and wide-eyed as he painted a vivid picture. 'Not while you're in the water. You just keep swimming and they go with you. Just bummin' a ride.' Davo's smile showed an uneven line of tobacco-stained teeth.

'Then when you get out the other side you just flick 'em off. Same with snakes. Seen lots of snakes in the flood-waters – spiders, everything that creeps and crawls.'

Davo loved to tell a yarn and he was a good storyteller. Nudding's eyes were huge and his mouth was slightly agape as he listened to the story. He kept glancing to his left and right into the inky night as if the fiends may be just out of sight. He seemed to relax when Davo got onto the story about the camel trains that used to pass through the district, labouring under their loads for strange Afghan men with swarthy skin and fierce black eyes. Tough men and animals that took on the unknown with a brave pioneering spirit and opened up the Australian outback.

Andy tossed out the dregs of his tea and stood up, stretching his aching muscles and announcing that sleep would be good. After rinsing their pannikins and saying goodnight everyone melted away into the darkness. They lay in their swags listening to the rhythmic grinding of the horses' teeth finishing their night feed. The air was still and strangely silent without the sound of busy crickets or hunting owls that would normally be heard if the land were not gripped by drought.

Davo threw back another half a cup of rum and settled down for the night. The others had moved well away from the cook's van with their swags but he could hear someone snoring and he smiled as he closed his eyes. It felt good to be able to help Andy out. He was enjoying his new role as saviour and the uplifting company for a change. Davo had known the Roberts' family all his life and had watched Louise and Andy grow up. He felt responsible for them since they had lost their parents. Davo sighed. They were good kids, Andy and Bec. They deserved a break. He stretched and yawned in his swag. The rum had numbed the aches and pains of age and, as he waited for sleep to come, the unmistakable sound of a dingo howling drifted to him from far away on the still night air, plaintive and mournful. Like the horrid black crows, the dingos had been thriving and feasting on the spoils of the drought. This one was a long way from water though and Davo deduced that it had probably followed them curiously, intrigued by the scent of his working dogs' spoor. *Every dog has his day*, he thought, and drifted into slumber.

༄

So the trip went on. The days starting at 3.30am and ending around 9pm, passing like cold honey falling from a spoon, so slow as to seem that time was suspended in the watery mirages that floated like illusionary lakes on the open plains. Steadily they led the cattle towards Balmacarra. Many hours were spent waiting out the heat of the day under the meagre shade of the stunted gidgee trees. The ever-present mocking *argh, argh, argh* of the crows the only sound as clusters of whirling dust devils circled about them like curious ghouls. Weary bodies waited for exhaustion to overcome their discomfort and bring them fitful oblivious sleep. Coley's comings and goings with the water tankers were always a welcome distraction and the dogs often provided amusement with their antics and squabbles. The cows were travelling well, the supplement in their water and the roughage of the hay were giving them sufficient strength to shuffle along each day as they crept closer to green grass and salvation. Rebecca was sure they knew they were going to a better place.

It was midday and the drovers and the mob were camped up to wait out the heat of the day when Bec saw the tall plumes of dust that announced a vehicle approaching. *Must be Gordon*, she thought, referring to the owner of Gungalla whose land they were passing through.

She kicked half-burned sticks into the coals and soft white ashes of the fire and filled the billy can in anticipation, looking forward to the visit to pass the time. Andy had gone back to Coolibah Creek with Coley in the truck to fill up with water and Davo had gone on ahead to feed his dogs that were guarding the hay further on. Nudding and George were dozing with the dogs on the other side of the herd. Bec's canine companions, Hopscotch and Tiptoes, Davo's German coolies, pricked their ears and sprang from their rest, trotting out and barking up the road as the vehicle approached. Drawing her bottom lip over her teeth Rebecca whistled sharply and the dogs stopped instantly and scampered back to her, sitting behind her legs.

The welcoming smile she had ready for Gordon vanished from her face and her expression changed when she recognised the car and the driver as they arrived, stopped and were subsequently enveloped in the billowing cloud of dust the station wagon had created. The busy, bustling figure of

Gail Burns, the new local stock route and lands protection officer, alighted from the car and strode purposefully out of the dust towards Bec, looking crisp and fresh in her immaculate khakis. The locals had already christened her 'Little Hitler'. An ex-police cadet who hadn't made the grade, she was a nasty individual with limited knowledge of her new role but a whole heap of bad attitude. Countless stories of her aggravating ways were circulating round the community but Bec had not yet encountered the 'wet behind the ears' enforcer.

'What are you doing here?' Bec murmured under her breath. Her eyes narrowed and her hands came up to her hips as she braced herself for what was obviously going to be some sort of confrontation.

Gail started shaking her pointed finger and gesturing towards the cattle before she reached Bec.

'You can't do this!' she said through clenched teeth.

Bec made an indiscernible signal with her hand and the dogs resumed their sitting position, leaning against her legs protectively, sensing the hostility of the visitor. Gail marched right up to her. She was much shorter than Bec, her complexion ruddy and her build stocky. She pushed herself really close and continued to waggle her finger right under Bec's nose.

'This is not a designated stock route! It's illegal to travel stock through here. You think you can do what you damn well like!' Gail ranted.

Bec just stood there, hands on hips, clamping her jaw shut as an incredible anger rose up inside her. She could no longer decipher the words still spewing from the official's mouth as she was overcome by a deep-seated wrath, anger about the drought grinding them into the ground, anger at over-educated 'experts' with no practical knowledge or experience of her cherished land, anger at the condescending attitude and the ridiculous regulatory power people like Gail Burns had been granted.

All Rebecca's pent-up fury transferred to her tightly clenched fist and she exploded like a match touched to petrol. Her work-hardened knuckles smashed into the left side of Gail's sneering mouth. The sharp edge of the official's eye tooth sliced through her lip and laid bare the snow-white cartilage of Bec's knuckle. The force of the blow knocked Burns backwards and she landed on her plump posterior, stubby legs thrown into the air, blood trickling from her already swollen lip and a look of absolute shock in her eyes.

Bec shook her jarred and bleeding hand. 'We have written permission from the owners, and a permit,' she said quietly, fuming as she raged within.

Regaining her wits Gail sprang to her feet and rushed at Bec, screaming and groping for her hair. Bec ducked the charge and drove her shoulder up under her foe's ribs, pushing forward with her legs in a perfect rugby tackle she'd learnt from her brother. Burns staggered backwards once again, losing balance and grabbing two handfuls of Bec's hair as they fell to the ground. The impact of the fall knocked the wind from the official's lungs and she loosened her grip. In an instant Bec was sitting astride her, ready to have another go.

Arriving at the scene, George grabbed her from behind and plucked her from her victim in one smooth movement. Nudding controlled the dogs that moved to run in and nip Burns' legs.

The inspector struggled to her feet, her breath rasping in her throat, her face bloodied and red, and her eyes full of venom.

'I'll get you, you bitch!' she screamed. 'I'll get you.' Still mumbling she stormed to her car wiping the blood from her mouth on her sleeve.

They watched her roar off down the road, grinding the gears and wavering off the road.

Rebecca loosened herself from George's grip and went to get water to wash her injured hand. 'Could get bloody rabies or God knows what sort of disease from that disgusting bit of gear!' she rambled to herself as she scrubbed the open wound. She took the first-aid box out from behind the seat of the car and poured Dettol over her still trembling knuckles then pulled the split skin together with a closure strip and bandaged it.

George, with his usual cat-like stealth, materialised at the door of the cook's van. 'You alright, Missus?' he inquired.

Bec cradled her hand in her lap and stared at him with unseeing eyes. Huge tears rolled down her face as she came crashing down from the mountainous heights of her anger.

George turned away, embarrassed by her bare emotions. 'I'll make a billy, Missus. You'll be right. Boss'll be back soon.'

He walked away and Bec heard him barking orders at Nudding.

'What you standin' there lookin' for, boy? Get round the other side of them cattle.'

Andy turned up an hour later and Bec told him what had happened.

'You what?' he asked incredulously.

'I flattened Gail Burns,' Bec repeated slowly, turning her face away and casting her eyes to the ground.

'But . . . When? What?' Andy stammered.

'Oh she came here all flags flying, yelling at me about how we couldn't travel the cattle this way and I suppose I just snapped,' said Bec, her head bowed to study the bandage on her hand, which she picked at nervously, feeling a little ashamed of her extreme reaction.

Andy took her injured hand and cupped it gently in his. He placed his finger under her chin and tilted her face up. Bec looked into his deep brown eyes and immediately recognised the merriment and mischief in them. He pulled her up off the chair and kissed her, hugging her to his chest.

'Can't leave you alone for a minute, hey boss,' he said and started to laugh. 'Talk about Saltbush Bill!'

Bec stiffened in his arms and pushed herself away.

'It's not funny!' she said sharply.

But Andy was still laughing and it was such a wonderful, contagious sound that a smile tugged at the corners of her mouth. When he started shadow sparring around her, she let go and started laughing too.

Chapter 11

On the road to Balmacarra no one brought up the subject of the fight. It wasn't something to be discussed by the men in Bec's presence but all of them had a quiet smile to themselves about the incident and their respect for Rebecca went up another notch.

They had the cattle watered and fed for the night and Davo was holding the floor again. He pushed back his old Akubra with the 'Slim Dusty' shape and style and lowered his gravelly voice almost to a whisper. George and Nudding, Bec and Andy all leant forward. It was the tactic of all good yarn spinners, to get an audience's full attention.

'Yeees,' Davo drawled. 'King Canute. Hey Andy, I don't reckon you should bring them fancy pants bulls of yours over to Balmacarra. Ol' Canute might be a bit rough on 'em,' he teased.

Andy had been feeding a group of his best bulls for a long time in anticipation of a break in the drought. He didn't want to lose their highly sought after and expensive genetics. Davo thought they were too pampered and sooky and loved to bait Andy about it.

'Who's this Canute bloke, Davo?' Nudding prompted, sensing there was a good yarn behind that name.

'King Canute was the greatest and bravest warrior of all the Vikings and king of England, Denmark, Norway and Sweden, all at the one time. That was a thousand years ago, Nudding, way over the ocean on top of the world,' said Davo before pausing for effect, raising his leathery old face like a Shakespearian actor, and booming out, 'Let all men know how empty and worthless is the power of kings, for there is none worthy of the name but God, whom heaven, earth and sea obey.'

Davo was quite the actor. 'Oh, I love history. So much to learn from it,' he said wistfully. And then, blinking and shifting in his seat, bringing himself back to the story he continued, 'King Canute. That's the name I gave the biggest, meanest scrub bull I've ever seen. He lives there at home, wanders the whole place. Fences don't stop him. Nothin' stops him,' he said as he rolled a smoke with gnarled and hardened hands.

'I only saw him once. I knew he was there 'cause I seen his tracks all the time, big as your dinner plate and deep into the ground. I even camped out on one waterhole that was almost dry and thought I might see him comin' in to water at night but he was way too cunnin' for me. I found his tracks a couple of days later, twenty kilometres away. No, it was just luck, the night I saw him.'

Davo took a long draw on the rollie between his tar-stained fingers. 'I was pokin' about down at Junction paddock lookin' for a roo for the dogs. There was a big full moon, bright as day, so the roos were a bit shifty. I pulled up to pour a rum and I s'pose I had a couple and dozed off.

'It was about three when I woke up. I was getting out of the car to have a leak when I noticed movement on the flat in front of me. I rubbed me eyes and stayed quiet and still, trying to see him in the moonlight. He had his head down feedin' and I thought I musta been in the horrors, 'cause he looked to be the size of an elephant. Then he lifted his head up. Well, me old heart turned over in me chest when I seen the size of him, and the horns!' Davo held both his arms out above his head. 'Like that! As thick as my arm but longer.

'He'd be six feet high at the shoulder, at least. Got a Brahman cross in 'im. But the strangest thing is his face. He's got a white blaze on his face in the perfect shape of a dagger. I tell you I could see it clear as a bell when he looked at me, that big bastard. Oops, sorry, Bec. Anyhow, I christened him "King Canute" because his big horns reminded me of the Vikings and he must be the king of them all.

'If we're lucky we might run into him when we muster. Or unlucky maybe; I wouldn't like to tangle with the big bugger. I've seen a few bulls pretty ripped up. Gotta be him. Then of course there's the ones you don't see, that don't live to show the scars of a run-in with ole King Canute. I'll show you, when we get there, where he's been tearin' down the mulga. I'll show you how far up the tree he can reach. You won't believe it. Naah, Andy better keep them pretty boys at home I think,' repeated Davo, winking at Nudding.

'Maybe you're right, Davo. I believe every word you say, mate. Not like some people who think you like to exaggerate to make a better yarn of it,' said Andy with a grin.

'Mmm. Well, we'll see,' muttered Davo, standing up wearily, his old frame feeling the strain of the big trip. 'Time for a nightcap. Night everyone.'

⁂

George wasn't sure why he woke but he lay on his back in his swag, suddenly wide awake. He sat up. A strange feeling came over him, a weird sensation, an eerie sort of thing. Mystified, he got up, pushed his bare feet into his boots and hobbled around the end of the cook's van towards where the mob was camped up.

He stopped dead in his tracks, rooted to the spot. A bobbing ball of fire was bouncing across the backs of the sleeping cattle. It looked to be about the size of a football. George saw that it wasn't fire, but in fact a sort of orange glow. Its erratic cavorting was mesmerising.

'What the . . .?' George whispered.

The cattle seemed not to have noticed the light. Yet it appeared to be landing on their backs and flitting from beast to beast like a honey bee feeding on a flower garden.

'Min min,' muttered George.

Not wanting to spook the cattle, he tapped gently on the side of the van and called lowly, 'Davo.' The light continued its merry dancing. 'Hey, Davo!'

After a moment George heard the rustle of Davo's bedding.

'Look, Davo, min min here!' George could hear the awe and fear in his own hoarse voice.

Davo padded barefooted to where George was standing at the end of the van.

'Oh yeah. Min min, George,' he confirmed.

As the pair watched, the glowing ball divided and then there were three orange lights hovering and darting randomly about, just above the cattle. The strange thing was that they seemed to emit no light. There were no shadows, nor were the cattle illuminated.

George's Aboriginal heritage took a firm hold of him, and Davo could see the whites of his eyes in his dark face rolling around in fear.

'Min min! Davo! Bad news!' George moved with a soundless, fluid grace and in the blink of an eye was inside the caravan, holding the door closed with both hands from the inside.

Davo chuckled and watched on, fascinated by the phenomenon. He'd seen min min lights before but he'd never seen them while he had a mob of cattle in hand. He'd heard yarns about how some mobs seemed to be entirely unaware of the light and tales of others that had rushed and stampeded, causing mayhem in the darkness. Min min lights couldn't be explained; everyone had a theory but nothing had been proven. He'd better get Andy.

Just as he was about to turn away, the three lights came together, colliding and forming a single glow again. Suddenly the orb was still. It looked like it was shimmering or vibrating. The hairs stood up on the back of Davo's neck as the light appeared to be 'looking' at him. Then, still immobile, the light intensified, gradually at first, then more rapidly. It got brighter and brighter until it was blindingly white. When it reached this bright, white state, it suddenly careered away, at an incredible pace, into the distance, and disappeared, leaving Davo standing there, barefoot and bare-chested, staring after it.

George's hands were still clamped around the door handle as he peered out through the window into the blackness of the sky. Davo walked to the steps and yanked the door open, almost pulling George out with it.

'Might as well light a fire, George. It's three o'clock. Show's over.'

'Yeah, Davo.' George cleared his throat and brought his voice down an octave. 'They don't come back, hey, them min mins. He won't be back tonight that bloke, hey?' he said, still standing in the doorway.

'No, he won't be back. Come on, mate. Let me in so I can get the wash dish,' said Davo.

George descended and melted into the murky night where, upon finding his swag, he jumped into it boots and all and pulled the tarp up over his head.

༒

The trip went on and to Bec's relief and delight everything had gone to plan. For some of the cows, though, the battle for survival had been too long. Andy had to destroy six head that got down and couldn't rise. It was a task that still broke his big heart, placing the gun to the animal's head, seeing the suffering in her eyes and pulling the trigger. It didn't ever get any easier but they had to push on with the strong. It was the night of the drover's final camp before the next day's walk to Balmacarra where the sweet, green grass awaited them. Andy and Bec were lying in their swag under the spectacular star-studded sky that had been their ceiling for over a month.

Coolibah Creek

'I didn't punch her because I thought she would try to stop us from taking the cattle on. I just lost it, Andy,' Bec said, out of the blue. 'I mean, your family has loved this land for over a century. We are the ones who make a living from it, who go through everything that nature throws at us every day and continue to learn and live with the land not just on it. Mongrels like Gail Burns just charge about with a three-day course certificate in their hand and a logo on their chest pushing people around. It's so demeaning and condescending. There's no respect. Surely we can work together if everyone could change their attitude. Guess I can't really talk after what happened. I just blew a fuse.'

'That's fair enough. We all do that sometimes,' said Andy.

As Bec talked on, Andy cradled her in his arms and lay quietly, realising that she needed to get it all off her chest and he just needed to listen.

'Dad was saying the other day that Justine Rand has started up an environmental consultancy business in Coombul. She's all trumped up with an honours degree, a new Porsche and a full head of steam. Apparently the word is that she's after some of the dollars around the environmental assessments for listing wetland areas for protection as well as taking advantage of all of the new mining exploration activity in the Telford Shire. Justine Rand, now that's one woman I wouldn't like to tangle with,' Bec said sleepily as the exertions of another day on the road began to take their toll on her.

'Our dream of the artesian project and organic production could strike a hurdle if all of this mining exploration comes into production. It would be horrible if the water was contaminated... It's our greatest asset – our unaltered natural landscapes, chemical free – if only we could all work together. Oh well, I'm just too tired to think about all of that at the moment.'

Bec yawned and snuggled in closer to Andy and he felt her surrender to the tide of exhausted sleep.

Chapter 12

Out on the endless plains close to Balmacarra a westerly wind blew fine grit into the faces of the drovers. The demands of the long drive were reaching deep into the dwindling reserves of them all and the straggly, road-weary group – people, horses, dogs and cattle – plodded on oblivious to the stinging dirt, the presence of the menacing, burning, orange sun and the surrounding sea of bare red earth. The ordeal of the trip had induced a state of suspended consciousness in them all, of placid acceptance of their conditions. Even the close proximity of their destination failed to drag them out of the doldrums.

Rebecca rode in the lead of the mob. Turning sideways in the saddle, she looked into the eyes of the lead cow. The ravages of drought had failed to diminish her elegance and the quality of her breeding. Bec hated the look in her eyes.

It was as if she was saying, *I trusted you. Where are we going? I have no choice but to follow.*

The deep black pools of her eyes were sunken in her white face. She was tall and, though emaciated, her frame showed superior spring of rib, a strong straight back and perfect legs and feet. She was a matriarch.

The driving wind stalled and changed direction slightly, swinging to the north. The leader lifted her head and flared the nostrils in her inky black nose, revealing a flash of scarlet. She pivoted slightly into the breeze, raising her nose high in the air and testing the scent. Her weary followers stopped behind her and, after a moment, raised their own noses to the sky, waving their heads from side to side, snorting and turning, smelling the hot air.

'We're almost there, girls,' Rebecca said to the cows. 'I knew we could do it.'

An hour later the cows could smell the fresh green feed, which was growing less than three kilometres away. The sweet aroma of the muddy creeks wafted on the wind and filled the cows' lungs as if it were a tonic. Like some heady drug, the scent-laden wind washed over the herd and brought a spring to their step, a change to their demeanour.

Rebecca and Andy could never describe the feeling of elation and triumph they felt when they reached the summit of a stony ridge on the Balmacarra boundary and looked out over the winding gidgee gullies lined with soft green grasses and juicy herbages. They breathed in the sweetness of what looked like a veritable garden of Eden to the drought-worn crew.

'Keep 'em movin',' called Andy as the cattle dropped their heads to the ground and stuffed their mouths with the smorgasbord of plants. 'We'll have to get 'em to the yards before they get too big a gutful of this green feed.'

Andy knew that the dramatic change in diet for the cows could be fatal, the juices from the green feed creating an overproduction of gases in the stomach leading to extreme bloating and an excruciating death. The herd would have to be gradually allowed on to the pasture, day by day. He had repaired the old yards so they could feed the cattle out during the morning and then lock them off the grass, allowing them a little more time out each day. Nudding had used the Toyota to drag a section of railway line through the yards until the thick mat of pigweed was uprooted and dried. The weed was highly toxic to stock on dry feed when consumed in large amounts.

Once they had entered the area where rain had fallen, sticky black flies greeted them in swarms, clustering in the corners of their eyes and crawling with clinging legs on their skin.

'It's even good to see the flies,' said Bec, riding up beside Andy, so close that their legs touched.

She smiled up at him, her hazel eyes dancing with excitement. They both felt a charge of sexual energy surge through them as their eyes met. Andy reached down from his lofty height on the tall gelding and plucked Bec from her horse. He swung her on to his lap and kissed her hungrily.

'Hey . . .' she protested without conviction, pushing herself away from him. But the hand she placed on his chest felt the hard muscle under his shirt and the heat of his body. 'Everybody's watching!' she went on before wrapping her arms around his neck and kissing him back with equal passion.

'We made it, love,' said Andy, suddenly very still in the saddle. The satisfaction and relief were evident in his voice.

'Never doubted you for an instant,' Bec replied and squeezed him a little harder, her heart filled with pride and admiration for the man she loved so much.

*

The spirits of the whole team had lifted and everybody was jovial and busy with the task of yarding the mob. The hungry cattle were almost impossible to drive through sweet pastures and Davo's dogs were working hard, barking and nipping at the cattle's heels. Their noisy chorus somehow added to the celebratory mood of the day.

Nudding took off his hat and wiped the sweat from his forehead. He smiled a broad white smile as he looked over and saw the boss and the missus canoodling on the horse. His thoughts drifted to the flashing eyes of a girl he knew back home.

The marauding flies swarmed about his sweaty head, drinking the moisture from his skin. 'Ow!' said Nudding as he felt a sting on his temple. 'Ow!' He swatted at the insects crowding around his hairline.

He rolled the squashed body between his fingers and held it out on his palm to see what had bitten him. It was a native bee. 'Honey!' he said, saliva forming in his mouth as he remembered the delicious sweet taste of the wild honey stolen from the native bees' nest.

He wasn't supposed to go after the honey. His mother always told him to let his brothers or cousins get it because he was allergic to bee stings. He thought that she was just an old worrier. The lumps that came up from the bites were itchy for a few days but they were a small price to pay for the bounty of the honey.

He replaced his hat and sat very still. It was going to be difficult to pick out the bees from the flies. They were about the same size but the bees had a mustard yellow portion on their body. However, with his keen eyesight he soon distinguished the faint line of bees that led a trail to their hive.

'Ah . . . I see you little bees,' he said under his breath as he touched his heels to his horse and set off after them. 'Take me to your house,' he said, already tasting the honey on his tongue.

He didn't have to go far before he came to the tree where he could see bees entering a hollow in the branch. He studied the height of the hollow trying to guess whether he could reach it by standing up in the saddle or whether he'd have to climb the tree. He decided he could probably reach it, so he dropped the reins and placed his hands on the pommel of the saddle, and in one quick spring was perched in the seat like a frog. He spoke to the gelding to steady him and then stood up in the saddle, face upturned, arm outstretched.

Nudding's mouth dropped open as he balanced on the saddle and stretched up to reach the nest. As he inhaled he drew into his throat one of the bees from the cloud that was surrounding the prize.

The bee stuck on his tonsils and bit him in the soft wet tissue. Nudding sat back down in the saddle and took up the reins, coughing all the while, spitting and hawking trying to dislodge the biting insect.

With growing agitation Nudding reached for his water bottle. He quickly unscrewed the top and filled his mouth with the lukewarm water, tossing his head back and gargling loudly before spitting the foamy liquid to the ground and taking another swig. His throat had begun to itch and he felt as if there was something stuck on one side of it. He tried swallowing hard in an attempt to relieve the itch. Then his scalp started to tingle and itch and he tore off his hat and dragged his fingers through his thick black hair, scratching at the rapidly increasing irritation.

Nudding realised something was really wrong. His eyes widened in panic and he dug his heels sharply into the gelding's sides and urged him forward.

Gotta find the missus, he thought.

※

Bec saw Nudding approaching at the gallop. She smiled and wondered if one of the numerous flying insects that were flushed from the grass by the moving herd had settled on him somewhere.

But the smile faded and died on her face when she saw the panic-stricken look in his eyes as his horse came to a skidding halt in front of her. She could see puffy bags of fluid forming along his jawline and heard the whistle of his windpipe as he inhaled.

Nudding couldn't speak but was gesticulating wildly with his arms and pointing into his mouth where his tongue was now so swollen that it was protruding and pushing his bottom lip forward. Bec put her two index fingers to her mouth and turned in Andy's direction. She whistled loudly and when he turned towards her, waved her arms to signal for him to come quickly. He and the others were just pushing the last of the cattle into the yard.

Coolibah Creek

Nudding had slid off his horse and was leaning against her shoulder, both hands to his throat as his lungs laboured to draw enough oxygen through the narrowing trachea.

'Try to be calm, Nudding. Everything's going to be okay. Just lift your arms up over the saddle,' she said, lifting them for him and leaning him against his mount to open up his chest and help make his struggle for breath easier. 'Now calm down, mate. Just breathe slowly, just breathe slowly.'

Bec could see the little hollow in the middle of his chest where the collarbones met being sucked right in by the labouring lungs. She resisted the urge to ask him questions; he needed to concentrate on getting air. The swelling around his neck made it obvious that he was having some sort of allergic reaction and she recognised he was in real trouble. Her mind raced as she tried to keep her voice calm and gently stroked the stricken lad's heaving back with her hand.

The Balmacarra homestead was thirty kilometres away. The UHF radio was probably out of range for the neighbouring property. They had to get to a phone and call the Flying Doctor. Bec remembered the time before satellite phones when every vehicle had a VHF radio in it – a radio that was powerful enough to contact the Flying Doctor channel – but as technology marched on, those radios had disappeared. All properties had a medical chest at the homestead, and Davo had one, but they were too far away for this situation.

Andy arrived and leapt from his horse. 'What is it? What's wrong?'

Nudding turned his head towards him and Andy was taken aback by the youth's grotesquely swollen face and the pleading look of panic in his eyes that were now almost closed by the gathering fluid. The whistling sound of his breathing was becoming more high-pitched.

'Go. Get the Toyota. Hurry,' he said to Bec, who immediately vaulted onto her horse and yelled at the mount, galloping wildly across the flat to where Davo was parked under a tree giving instructions to his dogs.

Andy spoke in a soothing voice to the stricken lad. 'You'll be right, mate. Try to take it easy. Something must have bitten you. Keep your arms up. Draw it in slowly.'

Suddenly the whistling stopped. Nudding spun around towards Andy and grabbed him. His terrified fingers dug deeply into Andy's shoulders. He tried to open his jaw further but his tongue was so large that it filled his mouth. There was absolutely nothing that Andy could do.

Nudding read the look of helplessness in the boss's eyes and, within the small area of his pupils that were still showing through the slits that were once his eyes, Andy saw the abject fear of the dying boy. Nudding sunk to his knees, clutching at his throat and then falling on to all fours heaving and convulsing for oxygen.

Andy got down with him. 'Hang on, mate. Hang on. You'll come right.'

Andy could see the Toyota bouncing across the flat. His mind was in turmoil, frantic. He knew what he had to do. He'd done it once before. He'd found one of his stud bull calves with a bone stuck in its throat, about to give up the struggle to live as the swelling of the tissue around the bone closed off its airways. It'd been easy for Andy at the time to unsheathe his pocket knife and puncture the windpipe, allowing the animal to breathe while he prised its mouth open and retrieved the obstruction from the back of its throat. But this was different.

It's just the same, he told himself as Nudding's body went slack and he slumped forward onto his face. Andy caught him and rolled him over. He sat flat on his backside on the ground and put one of his legs under the back of Nudding's neck, allowing the now balloon-like head to loll down between his legs. His fingers fumbled with the buckle on his knife belt as Bec and Davo screeched to a halt and came running up to him.

'Get the first-aid box. I need some antiseptic for the knife. Go! Hurry!'

Bec tore back to the car and grabbed the first-aid box from behind the seat. She jerked it open and all its contents spilled to the ground. She picked up the antiseptic and unscrewed the lid as she ran back to Andy.

'Pour it over the knife,' said Andy, his face anxious. 'Get a towel or a shirt or something.'

Bec tried to keep her rising panic in check as she ran back to the vehicle.

Davo sat down beside Andy.

'Gotta do it, mate. It's his only chance. Lucky you're a good man on the knife, hey.' Andy knew that Davo was trying to reassure him.

'Push his head down, Davo,' he said. 'It's got to be arched back to make the windpipe stick up.'

'Right,' said Davo, pushing down on the boy's forehead.

Andy took a deep breath and placed the finger and thumb of his left hand along either side of Nudding's windpipe. The incision needed to be vertical to avoid any chance of cutting the arteries alongside it. He pushed down gently with his hand to locate the gristly windpipe underneath the swollen tissue and with the sharp pocket knife, sliced the shiny black skin. His cut exposed the white ribbed hose-like windpipe lying in bright red blood. Without hesitation Andy made another incision and punctured the gristly substance. Immediately Nudding's oxygen-starved lungs expanded and sucked in the air through the opening causing the edges of the wound to vibrate and flutter.

'Get the pen out of the glove box,' Andy said to Bec, who was hovering nearby.

She quickly returned with the biro. Andy removed the ink stem and handed the casing back to Bec to douse with the antiseptic. Then Andy gently inserted the hollow plastic tube into the quivering wound. He reached up with his free hand and into it Bec placed the wad of cotton wool she'd found in the first-aid kit.

'Get me the bandage,' he said as he deftly wound the cotton wool around the pen to form a seal. With Davo's and Bec's help, he then bound the wound, comforted by the steady rise and fall of Nudding's chest.

'I've sent George back to the camp to take the truck on to Balmacarra and call the Flying Doctor. I wasn't sure what we could do here,' said Bec, plonking down on shaky legs beside the trio in the dirt, throwing one arm across her husband's shoulders, feeling him tremble.

'We'll give him a couple of minutes then get him into the back of the Toyota,' said Andy. The shaft of the biro looked a startling blue, protruding from Nudding's throat as it whistled rhythmically with his breathing.

The patient didn't regain consciousness until they reached Balmacarra, where they were greeted by George, who trotted out to the vehicle with the news that they were lucky: the Flying Doctor was in the air on his way back to town with a patient with a broken leg.

Coolibah Creek

'He should be here soon, Missus. They wasn't far away he said,' said George, feeling proud of himself for doing his part in the rescue mission.

'I'll go down to the strip and wait for him,' said Davo, climbing out of the back of the Toyota and walking towards the old camp truck. 'Put the billy on, George. I need a rum but I s'pose a cuppa tea'll have to do for the moment.'

He did have a rum, and another and another and quite a few others later that night when they had Nudding safely in the Flying Doctor's care. It had been quite a day. Davo was singing loudly when Andy and Bec left him to go to bed.

'It's amazing how being so close to the face of death makes you feel so much more alive,' said Bec as she lay cradled in Andy's arms. 'You truly amaze me, my darling. I love you so much.'

'Just something that had to be done and, hey, . . . I love you too,' he replied, pulling her closer. The comforting stroking of Bec's hands became something entirely different as she arched her body against his and kissed him.

Chapter 13

Taking over a billion years to form, under immense pressure one hundred and fifty kilometres from the earth's surface, close to the planet's molten centre, the diamonds had been catapulted violently upwards with an immeasurable force. A deep origin volcano's lava had ripped through thousands of layers of rock and earth with extraordinary power. This rare set of circumstances had led to an eruption so powerful that it forced continental plates apart and continued upwards over a hundred kilometres towards the surface.

Five hundred million years ago some of the diamonds were scattered about and set in igneous rock, while others clung to the edges of the volcanic tube that had propelled them upwards. Over eons the rock was eroded and broken down, freeing the impermeable hard diamonds. As the centuries advanced, plants and animals evolved and a rainforest formed above them. Constant rains washed and moved soil and pebbles but the heavier, denser diamonds settled and lodged in long lines along the edges of the stream, precious and concealed.

Time marched on and the rainforest was consumed by an ocean before the land once again pushed upwards to disperse the inland sea and expose itself to the sun. The diamond lode now lay at a depth of less than a kilometre in the form of a tee. A seam lay horizontal in the ancient riverbed buried way underground and the other seams ran vertically down either side of the volcanic tube crater. The crater formed a series of bathtub-type structures five hundred metres deep sealed on all sides with solid rock. Over the millenia, water had seeped through the sandstone above, filling the structures with filtered water: pure, soft, sweet water beneath the dusty Coolibah Creek plains.

༄

Justine was at a meeting with the Phosec board. They were at the Crown Casino in Melbourne.

'The water pooled over the diamond seams is the challenge we face,' the expert geologist explained. 'We won't know until we get down there, of course, but all of the indicators are pointing towards high-quality and good sized gemstones, a deposit that may well be the largest and most valuable in the world.

'With such a valuable resource we cannot risk using marine machines to dredge for ore and pump it up to the surface. We will need to use the Placer method optimally using hydraulic water pressure,' he explained and flicked to the next screen of his presentation. 'This diagram shows where we believe the stones are located. There is a seam of alluvial, where the diamonds are sitting in sand and soft sedimentary structures. Once the water level is reduced we should be able to quite easily access the diamonds with simple cone or box screens. If we can do this underground, production costs will be minimal as we will not need to bring large quantities of material to the surface, just the diamonds.'

'The diamonds down the mouth of the volcanic pipe are embedded in the rock, possibly around the entire surface of the bottom of the aquifer. This stage of the mine will require the full dewatering of the site.' He pointed to the next slide showing the basin-like structures and where he thought the diamonds were.

'Our information shows that recharge of the aquifer is relatively rapid in major rain events. This will be a limiting factor on production and costs but if the load is as good as we think it is, the recharge can be managed,' he said, bringing up a graph of rainfall patterns. 'As you can see from this slide, major rain events of the amount and duration required for a shutdown recharge event can be as long as thirty years apart. It's possible we could work through the full life of the mine without having to do a second major dewater. We would of course have the initial dewatering, which will take time. In closing, I would like to thank the board. This is undoubtedly the most exciting diamond find, maybe ever, even into the future. It has been my privilege to work on this project with you.'

Chairman Angus Dalgliesh rose from the padded black leather chair and moved to the presentation area, shaking the geologist's hand. 'Thanks, Pete. Well done. So, the time has come,' he said, his eyes gleaming with excitement. 'It's time to begin the Coolibah Creek project, possibly the richest diamond mine on the planet. The signing of the access agreement should be nothing more than a formality and we are not anticipating any resistance initially. Native title issues are progressing rapidly with the traditional owners so I trust you all have your share portfolios secured. By next week the beginnings of interest in our company will start. Get ready for a roller-coaster ride to riches, gentlemen. Miss Rand will join us for dinner where we can discuss the possible reactions we may encounter from the public and environmental groups,' he added, smiling. 'Meeting closed, gentlemen.'

Everyone rose and shuffled out of the room chatting quietly. The air was thick with the thrill of what the future might bring and the thought of incalculable wealth was electrifying.

Dalgliesh placed a proprietorial hand on Justine's elbow as he ushered her out of the room. 'I'm going to be a very, very rich man, my sweet,' he said as his hand brushed over the curve of her buttocks.

☙

Over dinner that evening with the board members, Dalgliesh spoke in glowing terms about Justine's credentials.

'Most importantly, Miss Rand has strong connections with SOWF – Save Our World First, the global environmental protection organisation. She has worked for them in opposing goldmining in South Africa and coal seam gas in the United States. She can give us an excellent insight into the areas where we may encounter opposition and advise us on how best to manage that. As a bonus, Justine was actually raised in the Queensland outback, so she has the added advantage of knowing this specific demographic and actual individuals who may need high-priority management to minimise any delay in the project. We've waited long enough, gentlemen. I'll let Justine explain how she believes we should proceed,' he concluded, refilling Justine's wineglass with Grange Hermitage.

'Gentlemen. Director Tate,' Justine smiled and nodded to acknowledge the female board member. They were all engaged. 'Obviously a dewatering project of this scale will cause a lot of concern in an area that is climatically arid. The proposal to pump the water into the existing waterways will be met with strong opposition from local and national environmental groups due to the change in water quality, turbidity and flow, all of which would be unnatural and could be detrimental to the unique flora and fauna. The area is part of the world-renowned Lake Eyre Basin, the largest inland draining river system in the world. It has been nominated for World Heritage Listing in the past but the bid failed largely due to residents' opposition and lobbying that got the government's attention.

'The fight against the proposed listing brought about a far greater level of awareness of the unique qualities and the fragility of the ecosystems within the basin. Whereas before, landholders only thought about the land within their boundary fences, there has been a major shift in thinking over the past decade. Though local resistance to the dewatering may be high, without the support of a larger more globally prominent group, there will be minimal disruption to the project as any protest will be a match in the wind and will gain little media attention.

'The other advantage insofar as controlling opposition to the project is that the entire area only has one MP. It's been a safe conservative seat for over sixty years, so there's no opportunity for political pressure whatsoever. The owners of Coolibah Creek, Andy and Rebecca Roberts, could lead the opposition, and they are well respected in the community. Our local MP, Stephen Hogan, is Rebecca Roberts' father, so there is a strong connection there.'

Justine spoke for a few more minutes, pausing occasionally to flick her almond eyes around her audience to make sure she had their attention. She could see that she was swimming with some big fish and she liked the feeling.

Chapter 14

The Coolibah Creek breeders settled in well at Balmacarra and Andy and Bec felt greatly relieved that they would be able to carry them through the winter, but they knew it was only a temporary reprieve. When the seasons changed, the exit of summer would take with it any chance of more rain. Winter rains were unusual in the region. Soon enough, cold southerly winds would be merciless and even drier. They would blow day and night, chilling everyone to the bone. Bec shivered just thinking about it. She knew they would be struggling to keep the embers of hope alive if they had to go into another dry winter with the chance of relief once again so far away.

At Coolibah, Sam grew a beautiful veggie garden with the underground bore water despite the continuing dry. The milker cow broke into it a couple of times, the electric fence could not keep her from the lush green growth, but the vigilant gardener was on to her straight away and little damage was done. Bec continued to find comfort in her garden. She was thankful that they had a good supply of bore water at the house. She was wasting away with the land, though, it seemed. She grew more and more depressed as the long summer days crawled by.

Andy got to the point where he could no longer bear to watch the remaining animals suffering in their bid for survival and found excuses to stay around the shed, sending George out alone to do the water run and hating himself even more for his cowardice and inability to change anything. George and Nudding, now that he'd recovered, castrated yearling horses and broke in the two year olds. They pulled down the old phone line poles and cut and welded them into gates and panels at the cattle yard. The fences were strained tight, the roads graded. There was no cattle work to do, leaving an empty void in their work days.

Bec and Andy drove to Balmacarra often. It was a salve to their battered spirits to see the cows and calves doing so well, contented and full. But then came the terrible sinking feeling, like a solid door closing on the happy place, when they drove home to the moonscape that was Coolibah Creek.

Bec found that it was impossible to share her father's optimism for driving the dream she shared with Andy for the artesian water project when everything around her was dead or dying. Her world became more and more insulated and desolate at Coolibah Creek, and she was unable to look any further ahead than the next day. A sombre Christmas came and went. They were trampled into the dust and dragged along by the scruff of the neck by the drought into

February. Bec tried to be grateful for the good things she had in her life – her family, her friends, her husband, her garden – but it was hard.

※

The rain came like a thief in the night. In the dusty twilight, standing at the garden fence, the old milker cow raised her nose and sniffed at the moist wind that blew from the northwest. Andy and Bec noticed it too but were past hoping, not able to cope any more with getting their hopes up only to have them knocked down again. They'd stopped anxiously hanging on the weather forecasters' unreliable predictions every twelve hours; it was just too much. Low and fluffy, the purple clouds silently floated over the moon. The cloying humid night air was sticky and uncomfortable. Andy ran a small generator for the fridges and freezers and turned it off at night to save fuel. There was no fan or air-conditioning, and no breeze. He and Bec had gone to bed and lay stark naked in fitful sleep, sweating. There were no mosquitos or crickets chirping, even the insects had succumbed to the drought. The night was pitch black and soundless.

The softest sprinkle of rain, velvety as snowflakes, stroked the hot iron of the roof. Precious, gentle droplets fell, as if the rain knew how raw the drought's wound was on the land. It was the smell that woke them, not the whispering sound of the shower: the unmistakable, glorious smell of rain on dry earth.

Andy opened his eyes but could see nothing in the complete darkness. He lay rigid in the bed, afraid to move in case he discovered he was dreaming. A full minute passed.

Bec stirred and the sound of water trickling into the gutters of the house was like joyous music to her ears.

Still they didn't move. The light shower continued. Andy turned on his torch. Bec pretended to be asleep. He pattered out to the verandah and held his upturned palm out to the sky. The rain was warm and he clenched his fist to capture it as if it were gold dust. He put down the torch, turned it off and stretched out both his hands, wetting them and then wiping the priceless liquid on his hot face. Bec appeared beside him. She did the same. She took his hand and they stood there in the darkness, breathing the splendid smell in deep breaths, filling their lungs with the aroma.

The shower, gradually, slowly like the hands of a patient lover got heavier and stronger. The couple held onto the railing and closed their eyes in mute and desperate prayer. Soon the gutters filled and flowed into the long dry rainwater tanks making a strange echoing sound as the water splashed into the empty chambers. Andy and Bec felt that if they moved the spell may be broken. In the darkness they couldn't see anything, just hear and smell and feel the luxurious rain.

A torchlight came on in the men's quarters. Andy suddenly grabbed Bec's hand and pulled her along, down the stairs and the unclothed couple ran out into the rain. The grass was soft and cool under their feet, the rain tepid and tickling on their skin. They started to laugh. Collapsing onto the spongy grass in each other's arms they lay flat on their backs offering themselves to the rain.

'Yes! Yes! Yes! Send 'er down, Hughie!' Andy punched the air and sat up. The rain was getting heavier, plastering the hair to his head and stinging his shoulders and face. 'It's here, Bec!' he said jubilantly as he crushed her to him. Before she could answer he was covering her face in kisses as he held it in both hands. He laughed again and licked the rain from her throat.

Bec was giggling and crying at the same time as she felt the rain wash away their pain. She threw her arms around Andy's neck, found his mouth and kissed him passionately. Andy responded fervently as their laughter ebbed and their craving for each other flowed. He tossed Bec's naked body down in the water, sucking her breasts and lapping the water that pooled between them. Bec clutched her fingers into his wet hair and pulled his face back to hers, pressing her body up to his with wanton desire. The pouring rain stung and prickled Andy's back and buttocks as they made ravenous love in the downpour.

※

The breakfast table next morning sounded like a bird aviary as everybody chattered excitedly over steaming cups of tea. The rain continued to tumble down, pounding on the roof and gushing out of the overflowing gutters and tanks. Everyone was silent, though, when the radio crackled as the early morning forecaster explained the unusual weather pattern that had developed so suddenly.

'At this stage we expect this system could expand and remain relatively stationary for some time,' the weatherman said.

'So can we expect drought-breaking rains from this system?' the interviewer asked.

'Well, I wouldn't like to go out on a limb and say that just yet. I know a lot of your listeners are desperate for rain but it's certainly looking very promising for good useful rain. We'll just have to wait and see if it delivers.'

Bec bounced up and down like a kid at a birthday party. The phone was ringing constantly and the news kept getting better and better. It was raining everywhere. Andy had spoken to Davo and half-a-dozen neighbours. Bec had been talking to her mum and dad in Coombul and the grocer in Telford.

'I better give Maggie a ring,' she said. 'I think Doug's still away.'

Maggie picked up quickly. 'Hello.'

'G'day, Maggie. It's Bec. How much rain have you had?'

'Doug always says it's bad luck to measure until the rain has finished, so I haven't measured it yet. It's been raining through the night, though, and there's a lot of water about this morning.'

'We've had fifty mils here and it's still raining hard,' said Bec. 'Isn't Doug home?'

'No. He's still away,' said Maggie. 'He's gone to bring home the boys from boarding school for the muster.'

'Oh well, Lance is there, isn't he? You need someone to look after you a bit now, Maggie. I hope you're taking it easy?' Bec knew that the stockman, Lance, was a decent and reliable man and she was pleased that he was there.

'Well, actually, Lance seems to have gone away again. He goes walkabout from time to time,' said Maggie. 'But I have the phone and the radio and it's still almost three weeks till my due date. Surely I'll get out before then.'

'Of course you will. I guess you have plenty of company with all your pets around the house. Make sure you give us a call if you need anything. Have you talked to Doug? Is he on his way home?' asked Bec.

'Apparently, but he thinks if it keeps raining, the creek might come up before he can get past it. We'll have to wait and see.'

Bec said her goodbyes and hung up. A tiny frown creased her brow. Maggie sounded very vague and odd. Perhaps it was all part of her pregnancy. She would have to keep in contact with her. Maybe it would rain for weeks. Oh how she hoped that it did.

Chapter 15

Gunmetal-coloured skies emptied their bounty for days and nights. For almost a week the rain kept falling, pushing into the already bursting waterways and flooding out over the plains until the rivers became rampaging torrents and the entire inland was awash.

Doug was stranded in Telford with their two boys. He called Maggie at 5am one morning, obviously in a foul mood, no doubt from a crushing hangover.

'Still raining there?' he asked.

'Yes. It's been raining steadily. We've had over a hundred and fifty millimetres now,' Maggie replied. *You'd think he'd be happy about the rain*, she thought.

'So are you alright? How high's the river?' he said.

'Well, I can't actually see the river yet; it's too dark. But Sheba is missing and I can hear her calling from that way somewhere. I was just going with the torch to have a look for her,' Maggie told him.

'Don't you dare go into the river after that mongrel cat!' he yelled. 'For God's sake, woman, you're about to spit a foal and you're not gonna try wading around in the bloody floodwaters! I knew you were stupid, but that's just ridiculous. It's a bloody *cat* for Christ's sake!'

Maggie winced at his loud voice and hurtful insults. She had long ago given up on him ever understanding her love for her animals, especially Sheba, her aging Siamese.

'No dear,' she said. 'I won't go into the water. I just want to see if she's alright.' *You're not here to know what I'll be doing, Doug*, she thought.

'Lance seems to have wandered off again,' she said.

'*What*! That yellow bastard! Are you sure he's gone?'

'Well, yes, I think so. He didn't come over for dinner last night. You know how when he goes walkabout he always goes at night,' said Maggie matter-of-factly.

'The bastard must be half duck if he's gone anywhere now. Shit! I'll have to come out there and pick you up in a chopper,' said Doug.

'*No!* Doug, no!' said Maggie. 'You know how terrified I am of flying, especially in a little helicopter and I'm so pregnant! Please no, Doug. I'll be alright. I've got the phone and the radio if anything happens.'

'Well, you just stay put in the house. No going off after that mangy cat. Damn that yellow bastard. You just can't rely on 'em,' cursed Doug.

Maggie thought to herself how Lance always became 'yellow' when something he did upset Doug.

'When the rain eases off I'll have to organise to get a chopper in to Coolibah and then Andy can bring me across the river in his boat. Anyway, I'll ring you tonight,' said Doug.

'Yes, alright. Don't worry, I won't go in the river. I'll be okay here,' said Maggie.

'Righto, bye.'

'Yes. Bye, Doug.'

Maggie hung up the phone. A flicker of anger rose in her chest at the way Doug had spoken about Lance and her cat, but she was too distracted to maintain her anger for long. At least the lie had gone off well, she thought.

༂

As she lay on her bed in the candlelight the constant drumming of rain on the roof rasped on Maggie's already raw nerves. The days of rain had at least brought the searing temperature down, but her forehead was shiny with sweat in the amber glow of the flame. She was in labour. Her shyness and the fact that she couldn't bear to look into his eyes prevented her from calling out to Lance, who was reading in his quarters. It had been so difficult being there alone with him given the situation. Maggie had put up an iron curtain between them since their encounter. 'Oh God. What have I done' she said out loud in the night as her face contorted and reddened with another contraction. The memory of the touch of his hand on hers, his lips, his mouth, his young strong body came bubbling into her mind like uncorked champagne, making her light headed. 'I love you. How I love you, Lance,' she whispered as the contraction passed.

Maggie was not sure whether Doug or Lance had fathered the baby she was about to deliver. That fact only added to her state of mental fragility. Part of her longed for a child with Lance, a precious product of their love, and yet despite her endless sleepless nights and long tormented days she had been unable to find a solution to her dilemma. Doug was like her, very fair with blue eyes and reddish hair, what was left of it. There would be no way that she could get away with having a dark baby.

She had been on the brink of confessing all to Bec. Her neighbour was so caring and kind, so down to earth and honest. Maggie felt she was a true friend, but she couldn't bring herself to divulge the details of her affair with Lance. Now the moment of truth was upon her.

She had been so relieved when the rains had come and kept Doug away. It meant that she could deliver the baby alone, away from the questioning eyes of her husband or the nurses and doctors in Coombul. As soon as she'd received the call from him saying he was stranded in town, she had drunk the thick, rank-smelling castor oil. She'd assured him on the phone that she still had a month to go, when in fact it was only a fortnight. Maggie was positive that her oaf of a husband would have absolutely no idea when she was due. Within hours the purge had begun to work. It was now almost midnight and her waters had broken just after eight when she'd heard Lance quietly close the door and retreat to his quarters. For months now she hadn't been able to sit at the table with him if they were alone.

The contractions were regular and strong. Maggie hoped and prayed that the delivery would be normal; she refused to think about all the things that might go wrong. At last the baby was almost here. How could she have done it? What madness had possessed her? How could she risk her boys' futures?

There was no way she could stay on at Lennodvale if she produced the bastard child of the Aboriginal stockman. What shame that would bring to her family. She loved Lance with all her heart, but she should have been able to sacrifice her right to that love for her children. How could she have betrayed them and been so selfish? How could she have taken the risk of hurting them? The guilt and worry were driving her mad.

Just after two o'clock when the candle had nearly burned out, Maggie bit down hard on the pillow and pushed with all her strength. The tendons in her neck stood out and her fingers dug into the soft flesh of her thighs as she craned forward in the sitting position. Stinging pain that made her gasp came as the baby's head crowned. Within seconds the crashing wave of the final contraction came and anchored her to the bed. A strangled cry escaped through her gritted teeth and she felt the hot rush of the baby slide out onto the bed. She felt a ridiculous urge to laugh and cry . . . and she did.

As she reached forward to pick up the infant, the flickering light from the candle went out. The darkness was complete. It distracted her for only an instant as she picked up the baby and felt for its mouth to make sure it was clear. Blackness enveloped them, and the rain hammered the roof. The new arrival let out a very healthy wail. Wriggling and crying, the infant was hard to hold. Maggie knew that she had to cut the cord and void the placenta. She had all the necessary things on the dresser beside the bed but she couldn't see.

Cradling the baby in one arm she felt around on the bedside table for the extra candle she had placed there.

Her hand closed over it and she put it between her blood-soaked legs and fumbled for the matches. She found them and struck a flame and held it to the wick. Holding the candle in one hand and the squealing baby in the other, Maggie could see that she had a daughter, a beautiful plump baby girl with a shock of straight black hair. She moved the feeble light closer and even in the dimness she could clearly see the coffee colour of the chubby little legs kicking against her snow-white belly.

She lay there frozen, the cord uncut, blood all over her, the candle held aloft in her trembling hand. A torrent of tears washed down her pale face. A gorgeous, gorgeous girl. Oh, a sweet baby girl. What was she going to do? What could she do? She shook her head from side to side and rocked the baby rhythmically back and forth on the bed. Eventually, her eyes stopped crying and glazed over, staring with a horrible blankness. She sat still and staring, as if hypnotised.

Somewhere, far away, she heard a noise. It was an irritating noise, an urgent noise. It was drawing her to it as she fought through the cloudy, tumbling maze of her shattered thought processes. Then suddenly her womb tightened again as it contracted to expel the placenta. The pain brought her back to reality with a jerk and she realised that the noise was the sound of the baby crying.

Now her movements were sure and precise. She tied and cut the cord, changed the pads underneath her bottom and set about washing the baby and herself from the two bowls of water she had placed on the floor next to the bed. The girl child in her arms was exquisite in every way with big almond-shaped eyes like her father. As Maggie cleaned her, she gently rolled her over onto her belly and gasped in surprise as she saw an exact replica of the birthmark that had been such a torturous stamp on her own neck and face. The blemish was comparatively much smaller and instead of being a beetroot red it was the colour of chocolate and it lay across the top of the baby's left buttock. Her mind threatened to slip back into a state of confusion but she forced herself to concentrate on the task at hand. She knew what she had to do now. If she stayed focused on her goal, her mind would stay sharp and clear. Everything was so much easier now she'd decided.

With mechanical movements, she nursed the newborn, calmly now, as she felt the thick yellow colostrum being drawn from her breast by the eager baby. She glanced at her wristwatch and saw that it was 3am. With the heavy cloud cover it wouldn't be daylight till six. Lance wouldn't come over to the house until she called him for breakfast, even though she knew he was always moving around early.

'Charlotte. That's such a pretty name. I hope you like that name. You're such a strong girl. You're going to be just fine. Good, strong, healthy baby. You'll be fine,' Maggie muttered. Stroking the soft skin of her baby's cheek she began to croon a lullaby. The baby had her fill and drifted off to sleep.

Maggie placed her in the cot and immediately set to work cleaning up the bed, rolling up all the soiled towels and pads in the bedspread. She found a torch, pulled on a robe and oblivious to the pelting rain and the cold, muddy ground, trudged out past the house yard fence to the old milking shed. The two-hundred litre fuel drum they used for burning waste was still dry under the corrugated iron roof of the open-sided structure. She shoved the bedspread and its contents into the drum then looked around and found the fuel bottle, doused the bundle and set fire to it. She hoped the wind would take the smoke away and it would burn without Lance noticing the glow. She just had to take that chance she told herself and frowned as she padded back into the house, not stopping to wipe the mud from her feet.

Maggie went to the pantry and collected an assortment of baby items. Into a box she carefully placed nappies, formula, a bottle and spare teat, skin cream and tiny little jumpsuits. She then went back to the bedroom and fossicked about in her wardrobe until she found the breast pump. She sat on the bed in the candlelight, staring at the sleeping child as she expressed the rich milk and filled the spare bottles she had found. The milk would keep. It was cool enough.

It was 4.30am. She looked at her watch as she finished the task and then took the expressed milk and placed it in the box. When she returned to the bedroom she brought the box with her and put it in one end of the cot. Then she went to her wardrobe again and from a pretty cardboard box, which was carefully hidden behind the piles of her underwear, she lifted a tiny bracelet. It had been her christening gift from her grandmother. The delicate piece was solid twenty-two carat gold inlaid with a garnet on the clasp.

She stroked the bracelet with reverence and tenderness before taking it and tying it around Charlotte's tiny wrist. Maggie didn't cry, there was more to be done. She returned to the pantry and found an electrical extension cord and moved towards the front door. She was running out of time. Maggie's hand did not shake as she calmly wrote the note.

'Dear Lance, gone to the creek to look for Sheba. If you come home please feed baby Charlotte.' She signed the note and sat the teapot on top of it on the dining room table. Their hands had first touched on top of that teapot, Maggie thought, and once again she fought back the gathering wave of sadness.

Darling Lance, I know you'll run with Charlotte. I know you'll love her and care for her, maybe even die for her. God grant you the strength to make it through the rain and the floodwater, she thought.

These were the words she knew were too risky to write. She would have loved to write how she couldn't bear to live without him anymore, how she would love him forever, how much she would have loved to share Charlotte's life with him, but she dared not leave any evidence.

She was about to pull the door open when she hesitated and turned back towards the bedroom. Beside the cot, bending over the sleeping baby, she kissed the infant's forehead then clasped her tiny hand in her fingers. For a moment she felt as if her whole body might crumple, but she stiffened her back, clenched her jaw with steely determination and doused the candle, felt the weight of the long cord in her hand and left the room, the baby and the house.

The ground outside was under a couple of inches of water and it was slippery. She pulled the roll of cord over her shoulder and across her chest so that she could use her arms to balance. Her legs were shaky and weak and she could feel a stream of warm blood running down the inside of her thighs. It wasn't far to the river.

The night was so dark it was difficult to make out the track, especially with all the water about. Maggie knew the general direction, though, and she marched on. The big coolibah tree that towered beside the river track well before the edge of the bank was surrounded by the angry swirling water and Maggie could hear it sucking and gurgling around the tree's base as it pushed and shoved in its race to get past.

She sat down in the water and spread her thin long legs and began to scoop up big handfuls of mud and place them in the billowing skirt of her nightdress. It was an exhausting task and she had to keep stopping to catch her breath but gradually she amassed a ball of several kilos of the sticky, heavy clay. She rolled it forward towards her belly and began to tie it to her body with the cord, careful to pull the skirt above the cord so that it wouldn't release the load.

With enormous effort, Maggie struggled to her feet and stumbled on into the raging torrent, carrying the bundle of mud in front of her.

The cord will loosen with the movement of the water. They'll never know I tied it around myself, she thought.

Without a tear or a moment's hesitation, she calmly marched into the rampaging floodwaters. When she fell for the third time, the water was deep and the current strong enough to take her. The weight of the mud dragged her under the tumbling water and she was gone.

Chapter 16

'There's still no sign of her.' Bec put down the phone at Coolibah.

The rain, finally, had stopped, after almost two weeks of persistent deluge. The summer sun had returned and drew moisture from the sodden soils each day, creating a tropical greenhouse atmosphere. As the river was dropping, the police and Doug flew the watercourse in choppers. SES crews searched in boats for Maggie. The rain had washed away any sign of her.

Doug presumed that she had gone into the floodwater trying to rescue her cat, that some sort of accident had happened and the river had taken her. The initial hot anger that he felt at the thought that she would do such a stupid thing had been a barrier holding out his grief, but as the days passed that barrier was falling and the misery that was pushing through was something he couldn't bear. The boys were bereft and he could give them no comfort. He knew that if he tried he would collapse himself and he had to stay strong. It was hard not to blame himself. He shouldn't have left her alone. He should never have trusted that yellow bastard to stay, he thought. His saddle was gone and his pet brown mare but he'd left the rest of his gear in his room. The wandering mongrel will expect to just walk back into his job when he's finished drifting around. Doug fumed. It was easy to transfer the blame on to Lance. Doug did so with a dreadful hatred that fed itself and grew like a tumour. They searched for ten days. There was no sign of Maggie. Nothing.

'It's just so tragic,' said Bec. 'Dear Maggie. We'll never know what happened. Her animals were her world and I don't doubt for a moment that she probably has gone out into the river to rescue her cat. Poor Maggie. And the baby. And the boys. It's just terrible.'

Bec and Andy were sitting on the verandah drinking coffee and counting their blessings. They had run out of tea, just as they had run out of most things, being caught unawares by the extended rain period. Sam and George had been killing the chooks for meat and Bec had been making damper. At least they had some green vegetables from the garden and milk from the cow, but no potatoes or onions. The landscape beyond the greenery of the garden resembled mudflats at low tide. Where it had been bare before the rain it was positively glassy now. Bec and Andy waited with contented patience. They knew what was going to happen. The rebirth of the land would be a miracle to be witnessed.

'Apparently Doug wants to keep looking for another couple of weeks before he gives up entirely,' said Andy. 'It must be terrible to not have a body to bury. He's still blaming Lance, of course, but Doug would have been at Lennodvale himself if he hadn't been on a bender up at Coombul. Wonder where Lance went? They still haven't found him either, hey.'

'No. They reckon his grandmother, old Peggy at the mission, said he took his swag and hitched a ride on the highway. Sick and tired of Doug, she reckoned. I could understand that,' said Bec.

Just as suddenly as the rain had come, as if by magic the green appeared overnight. On the fourth morning of sunshine, the golden orb of the sun broke through a salmon-coloured sky, its rays brushing the heads of a million battalions of the green army. All manner of grasses and herbages had germinated and unfurled out of long-dormant seeds, pushing upwards through the mud. So great was their number that the plants jostled and squeezed against each other as they grew. From barren, parched nothingness the earth's metamorphosis was a marvel to behold.

On the first day the new growth resembled a tightly woven carpet of the most beautiful, brilliant green shade. Then it re-formed into shag pile and then into a waving ocean of luxuriant tender growth. All around the horizon, as far as Bec and Andy could see, was green. From out of nowhere came insects of every size, colour and description, the buzzing black flies, the birds and at night the crazy cacophony of sound as frogs and bush toads called loudly for mates. The coming of the rains was one huge celebration of life, which made the tragic loss of Maggie and her baby's life so much more acute.

As the land was reborn, so too was Andy. He was once again full of energy and enthusiasm. Contained by the boggy roads and swollen creeks, he paced the verandahs and invented all sorts of tasks for the men. One morning Bec came outside after spending a couple of hours on the bookwork to find that they'd landscaped a new area of garden in the backyard and put in a barbecue.

'What do you reckon?' Andy's face broke into that wide, charming grin she loved.

'It's fantastic. I love it,' said Bec, beaming.

They talked about what to plant where before going inside for morning smoko.

'Dad called. He's pushing for us to get the artesian water project down on paper. He wants to take us to the international sustainability conference in South Africa. They are offering a global enviro stamp of approval for selected projects as well as partial funding. He said the first thing we need is a title, so we have to come up with a name for the project,' said Bec.

'It would be a great trip for sure. If anyone can help us get the project up, it's Stephen. He's never lost sight of the big picture throughout the drought and he's a smooth old fox,' said Andy.

'Well, if the environmentalists are fair dinkum in any way they'll get behind the project; it's almost certainly a unique opportunity to get things right from scratch,' said Bec.

'That's right,' Andy agreed.

'Lord knows the big international environmental organisations have got plenty of cash if they're interested in making a difference as well as making a noise,' said Bec.

'Do you want to go?' asked Andy.

Coolibah Creek

Stephen had offered to shout their fares over as part of the group attending. He felt they had a lot to offer in communicating the concept to delegates.

'There's no way I want to be anywhere but right here at the moment. Do you think I could bear to miss this?' She threw her arms wide to indicate the verdant property. 'Dad's considering engaging Justine Rand to present the environmental angle and facts to the summit. Can't say I like that woman, but she would be a pretty powerful ally,' said Bec.

'Oh well, if she's going . . .' Andy winked at Bec and smiled.

'Oh stop it, you tease. If you so much as look at that redhead I'll know about it!' Bec protested but Andy was skipping out the door laughing.

The phone rang and she picked it up.

'Hello. Coolibah Creek. Bec speaking.'

'Yeah, it's Doug,' a croaky voice replied. 'They've found her. Way down the river.' His voice broke and she heard him struggle for breath and control.

'Oh Doug, I'm so sorry. Where are the boys? Can I come down to be with them?' said Bec, her mind racing.

'Yeah, the boys are here at Lennodvale. I don't know what to do really. Just don't know . . .' His voice trailed off.

'Just stay put, Doug. Andy and I will be there this afternoon. You just hold on,' she said as she heard the phone hang up from the other end of the line.

Bec hung up and then picked up the receiver again to order the chopper.

Maggie's funeral was small. The autopsy had confirmed that she had given birth before drowning but no trace of the baby had been found. Dreadful images came to Bec's mind of Maggie clinging to a tree in the ravaging floodwater, giving birth before being engulfed and dragged under. She felt for Maggie's sons, Sean and Daniel, who were unlikely to receive much emotional support from their father.

Bec and Andy had agreed to approach Doug at an appropriate time to see if he would allow the boys to go with them to muster Balmacarra. They were great kids and Bec would have liked to take them home with her immediately just to give them a big hug and tell them it was okay to cry. At least Doug had sobered up for the funeral but the gossip was that he had been hitting the bottle pretty hard.

During the drive back from Telford, Andy talked at length about the upcoming Balmacarra muster and how long he intended to allow the country to grow before he restocked Coolibah Creek.

'Can you believe that Louise?' he asked, changing the subject. His sister had flown in for the funeral. *Not to show respect*, Bec thought, *but as an excuse to ask Andy for money again.*

'Coolibah's growing grass not hundred dollar bills! She just never lets up. I tell you, she'll never change. I'll be so glad to be able to pay her out. That'll be a day for celebration, love,' said Andy, reaching across and squeezing Bec's thigh.

'One day, sooner rather than later now.' Rebecca smiled and covered his hand with hers. 'You must remember to call Nudding when we get home. He's been on the phone a couple of times.'

Nudding had gone home to see his girl and family when he had been able to get out from the sodden Coolibah Creek. The rains had gone on so he'd taken a job in the copper mine. 'I don't think he likes being down the mine, no matter what money he's on,' said Bec.

'No. He won't want to stay there. I'll ring him. Get him back out before we go to Balmacarra. He's a good man. Handy to ride out those colts. They'll be nice and fresh now. There's bound to be plenty of action over there, too. I want to clean up all those scrub bulls running in the paddock; don't want them in amongst our good cows.'

Andy slowed the car as they came to a creek where the water was still flowing pure and clear across the road. He thought about Maggie's boys, how he wished that he and Bec could start a family soon.

'Poor Maggie, we will never know what happened,' said Bec. 'The river holds her secrets now.'

Chapter 17

The Coolibah Creek mustering crew were full of excitement at getting back into some cattle work as the first muster of Balmacarra began since the rains. Andy and Bec had recruited Sean and Daniel O'Donnell, along with George and Nudding, to muster the paddock. Andy's lifelong Coolibah Creek Aboriginal friend, Clarry, was flying the chopper for the muster and Andy couldn't keep the smile off his face. There had been so many times when he wasn't sure a day such as this would ever come.

He wanted to get the wild inbred scrub bulls out of his cows and Davo reported that there were a number of big old piker bullocks that would be prime fat and saleable. They needed to get the fat cattle together and draft off some for sale, brand the young calves and truck some of the cows back to Coolibah. The team had set out at dawn; George

Coolibah Creek

and Bec on horses; Nudding, Sean and Daniel on motorbikes; Davo in the Toyota with water and lunch; Andy in the bull-catcher vehicle; and Clarry in the chopper. Andy had modified the old short wheel-base Toyota himself to use for chasing and controlling wild cleanskin bulls. It had a strong angled bull bar across the front as well as side rails and a roll bar behind the hood. He had swapped the original motor for a powerful V8 to give the bull-catcher power and speed.

It was just breaking day and Andy was giving directions. 'Sean and Daniel, we'll go to the back of the paddock and follow the channels down. Clarry will need a hand to get some of the rogues out onto the flats. Bec, you, Nudding and George go to the plain on the western side of Pituri waterhole. Clarry can fold them in to you from the other side to hold there while we get the cattle from the northern end. All on channel 7?' he directed and they all checked their two-way radios. Andy spoke directly to Sean and Daniel as Bec began to unload the horses. 'The channels here are steep and there are dozens of them, so it's easy to get yourself into a situation where you can't get out on a bike. Make sure you pick a path and don't do anything stupid,' he instructed sternly. The eager young men were susceptible to getting hot blooded in the chase. The faint sound of the chopper away in the distance set the musterers' hearts racing in anticipation of what the day might bring.

'Got a visual on you, Andy,' Clarry's voice boomed over the radio, and the men started their bikes. The bull-catcher's ignition fired and the big motor growled like a living thing, shattering the stillness of the morning as the team set off in search of the herd.

The chopper flitted and danced in the apricot dawn like a dragon fly and the glossy fat cattle streamed out of the channels and gullies into the care of the crew. Andy's heart sang as he saw the fat cows trotting out, looking in such splendid condition, some with chubby calves at their heels, balloon-like udders full of milk, swinging from side to side. The cattle were unrecognisable to the untrained eye as the ones that had come to Balmacarra just a few months ago. He marvelled at the ability of the land to produce such high value pasture naturally. Best country in the world. Just add water, he thought. A broad smile broke across his face when he recognised the matriarch lead cow striding out to the front of the mob. It was like seeing an old friend in the crowd. He looked across at Nudding and saw that he was smiling too.

'These are all heading in the right direction. Nudding, you stay with me. You boys keep heading up the river until you reach the boundary,' Andy directed the lads. Sean and Daniel rode on close together, carefully picking their way through the terrain.

'No worries,' Sean replied.

'There's only a few left up here in the corner.' Clarry's voice came over the airwaves. 'You can cross the channels if you get onto the next big cattle pad a couple of hundred metres in front of you,' Clarry said. The boys went on a little faster to where they found the pad and turned east to follow the cattle's footsteps and find the crossing.

Sean and Daniel couldn't believe their good fortune when they saw the massive brindle bull race out of the scrub. He was unbelievably huge. They turned their bikes to follow, hearts racing, excitement drying the saliva in their mouths, fear clutching their bellies.

Coolibah Creek

Most of the time, the musterers only saw the dust of the scrubbers as the nervous animals heard the bikes approaching and fled, only to be ensnared by the mob in their path. But here he was, this gargantuan beast, right under their noses. He was undoubtedly the legendary King Canute that Davo had mentioned before they set out.

Sean's frantic fingers fumbled with the button on his radio as he dodged the low-set turkey bush and kept pace with the bull.

'Copy, Andy,' he said, trying to moisten his tongue so he could speak.

'Gotcha, Sean,' came the reply.

'It's him. King Canute. He's just broke outta the scrub right in front of us.'

'Keep off him, Sean. Let him run. Which way's he headed?' asked Andy.

'He's headed for the creek west of the river about a kilometre north of the junction, but he don't look like he wants to keep goin' that way.' Sean's voice was distorted by the wind in the mike.

'No. He'll swing,' Andy's voice crackled on the two-way. 'Either south for the junction or straight back over you to the river. Just keep off him a bit, but keep him going. Don't give him time to think. He's never seen a bike, so you've got the drop on him at the moment. Is he still running?'

'Yeah, Andy. He's headed south.'

'Way to go. Keep him coming. I'm here at the junction with the bull rig. Let him run this way. When he gets here we'll try and bend him out over that creek to the west, okay?' said Andy.

'Righto,' screeched Sean in a shrill voice that sounded odd in his own ears.

The bull kept running south. Where the creek met the river there was only a narrow band of trees either side. West of the creek was a large area of spinifex and turpentine covered ridges. If the bull made it there first, he would easily crash through the woody vegetation and spiky surface and it would be impossible for the bike or the bull-catcher to follow.

'Clarry! Where are you?' Andy called the helicopter pilot.

'I'm out on the southwest side, running some in to Bec,' said Clarry.

'Better get back here. The boys have flushed out King Canute,' said Andy.

'Righto. I'm comin'.' Andy heard the eager anticipation in Clarry's voice.

'Bec. Copy?' asked Andy.

'Yep, gotcha,' she replied.

'Bring those coaches back. Straight up the river to the junction,' said Andy.

'Righto, we're about a k away,' said Bec.

'Good. Trot 'em along, love. Sean, when I tell you, you blokes come out to one side and see if he'll veer out to the creek. If he keeps coming on I might have to bump him but I don't want to take him on till we get him clear of the river,' said Andy.

'All okay,' said Sean. Every muscle in his body was clenched and rigid, his eyes were locked on their quarry.

Andy scanned the ground ahead, looking for gullies or stumps. The bull-catcher's V8 engine burbled quietly, like a purring tiger resting before the chase, as he lay in wait for the bull. In his head he heard Bec say, 'Put your seatbelt on. There's no windscreen and if you hit that mesh it'll turn your head into chips.' If this bull was King Canute, he might need his seatbelt. Still scanning the horizon, he clicked the belt into place.

Then he saw the bull and took in a deep breath, taken aback by the animal's size and the incredible rack of its horns.

'Holy shit!' he muttered.

Driving a bull-catcher well was like dancing. It was all about quick thinking, anticipation, coordination and timing: about moving your feet and hands smoothly, gliding, drifting, starting, stopping. Andy was good at it. Very good. And he relished the challenge before him.

As his adversary approached, the nature of the bull's gait told Andy many things about the beast. The experienced cattleman could tell that the bull was in 'flight mode'. His head was forward and down low. He was cantering but not at full speed, just keeping his pursuers at a safe distance. His ears flicked back and forward constantly, telling Andy that he was looking behind at the bikes, not running in blind panic. His foamy pink tongue curling out of his mouth indicated that he was becoming stressed, yet his stride was strong and steady and there was none of the body rolling that tells a bull-catcher that the animal will be easily knocked off its feet.

'Haven't even thought about fighting yet, ole man,' said Andy. 'Come round, Sean,' he ordered.

Sean's hands were fused to the grips of the bike's handle-bars and he didn't let go to press the button and reply. He pulled out to his left, glancing back over his shoulder to make sure Daniel did the same. Still about fifty metres away from the bull, Sean roared forward until he was just behind the animal but still a good distance out to the side. King Canute veered right, but only slightly, maintaining his loping run towards his goal.

'Come in a bit more on him, Sean. He hasn't spotted me yet. You've got his full attention,' said Andy.

Sean wasn't at all sure he wanted the bull's full attention but he came closer and the beast veered a little further, but he also started to lift his head and slow his pace, a signal that Sean read clearly: 'Don't come any closer!'

Nudding's voice came over the radio. 'Copy, boss.'

'Yeah, Nudding. Where are you'? said Andy.

'Just up the river from you, boss. This mob's just poking along the right way now. Do you want me to come down to you?' said Nudding, not wanting to miss the action.

'Nudding, you go wide to the east, roar down here past me at the junction with that creek that comes in from the west, you know, Sandfly Creek. Get down in the creek and if the bull comes down the creek you ride in front of him, stay well ahead and try to make him change his mind. Daniel, you get in the creek above him. Sean and I will try to convince him to go across.'

'All okay,' they replied in unison.

Nudding's face broke into a huge smile and he gunned the 600cc motorbike in the direction of the creek. He was afraid of insects, but he wasn't afraid of bulls.

'We're running out of room, Sean,' Andy spoke into the mike. 'You're going to have to come right in on him now. See what he does. Don't get too close and don't fall off.'

Andy knew that Sean was an incredible motorbike rider, one of the best he'd seen, but he also knew that any mistake could mean death.

Sean knew that too as he took a deep breath and raced the bike as close as he dared alongside the bull, revving the motor and shouting.

'Don't let him think!' Andy yelled to Sean. 'Keep him going.'

The brothers had turned the bull enough to have him almost facing west and the creek was closer than the junction. It was Andy's aim to make him choose the creek. He could tell the bull still had plenty of strength in reserve so was likely to want to flee if given the chance. The musterers all revved their engines and Andy laid on the horn but stayed far enough away so as not to engage the bull. Andy had outwitted him and as he trotted away from them he was getting further and further from his escape and had only one option: go for the creek.

Andy saw the bull make that decision and he called to Nudding and Daniel.

'Here he comes, boys!' said Andy. 'He'll come your way, I reckon. Nudding, try to get back around to the river. Sean, you break back behind me and back up Nudding.'

The bull dropped his head once more and charged for the creek with Andy behind him. He didn't slow down when he reached the steep banks and in an instant had disappeared over the edge into the creek. His post-like front legs drove deep into the sand and in an amazing feat of strength and agility he pushed up from his nose and floundered in the heavy going with his powerful hind legs. He immediately turned north.

Andy couldn't cross the creek in the bull-catcher; the banks were a sheer three metre drop. He pulled up near the edge and got out of the vehicle to see where the bull had gone.

'You tricky ol' bastard!' he said, seeing the tracks heading north.

He clambered back into the rig and yelled the warning into the mike. 'He's coming your way, Daniel! Nudding, come around! Sean, stay in the creek and get in behind him!'

Daniel had been nervous before but now he was petrified. The creek bed was narrow, only about four metres wide and the three-metre high banks rose vertically. There was no way he could get his bike out of the creek bed until he came to one of the places where the walking cattle had broken down the banks and made a pad to cross. The bikes were sluggish in the dry sand, tending to bog. If he got the wrong gear and stalled, in this situation he would die.

Daniel was white with fear. One of his legs started to shake uncontrollably and he slapped it to try to make it stop as his gaze became fixed with horror on the bend about sixty metres back. He had chosen this place to pull up because of the bend and the cattle pad that crossed the creek just below him. He hoped to bluff the bull into taking the pad out of the creek to where the others could get a go at him. But not even the image his fear-filled mind conjured up could compare to the actual sight of the massive creature rounding the bend.

Glistening, towering horns waved menacingly from side to side, and red eyes, wide and staring, fixed on Daniel. The bull seemed to fill up the creek bed with his bulk and deadly presence. He was charging.

Daniel snapped out of his stunned terror and spun his bike in a screeching circle. The engine screamed. Daniel wasn't sure if it was he who was screaming as the tyre bit into the sand and sent up a plume of tiny missiles that sprayed out ten metres towards the bull. Daniel was hoping to scatter sand into the bull's face and make him baulk.

Coolibah Creek

When he was facing north, he pulled out of the slide and took off, checking back over his shoulder to see the charging bull still coming on. He didn't see the log. The front wheel of the bike hit a solid black stump, which was protruding from a fallen tree buried in the sand. The collision shot his front wheel sideways. Daniel held firm to the handlebars and frantically geared down to try to power out of the dive but he struck neutral. The motor screeched and smoked but the bike didn't move. Daniel looked behind him to see the tiny bubbles in the frothy spittle dripping from the bull's open mouth. He screamed in terror and as the bike came over he tried to get behind it as he fell. He knew the bull was going to kill him. Its steely horns were lowered down to the ground, racing towards him. He flung his arms over his head, his screams tearing at his throat as he waited for the impact.

Nudding launched the big bike off the top of the creek bank and flew through the air. He sailed over the bull's back and landed just in front of Daniel. He brought the bike down on its back wheel and knocked it back a gear. He gave the 600cc full throttle. The engine grunted and sand blasted the bull and Daniel, cutting into the bull's eyes and filling his nostrils. Canute threw his head up and Daniel curled into a ball as the bull thundered over the top of him, stepping on the seat of his bike and crushing it but miraculously missing him completely. Nudding yelled at the bull, goading him and keeping him moving away from Daniel. Suddenly Andy was there, dragging the stunned Daniel up the cattle pad and shovelling him into the bull-catcher.

'You right?' asked Andy.

'Yeah, yeah . . . Nudding . . . he came . . . jumped over the top . . . hit a log . . . I stalled her.' Daniel's body was flung back against the seat as Andy accelerated away along the edge of the creek, dodging trees and gullies.

'Seatbelt,' he said, clipping up his own.

Nudding was still in front of the bull, yelling at him and slowing him up by spraying him with sand. Andy had called Sean and he rode along beside the bull-catcher.

'Go to the next pad crossing,' he instructed. Andy turned the wheel and took the rig away from the creek to the better going out on the plain, tearing across the rough ground to get to the next pad ahead of the bull. Even if they wanted to, Nudding and the bull could not get out of the creek. At this point, the bull was trotting along behind the bike. Andy had to get the bull out of the creek.

He and Sean reached the next crossing as Nudding and the bull came on steadily.

'Clarry, where the bloody hell are you?' called Andy.

'I'm at the junction. I can see the rig now.' Clarry's voice could be heard over the welcome thudding of the chopper blades.

'I'm going to put the rig in front of him in the creek and send Nudding out the pad. You can get down on him here. It's pretty clear. I want you to stay high then bomb him so he doesn't just see me and turn back the way he came. That way we can force him to follow Nudding up out of the creek,' said Andy.

'All okay, Andy,' confirmed Clarry.

'Got that, Nudding?' Andy called to the stockman in the creek, churning along in the heavy sand, the massive bull coming on behind him.

There was no reply and Andy knew that Nudding was too busy riding to talk. He was certain he would have heard, though.

Coolibah Creek

'Sean, you go across to the other side and try to take him out as far as you can into the open. Just get his attention, keep him on your tail, until I can get the bull-catcher out of the creek,' said Andy.

Sean crossed the creek to the other side and Andy waited back off the edge of the bank. He could hear Nudding's bike and he leant forward in his seat to watch for the pair. He saw the horns first, swinging from side to side above the grassy edges of the creek. In the creek bed, Nudding was slowly narrowing the gap between himself and his pursuer, engaging the bull. With immaculate timing, Andy drove the bull-catcher over the side of the bank directly in front of the pair. Nudding veered off up the opposite bank and the bull turned his head. At that precise moment, the chopper fell from the sky, dropping in on his right side. King Canute followed his head and trotted up out of the creek on the western side. Andy reversed to get a run-up to get over the bank on the other side.

The chopper banked and got in behind the bull, hovering low, whipping the grass and belting up curling clouds of dust. The bull stopped dead in his tracks, his great ribcage rising and falling, his eyes mad with fear and rage, his nostrils and mouth dripping thick strings of mucus and foaming saliva. He swung around, pivoting on his front feet, his massive weight auguring a hole in the hard red soil. The pursuant men didn't want him to bail up yet. They needed to keep him moving till they could get the bull-catcher out of the creek. As the chopper rose and fell above him the bull spun around and launched his huge body into the air. One of his horns connected with a strut as he tossed his massive head, trying to gore and rip his opponent.

Clarry had misjudged the bull's height. He was shocked that he had been hit. This close to the ground, with no air under him, the chopper lurched dangerously sideways and the blades belted through the dusty air, perilously close to the ground. Clarry heaved on the stick and powered forward to try to get some air under the rotors. Only his quick reflexes and years of experience saved him.

As the chopper rose away, the bull turned on the bikes. He set the circling pair, raking the ground with his plate-sized hooves and tossing his head. He snorted his challenge defiantly, blowing streams of white foam through his dilated red nostrils.

Suddenly, Andy was there and the chopper went high. They wanted to hold the bull here or move him back towards the coach cattle that were still coming up from the south. The bikes came back around to the bull-catcher, leaving the way open for Canute to go further out on the plain or away to the south towards the approaching cattle.

The King pivoted and tore at the dirt, his dusty hide quivered and twitched. Andy watched his trophy intently, all his senses on full alert. He knew it was impossible to predict what the animal would do but he was looking for body language, signs that would give him those crucial few extra seconds to position the bull rig and the men when the bull made his move. No one spoke. They all just waited. The tension built.

The dangerous, agitated creature continued to pirouette on the spot. On horseback, Bec and George were close now with the coach cattle. Andy could see them approaching. He hoped the bull would either stand his ground until the herd enveloped him or move towards them, but he didn't really expect the cunning Canute to choose either of those options.

Andy's thoughts were rapid but his movements were slow and smooth as he unclipped his seatbelt and took off his shirt. Hastily, but with no sudden or jerky movements, he wound the shirt around one end of the metre-long cattle prod he'd withdrawn from its place between the seats.

'Nudding, he's going to turn for the ridges.' Andy spoke quietly. 'Pull the fuel hose off your bike and soak the shirt.'

Nudding carefully slid from the bike in one fluid movement that drew no attention from the bull.

'When ole Canute makes his move only a bullet will stop him, so I'm going to race in front of him on the bike and light the spinifex across the base of the ridges. With this south wind it'll explode and make him turn back. Sean, you follow me with the rig to where I stop so I can bring him back into the mob with the vehicle when he turns.'

Nudding replaced the fuel hose on his bike, making sure it was tight. This was not a situation where running out of fuel would be a good thing to do.

Andy thought briefly of the fact that he would be ruining a perfectly good cattle prod but he couldn't risk the movement of the bikes or the rig to hunt for a stick. He had to stand his ground. The King would be worth over a thousand dollars for Davo and Andy, but this was not about the money. A rogue bull like this would be a constant danger to stockmen and would teach other cattle his own ways of hiding and avoiding being mustered.

A discord of lowing from the approaching cows calling to their misplaced calves was clearly audible now. Just as Andy threw his leg over Sean's bike, Canute made his break.

As Andy had predicted, the beast set a course straight for the shrub-topped ridges. Andy opened up the throttle. The big bike reared and snarled and tore across the plain at over a hundred k, easily overtaking the escaping bull. Canute never deviated from this line as Andy passed him and veered southward.

At the base of the ridges, where the prickly spinifex bushes grew closely bunched in clumps like an army of assembled pincushions, Andy slid to an abrupt halt. He got off the bike, threw the makeshift firestick on the ground and knelt down beside it, nervously looking back to the bull that was thundering towards him. He cupped his hands into the wind and struck a match. With a pop, the petrol ignited and wind fanned the flames. Holding the torch in his left hand, Andy swung his leg over the seat and gunned the bike forward to the north. Riding at about 40 ks, he brushed the tops of the spinifex with the burning shirt. Behind him the grey-green clumps exploded, the combustion of their tarry resin making a wall of leaping flames.

He met the bull as it moved back to a trot and tossed its head from side to side assessing the wall of fire towering in front of him and to the north. The coaches were still coming up behind from the other direction. The bull stopped and looked from the fire to the coaches, then back to the fire and to Andy.

'He's going to take it on!' thought Andy, his heart leaping as Canute lowered his great horns, closed his eyes and charged straight into the fire.

Immediately Andy spun the bike around and raced away towards the end of his trail of flames. When he reached the end of the flame wall he turned in behind it and continued at breakneck speed to the west, showing no quarter or caution as he bounced dangerously across the spinifex clumps and hidden anthills striving to get in front of the bull again.

Glancing to his left he saw King Canute lumbering along almost parallel to him. Andy gunned the bike, hoping his torch would stay alight in the wind. When he was far enough ahead, he slowed and turned back towards the bull. He was relieved to see the torch pop back into flame and he rode along touching it to the tops of the spinifex, setting another line of fire to try to turn the bull back.

He intersected the bull's line of flight when the animal was only about thirty metres from him. He flinched when he saw him come trotting out of the turpentine bushes. The spinifex exploded into tall flames behind him and the bull slowed to a walk and then stopped. Andy stopped too, his right hand clenched to the throttle, the bike idling ready to go. Fine hairs around the bull's eyes were singed to two bald pink patches. The coarse curled hair on his poll and neck looked as if it had been clipped. His great barrel chest heaved and fell as he assessed the new obstacle in his path. Then Canute turned back into the turpentine and crashed back along the path he'd come through.

Andy followed, dragging his torch behind him to keep the fire going but keeping a good distance between him and his retreating foe. He saw that Sean was bringing the bull-catcher steadily towards him and rode over to meet him.

'Here, ride this out,' he said jumping off the bike and into the vehicle. 'I can follow him out in the rig from here. We've got him now!'

Chapter 18

Bec's heart fluttered with anxiety and excitement. It was frustrating not being able to see what was happening. She knew Andy was still with the bull when she saw the second lot of smoke. She could hear the burble of the bull rig now, low geared and idling. She was just thinking Canute must be bringing himself back when the bull appeared from the scrub on the ridge. He hesitated before taking tentative steps towards the mob.

Bec felt the mare she was riding come up on her toes. Mischief tossed her head and flicked her ears back and forth as she pranced on the spot. Bec gasped involuntarily as the giant bull, its horns high and menacing, its mad red eyes glaring, shouldered its way into the mob. His sheer bulk at close range was frightening as he trotted along, oblivious to the other cattle melting away from in front of him.

Behind, Andy wasn't sure whether the bull would turn and make another run for the hills, take a breather in the middle of the mob or go through and make a break for the creek. As he watched, it quickly became clear the bull was gathering himself for a break, straight through the mob and out the other side. Andy spun the bull-catcher around to get to the other side of the mob.

Bec could see that the lumbering monster wasn't going to be calmed by the presence of the coaches as he made his way through the herd. In an instant, his colossal head jerked towards Bec and her mount and he set them like a missile locking on to its target. His head lifted higher and his gigantic neck expanded, rippling with great chunks of angry muscle. Within seconds the huge bull was at full gallop, charging towards her.

Bec's heart thudded in her chest, her hands were sweaty on the reins and she dug her heels into the mare's ribs all the while keeping her eyes on the beast thundering towards them. Mischief lunged forward and in a couple of strides was at full speed, racing away from the terrifying foe. Unseen, in Mischief's path, the goanna hole had been dug deep into the claypan and as her front hoof fell into the cleft she threw her head down, scrambling for balance. The reins were reefed through Bec's sweaty, grasping hands.

Andy was flying around the outside of the mob when he saw the bull set his wife. He pushed even harder on the already flat accelerator. Bec and Mischief were a very capable pair, but this bull was different. Panic coursed through his body when he saw Mischief stumble and the pair were sent sprawling onto the ground. The bull was almost upon them. Motor screaming, his foot jammed hard on the accelerator, Andy hurtled forward just in time to squeeze the vehicle between the lethal charging tonne of bull, the mare and Bec. With lightning reflexes the huge roan bull tipped his head to the side and drove one of his metre-long horns into the side of the bull rig with all his might, lifting two wheels off the ground as the vehicle skidded to a halt in front of him. The horn, being driven by such incredible force, pierced the steel side of the vehicle with ease. The dreadful curve of the iron-like spike, once through the side of the car, sliced through the bottom of the driver's seat and shafted upwards into the underside of Andy's leg, which was rigidly jammed on the brake pedal. The force of the impact snapped his thighbone like a dry twig. Splintered shards of bone sliced through the femoral artery as the inertia of his sudden stop drove the razor-sharp fractured bone up into his groin.

The bull-catcher lurched violently, Andy's body was held fast by the seatbelt but his head was whipped sideways and cracked against the side of the window. His vision blurred with the shock of the impact and he heard the awful sounds of the bull roaring as it shook its giant head in rage. Through blurring vision he watched in horror as the bull's horn cracked away from its skull and remained embedded in the car and his leg. The dreadful beast was free.

Andy swung his head around to see where Bec was. As the dust drifted past, he saw her racing back towards the rig on Mischief, yelling and screaming at the bull. She flew past Andy, thinking he must be having trouble with the vehicle not realising he was skewered to the seat, his lap already awash with blood, his leg useless. The bull lunged towards Bec's galloping horse, his mouth open and bellowing, one of his horns now a naked bleeding stump making him look lopsided and sickening. Bec leant over the mare's neck and urged her forward, resisting the temptation to look back over her shoulder as she led the charging fiend away from Andy and the vehicle. Once clear of the mob, the horses and vehicle, the tormented bull headed towards the river.

Knowing the fight with the bull was over Bec swung her horse back to the bull rig. Nudding and George were there gawking, hands hanging at their sides. Inside the vehicle, Andy's face was grey-white. There was a fine sheen of sweat over his face and the skin around his mouth was blue.

His eyes were wide and staring as with trembling hands he tried to stem the gushing flow of blood in his lap. The point of the horn had driven straight through his leg, exiting on the inside of his thigh. If it had remained jammed fast in the limb it may have steadied the flow of blood from the ruptured artery, but the bull had pulled the horn halfway out of Andy's leg when he'd tossed his massive head to free himself. Andy's life force was flowing away. With the artery severed, he was losing blood fast. His body was going into shock, the extremities turning blue and cold as his body drew all its energy to its centre to keep the organs functioning. A huge blue lump swelled rapidly at his temple.

Bec wanted to scream but there was no time. She knew that she shouldn't remove an embedded object from a wound but it was obvious that she had to get Andy out of the bull rig. Had to get him on the ground and elevate the wound. Had to locate the artery and pinch it off, get the Flying Doctor immediately and get Andy back to the strip at Balmacarra.

She started yelling instructions at the men to jolt them into activity. The impact of the hit had buckled the door and it was jammed shut. Despite their frantic efforts they could not get the horn out of the door. It had snapped off close to the outside of the door and they couldn't get hold of it and as it was still stuck well into Andy's leg, they couldn't lever or burst open the door to get him out. Time was running out. Fast. All the while Andy's blood gushed out of his leg and spilled from his lap onto the floor. It dribbled out through the buckled door into the grey dust of the claypan.

'Get him out the other side!' Bec screamed at them.

'We'll have to get the seatbelt off and lift him off the horn.'

'I'll do it,' said Nudding, pushing past the others, knowing that Bec wouldn't be strong enough to lift Andy and only one person could fit inside the cab of the car.

Andy was slumped forward onto the strap of his seatbelt, unconscious.

'Hurry up! Hurry, Nudding! Quick! Get him out! Get him out!' screamed Bec.

George grabbed her by the shoulders to stop her from clambering into the vehicle.

Nudding carefully eased Andy's shoulders back into the seat and unclipped the seatbelt. He knelt across the seat with one arm under Andy's limp legs and the other under his arm, and with super-human strength wrenched the stricken man up and off the steely horn. Scuttling backwards across to the passenger side he gently caught Andy's lolling head as he toppled sideways. The broken right leg fell at a horrible angle across the other and the entire seat and floor were covered in sticky arterial blood. George and Bec stepped forward quickly and helped to drag Andy from the car and onto the ground just as Sean arrived.

Coolibah Creek

'Sean, call Clarry!' ordered Bec. 'He can get up out of the timber and get reception. Get the Flying Doctor on the radio. Call anyone you can get on the UHF and ask them to ring the doctor, we need an aircraft immediately to Balmacarra: broken femur, head injury, blood type A positive. Blood type A positive. We don't have much time,' Bec screamed after Sean's disappearing back.

'Get his backside up,' said Bec returning to the task. 'Move him forward so that his legs can prop up onto the car.

'Pull the saddle off Mischief, George. Quickly, quickly! He's dying!' Bec's words were filled with urgency and dread. She put the saddle and padded blanket under Andy's backside.

'Nudding, you'll have to hold his injured leg up.'

In a flash Nudding was up inside the car, both hands around Andy's ankle.

'George, tie your belt around his leg. Tight. A tourniquet. Hurry! Hurry!' Bec was wracked with dread.

She had unsheathed her pocket knife and was frantically hacking the strong denim fibre of Andy's jeans away from the wound. Blood was pumping out of both sides of the leg not far from the groin. There was a jagged hole about ten centimetres long in the back and a smaller exit wound on the top.

'Davo, go and break off a couple of saplings for splints.'

'Pull his leg up, Nudding,' said Bec. She grimaced as she saw how severe the injury was – the thigh grotesquely distorted by the trauma. Bec knew that she needed to find the artery. The opening on the top was too small so Bec pushed her forefinger into the wound at the back. Tears sprang to her eyes and her agitation grew as she felt the grinding sharp points of many pieces of shattered bone. She felt through the hot, twitching flesh for the pumping artery and realised the torn vessel wasn't severed cleanly. The shredded muscle was swelling and closing in defence and the crisscross of bone chips made it hard to get to the source of the bleeding.

The tourniquet was beginning to stem the flow but still the blood ran out.

Davo eventually arrived at the scene. He had to navigate across the deep channels in the Toyota to get to the accident. 'Running to the ute, Bec grabbed the first-aid box and Andy's coat.

Andy was still unconscious and alarmingly pale. Bec covered him with the coat and felt the side of his neck for a pulse. The pulse was very weak and rapid, indicating he was in shock. She looked away, afraid that her emotions would overcome her and she wouldn't be able to function.

Bec told George to get the broad snakebite bandages out of the first-aid box. Working as quickly as she could, Bec bound the bandages tightly over the gushing wounds. Chest heaving, chin quivering, with blood stuck to her hands and face and in her hair, Bec stood up and stared down at her husband. The blood was no longer flowing and the thick wide bandages were white and clean, almost as white as Andy's face as he lay in a large puddle of his own blood. She dropped to her knees beside him and with all her inner strength held back her tears and her scream. She touched her trembling dry lips to his clammy forehead just as the chopper came in low overhead.

Clarry landed and came running over to where Bec was holding Andy's head in her lap.

Coolibah Creek

'Hang on, my darling,' she whispered, almost choking on her words. 'Hang on. I love you.' Her bloodied hand stroked the sandy hair back from his forehead before sliding down to his throat to check his pulse again. It felt like a fluttering moth under her fingers.

Clarry was hysterical and babbling the bad news that the Flying Doctor was up in the Gulf on another emergency.

'Alright. Get that splint on, George,' barked Bec. 'Can we strap him into the chopper, Clarry? We've got to get him back to the town, to hospital.'

With as much care as they were able, the trio lifted Andy's limp body into the chopper. There was little room in the cockpit of the mustering helicopter, just two narrow bucket seats.

A terrible panic gripped Bec's chest. She took Clarry by the shoulders and her fingers bit into his flesh. 'Andy's bleeding to death. I want you to try to call all the helicopter people and see if there's an emergency chopper or plane anywhere close by. Go! Go to Coombul!'

'I might not have enough fuel,' said Clarry.

'Go as far as you can. There's no time to go back to fuel up. Maybe you can pick up someone on the radio with an aircraft nearby or you might have to land at someone's place on the way, most people have av gas. Fly the road; there wouldn't be that much difference in distance. We'll get an ambulance coming out the road to meet you.'

Bec's mind was racing, searching for the best options. It was a matter of life or death for Andy.

There was no room for her in the chopper. She needed to take the bull-catcher. Nudding grabbed a sledgehammer out of the back of the Toyota and swung it at the door until it popped open and fell off its hinges. Then with one swift and well-aimed stroke he hit the ghastly blood-soaked horn and it dislodged from the seat. Tossing the hammer into the back of the vehicle, he quickly reefed the bull's horn out of the seat of the car and dropped it on the ground.

'I'll drive,' said Bec, pulling Nudding back and jumping into the driver's seat. She felt Andy's blood soak through her jeans as she threw the vehicle into gear and gunned the accelerator. Nudding just made it into the passenger seat in time.

'Hang on, Andy. Please. Hang on. We'll get you out,' she said.

On the radio, transmission was crackly and unclear as Bec spoke with Barb from Gungalla. Barb had been able to pick up their frantic calls. Clarry had also been able to get through to her once he was airborne.

'I've got the doctor on the phone.' Barb's voice came through over the top of the racing vehicle. 'He's still in the plane and on the sat phone, so he's a bit hard to hear. I'll relay.'

Bec gave all the details as clearly and as calmly as she could into the radio mike while driving with one hand as she tore along the bush track towards the main road. 'The thighbone is broken. Shattered. There's a major wound right through the leg. The artery has been cut. We have a tourniquet applied to the groin and a splint on the limb. He has lost a lot of blood. Over.'

Bec's voice was steady and strong as she relayed the information.

'Does the patient have any other trauma? Is there any other injury? Over,' the doctor asked.

Coolibah Creek

'Yes. He has a big bruise on his temple. His pulse is rapid and weak and he's cold to touch. Over,' said Bec, starting to shiver.

'How far are you from the nearest hospital? Over,' he asked.

'It's three hours from here by road but the patient is in the chopper. Over,' Barb replied.

'The patient we have on board is also critical. We cannot land before he is evacuated. Have the chopper follow the road. We will send an ambulance from Coombul to meet you. Over.'

'His blood type is A positive. Repeat A positive,' Bec said, swerving to dodge a kangaroo that jumped out in front of her.

In the helicopter, Clarry could see that the leg was now a very bad colour, blue from the tourniquet. Blood had seeped through the bandages and was dripping onto the floor. If Andy were to wake, the pain would be excruciating. His face was so pale and his hand felt cold. It was as if he were dead. Clarry's fingers pressed firmly on Andy's neck as he prayed for the pulse to be there. It was only a flutter. 'Hang on, mate. Hang on.'

'Ambo's left Coombul. They have blood on board,' Barb relayed the news to the pair of frantic travellers.

Clarry followed the route of the road in case he had to land urgently, cutting corners where he dared. He knew the country well and surged on at full speed. If he had to put down he would still be on the road where the ambulance would reach him.

Bec and Nudding followed in the bull rig at breakneck speed. She didn't know the road very well but she was a fearless and excellent driver. Wind whipped her hair across her face, stinging her cheeks and brushing away her tears. Awful images of the hunting dogs dying from being gored by wild pigs drifted through her head. They just sort of 'went', the dogs. No thrashing, no struggle, just staggered, fell and died. Not Andy. He was so strong, so healthy and young. Not Andy. No. No. No.

Bec felt numb in her seat and she shook her head trying to get rid of the images.

With the chopper at full throttle, Clarry was speeding north.

'Chopper to ambulance travelling to Balmacarra. Copy?'

'Copy you loud and clear. Go ahead,' the ambulance officer replied. 'What's your current position?'

'I'm around eighty ks north of Balmacarra, just coming over the bitumen now,' said Clarry.

Bec and Nudding could hear the two conversing on the radio. They were hurtling towards a fork in the road and Bec was unsure which way to go.

'Clarry. Fork in the road. Which way? Over,' she called shrilly into the radio mike.

'Go right, Bec. It's the short cut. Be careful, though. It's rough, but not far to the bitumen. Over.'

Bec swung the wheel right and spun the tyres as the V8 growled and lunged forward. Nudding grabbed the panic bar in front of him and leant forward with wide frightened eyes.

As they bounced along, Bec struggled to pluck the radio mike from its carrier.

'Clarry, is he still unconscious? Over.' Bec was afraid of the answer.

Clarry glanced across at his patient. Andy was slumped forward, still unconscious, and Clarry had to keep reaching across and tipping his head back concerned that his feeble breathing would be restricted. He kept his voice upbeat as he replied, 'Yes, he is. Might be for the best at this stage. But we're travelling okay. Over.'

Bec didn't answer; she was too busy driving like a demon over the rough winding track. Although they were travelling at high speed, Bec felt like she was standing still. After what seemed like an eternity, Clarry's voice broke the airwaves again.

'I've got a visual on you now, ambo,' he called.

'Okay. Thanks, Clarry. We'll pull up and get set up to receive the patient. Over and out,' the ambo replied.

Bec snatched up the radio mike. 'Where are you, Clarry?'

'Just coming up to Dingo Creek, Bec. Over,' Clarry responded.

Bec drove the dusty bull rig out of the side road onto the bitumen and turned north. Further up the road to Coombul, paramedics had Andy inside the ambulance. They struggled to get a vein to insert the drip, working one on each side, trying every different point. Ignoring their protests, Clarry clambered inside and pushed forward to grab Andy's cold hand, the tears now streaming down his face.

'Hang on, mate. Just hang on.'

He squeezed his friend's hand and backed out of the ambulance.

The paramedics found the vein and rigged the blood bag. 'Full sirens,' they called to the driver and the vehicle sped off up the road.

Chapter 19

Bright light from the floodlights in the emergency area poured onto Andy as the back doors of the ambulance were flung open. A bustling group of nurses and a doctor rushed forward and he was taken straight through to emergency theatre.

Fifty kilometres out of Coombul, the bull rig spluttered and coughed. Bec saw they were running out of fuel and quickly put the car into neutral and shut down the motor. The ensuing quiet was eerie after the continual revving of the motor for the last couple of hours. The only sound was that of the tyres crunching on the gravel on the shoulder of the road.

'Fuel in the back, Missus. I'll get it,' said Nudding.

Bec had almost forgotten he was there. 'There's a torch in the glove box,' she said, stepping out of the vehicle, her jeans soaked in Andy's blood.

Coolibah Creek

Nudding got the torch and went to the back of the rig to untie the jerry can.

'Let me hold that torch for you,' said Bec, anxious to get going again.

The car had enough fuel in the line to start immediately and Bec took off again at top speed. The suspense of not knowing if Andy was dead or alive was almost unbearable, but Bec focused hard on the road ahead.

As soon as they reached the hospital she jumped out and ran towards the entrance. For some strange reason she noticed that the stars were brilliant in a moonless sky. So many times she and Andy had made love underneath them, talked about their dreams underneath them...

Bec entered the building and headed for reception. She stumbled towards it and placed her quivering hands, still caked with dried blood, on the clean, smooth surface of the counter. There was no one there. She pushed the buzzer, looking around to see where a nurse might appear from. A matronly form waddled down the hallway towards her, her shoes making squeaking noises on the polished linoleum. Bec rushed to the nurse.

'I'm Bec Roberts. My husband, Andy, he's been admitted. The ambulance brought him in . . .' she was babbling.

The kindly matron took her by the arm and led her through to a small consulting room.

'Yes, Mrs Roberts. Your husband has been admitted. He's been taken through to surgery. Dr Anderson is in theatre. He has contacted a neurosurgeon in Brisbane. That is all we know at this stage,' she said in a calming voice as she sat Bec down and poured water from a cooler into a small paper cup.

'He's still alive? Oh, thank God.' The relief was enormous. But a neurosurgeon . . . ?

'Please, Mrs Roberts. Drink this water. You're going to need to be strong,' the matron said pushing the tiny cup into Bec's hand.

Bec swallowed the water in a single gulp.

'You said neurosurgeon? What's . . . Is he . . . ?' started Bec, struggling to find the words.

'Mr Roberts does have a significant head injury. Doctor will stabilise him first before attempting surgery on his leg. They need to get control of the bleeding. Then they will have a good look around, do some scans and make some decisions after they have more information,' the nurse explained. 'Is there anybody you would like to call, Mrs Roberts? I can give you access to an outside line.'

'Yes. Yes, please. I need to call Coolibah,' said Bec.

'This way,' said the nurse, motioning for Bec to follow her.

When Bec heard her mother's voice she broke down, sobbing great, rasping sobs, crying uncontrollably. It was in this state that Stephen found her. He cradled her in his arms, stroked her hair and kissed her forehead till gradually Bec started to regain her composure.

'Come on, Beccy,' said Stephen. 'There's nothing we can do here just at the moment. Best to get you a good hot shower and a meal.'

'I'm not leaving,' said Bec, adamant.

'You can have a shower here, Rebecca,' said the matron. 'I'll find you a theatre gown to wear until your father can get you some clothes.'

Touching Bec's arm, Stephen turned and left to go.

Coolibah Creek

'Dad, can you give Nudding a lift to his aunty's place. The bull rig isn't registered.' As soon as he was outside he rang Katherine. She directed him to where he could find some suitable clothes for Bec in her wardrobe at home. He met Nudding, who materialised from somewhere in the darkness, and they left together.

Bec shed the bloodied clothes, suddenly aware they had developed a sickly smell that coated the back of her throat. She bundled them up and stuffed them into the bin in the corner of the bathroom. Stepping under the hot needles of the shower, she felt her clarity of mind returning and the state of blind panic she had been in for the past five hours began to recede slightly. The pungent odour of hospital body wash was strong and it felt good to wash the blood from her skin and run the cleansing water through her dusty hair. She slipped into the theatre gown and padded back out to reception.

'My name is Sally,' said the matron. 'Here, put this around yourself and I'll take you up to intensive care.' She handed Bec a cotton blanket.

In the intensive care ward, the nurses told her Andy was still in theatre. They set Bec up in a reclining chair near the bed that was ready for Andy and gave her a cup of tea and some biscuits. She stared at them vacantly, unable to concentrate.

༄

Bec spent the night tossing in the chair and pacing around the room, waiting for news. She dozed off just before dawn and the clatter of trolley bed wheels woke her with a start. A wardsman, two nurses and a doctor wheeled Andy into the room. His head was swathed in bandages and an oxygen mask covered most of his face. A blood bag was attached to one arm and an intravenous drip to the other.

Bec bounded out of the chair and got out of the way as the group lined the trolley up with the bed, transferred Andy into the bed and checked a flashing, beeping monitor. Once they were satisfied that all was well, the wardsman and the nurses left.

'Mrs Roberts?' asked the doctor.

'Yes,' said Bec, resisting the urge to throw herself across Andy's chest and hug him.

'I'm Dr Anderson. Mr Roberts has had surgery to repair his femoral artery and pin his femur. We have had to shorten his right leg a little in the process, but other than that I believe the surgery went well.

'He has suffered a massive blood loss, and this has not been good when combined with the head injury,' said Dr Anderson before pausing. 'I will be doing more CAT scans, but I do have concerns about Andy's brain injury and condition. There's a possibility he may remain in a coma for some time.'

'What do you mean by "some time"? He will wake up, won't he?' asked Bec.

'Unfortunately we just don't know. With a brain trauma of this type, we can't make any accurate predictions at least until the swelling has subsided. Mr Roberts' blood loss has complicated things. He's extremely lucky to be alive and whoever administered first aid to him saved his life.'

Bec nodded as he continued. 'Please talk to him, touch him, play music. Even though he can't respond at this stage, we cannot say whether or not he can hear you. I'll be back at around nine o'clock and we'll talk further then.' Dr Anderson turned and left the room.

Bec felt overwhelmed by grief and worry. An awful roar of anguish lodged in her throat but she fought it down. Her tears drenched Andy's skin as she stroked his bare arms.

She gently touched her lips to his and whispered in his ear, 'I'm here, my darling. I love you. Stay with me, Andy. Stay with me, darling. I love you.'

There was no response, only the purr of the oxygen machine and the steady beeping of the monitor. Bec tucked the blankets around him, pulled her chair as close as she could and lay her head and arms beside him.

She began to pray.

Chapter 20

Andy was evacuated to Brisbane once he had been stabilised. In the beginning, Bec was filled with high expectations about Andy waking up and she spent almost two weeks speaking with specialists who were doing test after test at the Mater Hospital. Some were polite, some were abrupt, but all of the doctors and nurses were professional and caring. Bec thanked God that she had resisted the temptation to stop paying for health care insurance due to the financial pressures that the drought had brought. She was confident that Andy was receiving the best diagnostic and treatment care available.

Dr Arriotti stood beside Andy's hospital bed. He was the kind one. He had a head of tousled dark curls and big soft brown eyes. Despite being almost forty, he still looked like a uni student. His expression was sombre as he spoke to Bec, who was sitting in the chair she had been in 24/7. 'Rebecca, I'm sorry, but the injury that Andy has is such that we simply cannot predict what the future holds as far as the possibility of a recovery. We have come so far in the field of coma recovery but there is still so much we don't know. Andy has stabilised, the swelling has subsided. I am recommending that he be transferred back to Coombul. There is nothing further we can do here. I'm afraid that all we can do now is wait and see. That will be easier for you and your family at home.' Dr Arriotti's face was full of compassion. Bec felt the anticipation and hope she had used to shore herself up drain out of her like Andy's blood had done. As the buffer of hope disappeared, a raw and agonising grief was exposed. She slumped forward, onto the bed, her head cradled in her hands and began to sob.

At Coombul Hospital days rolled into weeks and then a month and still Andy remained in a coma. Bec had pushed through her grief and helplessness and reached deep inside for the strength to stay positive, to hold on to hope for a change in Andy's condition. She stayed by her husband's side and took care of his bathing and grooming. She talked to him all day. She read books to him and had a TV going in the room.

She played his favourite music to him. She cut his toenails and gently combed his hair. The prognosis was not encouraging but there were no certainties. Andy's leg was healing well but his brain injury wasn't allowing him to wake from his coma. The physiotherapist and staff at Coombul were exceptional and twice daily they massaged and moved Andy's body to minimise muscle wastage and stimulate circulation.

Andy's childhood mates, Clarry and Henry, as well as George, Nudding and Maggie's elder son, Sean, took over the running of Coolibah with lots of instruction from Davo. Katherine spent most of her time cooking and cleaning and trying to bring a sense of normality back to the homestead. It broke her heart to see Bec suffer and Andy lie motionless in hospital.

Bec's friends and acquaintances sent or brought a constant stream of fruit, chocolates, books and DVD's in an outpouring of support. At night, the strain of staying upbeat and cheerful for another day was released and Bec cried herself numb before falling into an exhausted, restless sleep. When she did sleep she was haunted by dreams about all the blood, so much blood, and Andy's pallid face. The terrible helplessness that had consumed her on the day of the accident lingered in her mind.

As she slept, Bec stirred and mumbled in her recliner at the hospital. In her dream, she could see Andy, just across the rodeo arena. He was talking and laughing with his friends. Her heart surged and sang in her chest and she was awash with yearning to touch him and run into his arms. She waved and called out but he couldn't see or hear her. She started towards him and noticed the sky turning dark with swirling clouds. The group were talking and laughing, unaware of the storm that was rushing towards them. Bec called again, trying to warn them, and ran towards Andy. Her legs felt heavy and constrained, like she was waist deep in water. Andy turned towards her and saw her. His face lit up and his beautiful smile was just for her. Bec could see the love and longing in his eyes. He ran to her and scooped her up, carrying her away to shelter from the tempest, speaking her name into her ear. The hardness of his strong chest and arms and the wonderful smell of him filled her with a euphoric sense of completeness. Bec felt warm tears of happiness on her cheek as she hungrily kissed him and clung to him, relishing the feel of his skin under her hands.

Then she woke up. As the reality of her surroundings drifted into her consciousness and the beautiful image of the dream receded, Bec realised that she was crying. She closed her eyes and pulled the blanket over her head, desperate to return to the dream, where Andy was awake and loving her again. Briefly, she was able to claw back the feeling. Her heart felt warm and full and her lips curved with the ghost of a smile. The sweet tears of happiness turned to the acid tears of despair as she watched the first grey light of a cold new dawn. Strangely, the dream stayed with her throughout the day. Feelings of the fantasy lingered and she found herself holding her arms across her chest and whispering Andy's name, clinging to the memory of the dream.

Lately it took all the feeble willpower Bec could muster just to face each day. She had to go to a doctor's appointment today. Her mother insisted she go. Katherine was worried about her. It had been almost two months since Andy's accident and it was like the light had been turned off inside her. Bec wasn't sure what a visit to Dr Morris would achieve but she did know that she needed something.

The walls of the waiting room were stark blue and white. As she had been since the day Andy had left her in almost every sense, she was only vaguely aware of her surroundings. A pale old man with a gravelly cough and a distraught-looking young mother rocking a grizzling infant back and forth were the only other people waiting.

'Bec.' Dr Morris poked his head around the corner and called her name. In his rooms, he spoke in soothing, sympathetic tones, gently asking questions and talking about tests and medication. Bec found it difficult to concentrate on what he was saying.

'How long since your last period?' he asked in his soft, whispering voice, as if he was asking her to tell him a secret.

Bec's attention was drawn to his kindly face as she pondered the question. She couldn't remember. When was her last period? Everything seemed to be a jumbled blur in her life.

'Don't worry, Bec,' said Dr Morris. 'Sometimes, in such trying circumstances you may stop cycling. I would like to do some blood tests so we can have a look at how we can help you with some supplements. Looking at your current weight, I'd say that nutrition hasn't been high on your agenda for a while.'

Dr Morris had his nurse take the blood samples and asked Bec to make another appointment for early the following week. She could not be persuaded by Katherine to go to the café, insisting that she had to get back to Andy at the hospital. Bec couldn't stand the pity in the townspeople's eyes, the way they turned their heads away, as if her grief was too hard for them to look at.

She knew there was much to do at Coolibah but she just couldn't find the strength to leave Andy. The burden of her situation was like a leaden weight on her life, too heavy to bear. She had no energy and no desire to do anything. All her dreams had evaporated.

Katherine chatted away cheerily as she drove Bec back to the hospital, though she knew her daughter wasn't really listening to her. When they arrived, she parked the car, turned to Bec and said, 'Bec, you need to come home to Coolibah. There's nothing more you can do here. The doctors and nurses are giving Andy the very best of care. You can't stay here forever. It's time to get back to your home. It's what Andy would want you to do. The bank manager has been calling. He needs to speak with you. I can't keep putting him off. Andy is taking a little time out but you need to get back in the saddle, Rebecca, and take the reins. Coolibah needs you,' Katherine implored. 'And you need Coolibah.'

'No, Mum. Andy needs me,' said Bec, getting out of the car and walking towards the main door of the hospital.

As Katherine watched her daughter walk away, her mobile rang.

'Mrs Hogan, this is Dr Morris. I can't seem to reach Rebecca on her mobile. Could you please have her give me a call at the surgery when she can?'

'I've just dropped her off at the hospital. She must have her phone turned off. I'll follow her in and get her to call you in the next few minutes,' said Katherine.

Dutifully, Bec dialled the number and was put through to the doctor.

'Hello, Mrs Roberts,' said Dr Morris.

'Hi,' she replied.

'Is your mother with you, dear?' he asked.

'Yes,' said Bec.

'It's just that I have some of the results back from the tests and I have some news for you.'

'Oh, okay,' said Bec.

'You're pregnant,' said Dr Morris gently.

Bec was stunned into silence.

'Are you alright, Rebecca? Please answer me.'

'I'm here,' whispered Bec, her head was swimming.

Katherine took one look at her daughter's pale face and rushed to grab her before she fell.

'Bec! What's . . .? Are you alright? Just sit down now. Big breaths,' said Katherine, lowering her into the chair and picking up the phone Bec had dropped.

'Hello?' she said into the phone.

'Katherine, I'm afraid I've given Rebecca a bit of a shock, but it was such wonderful news that I just had to tell her.'

'Tell her what?' asked Katherine.

'Rebecca's pregnant, Katherine.'

Katherine stood very still. She raised her head to the heavens and said softly, 'Thank you, Lord.'

'Thank you, Dr Morris. That's just wonderful news.'

'I'd say that she must be about ten weeks, so she's almost past the danger time, but I'll be in touch and I'd like to see Rebecca again as soon as possible for a scan.'

'Thanks again, Doctor. Yes. Goodbye.'

Katherine sank to her knees in front of Bec, gripping her hands tightly. 'This child is a gift from God, Bec. A gift from Andy.'

In Bec's eyes she saw the first slight flickering of a flame, a tiny glimpse of hope. She raised her daughter's hands and placed them on her pregnant belly.

Bec was remembering the night she and Andy were on the verandah at Coolibah when she'd brought up the idea of fertility tests and Andy had vehemently refused to go. She remembered the beautiful love they'd made after the argument, Andy claiming all they needed was more practice.

The precious nature of the gift she'd been given could not be described, could not be measured. She felt her strength and life force flowing back into her veins. It was a miracle. A sharp pang of regret that she couldn't share the happy news of the baby with Andy was not enough to quell the rising fountain of hope in her heart.

She had to get home.

Chapter 21

Far from the rolling plains of Coolibah Creek, Louise Connors was in her element. This was what she enjoyed most in life: entertaining, and entertaining the right people, of course.

Everything was going perfectly at her home in the exclusive Melbourne suburb of Toorak. Louise's parents' money had ensconced her in the highbrow neighbourhood, but her own earnings from the boutique and the income from Laurie's IT business only just kept her in the game. Constantly craving the society's inclusion and acceptance as one of them, she was excited and panicky that the people on her guest list had actually accepted for such an intimate party and were presently lounging with champagne on the terrace. *The* hottest new fashion designer in the country, Jennifer Paleos, the immensely rich and highly successful real estate magnate Rod Franklin, bank manager Trevor Gibson and diamond dealer Suzie Faulkner, who knew everybody who was anybody and everything about the social scene.

Louise loved to invite Suzie to her parties. She was a little overweight and loud. Her dress sense was outrageous and she was attractive and amusing, but not so much so as to outshine Louise. She had been 'friends' with Suzie for a few years. They both had businesses in the same building. Rod Franklin owned that building. Louise was dreadfully attracted to him; so young and virile, so ambitious and ruthless. Trevor Gibson was their new bank manager. He was new to town and single. Jennifer Paleos had no immediate family of her own but was related to Louise's husband. She saw Louise and Laurie as all the family she had. It was a distant family relationship but one that Louise was very quick to pick up on and utilise. She had even been able to persuade Jennifer to allow her to stock some of her fashion lines in her boutique.

Louise couldn't cook. She had ordered in from a fabulous restaurant three blocks away. All she needed to do was serve the magnificent courses. On the terrace, Suzie was holding the floor as usual, telling tales of her trips around the world buying diamonds. Fascinating and charismatic, she had a way of making most people feel awfully boring.

'Tell me, Rod, what's hot in Toorak real estate at the moment?' asked Suzie, waving her champagne flute about, flashing assorted jewellery on her fingers and wrist.

'The market has recovered a lot of ground since the crash, but property is still undervalued at present,' Rod answered. 'We've got a long way to go to get back to the top of the market. It's a once in a lifetime opportunity to get into property in Toorak,' he explained, ever the salesman.

Buying and selling real estate seemed to Louise to be such an easy way to make a lot of money, but she needed a sizeable chunk of investment capital to get into it. French champagne and delicate canapés loosened the guests' formal demeanour and the conversation and laughter began to flow. A delighted Louise and Laurie soon led their guests back inside to the dining room.

'So, Trevor, where did you come from?' asked Suzie.

'Oh, I've come over from Perth. I'm only relieving at this branch,' he said.

'I love Perth,' Suzie gushed. 'It's one of the loveliest, cleanest cities in the world.'

'My posting here won't be a long one,' said Trevor. 'I'm being transferred to a branch way out in the backblocks of Queensland somewhere. There are a lot of foreclosures to be done. Apparently it's been very dry up there and most farmers have little or no financial planning skills. The recent rainfall means that the properties have grass and water, which is worth something and it gives the bank a good opportunity to move those assets on and recover substantial amounts of debt. It's the bank's policy to remove the incumbent branch manager before we begin the foreclosures. I'll go in, do the dirty work, then move on. There'll be a relocation to a branch of my choice once it's all done,' he told them.

Louise was immediately alert, thinking about Coolibah Creek.

'Do you know exactly where you will be posted?' she asked casually.

'Coomtown or Coomvale, something like that,' he said. 'It's way out west. I'll have to buy an Akubra and some RM Williams boots.'

Louise knew that Trevor was probably referring to Coombul. *Interesting, very interesting*, she thought. She knew that Bec was in a lot of financial trouble. Despite her genuine concern for her brother, since Andy's accident Louise had been trying to think of a way to make her sister-in-law sell Coolibah so that she could get her share of the money. The clause in her parents' will stipulated that Andy was only required to make payments to her when Coolibah's financials were showing sound profits. Louise was becoming more and more frustrated with the situation and she knew it would be some time before the Coolibah Creek business showed a profit again. She wanted her money now. Rod was offering her the inside information on some property coming up for sale. She'd already let him know she was very keen to secure the property. It would be a complete loss of face if she couldn't come up with the finance. She had fabricated and woven a wonderful image of herself for Rod's benefit.

'You know, speaking of foreclosures, a dear friend of mine lost her husband recently . . . Well, he didn't pass away, but he's in a coma and doesn't look like coming out of it. She's quite bereft because it seems the bank has decided that, as her husband is the owner of the assets and he is now incapacitated, they do not have to extend the loan agreement to her, even though, if he had died, she would have inherited everything. Would that be true, Trevor?' Louise asked as casually as she could.

Trevor straightened up in his chair. 'Oh yes. That's entirely correct. The bank is quite within its rights to not extend the loan agreement to the spouse if the partnership becomes defunct. The bank may argue that they don't believe the spouse has the necessary business acumen to control the assets, and the funds and the loans would have to be renegotiated.'

Louise felt her pulse quicken. She smiled and was careful to show Trevor that she was suitably impressed by his knowledge. Her mind raced with thoughts about how she could ensure Trevor made a foreclosure on the Coolibah Creek loan. He looked quite pleased to be at the dinner in this company. Perhaps he would be interested in helping her out in return for some favours. She would begin immediately to bring him closer into her circle, make a friend of him. Then she would be able to sell him a story about how her wicked sister-in-law was holding what was rightfully hers. She could let him know that Bec had absolutely no financial management training and was simply a bush bumpkin who would lose everything in the end, including Louise's inheritance. After all, the financier would never believe that a woman could run a large outback cattle station on her own.

'More wine, Trevor?' Laurie asked, and exchanged a knowing glance with Louise.

༄

At Coolibah, it was as if the land had been fully sated, released from its tormented starvation and, after expending so much energy to revitalise, was now reclining with a sigh of relieved contentment. Bec's life was hectic as she managed the property and made the six-hour return trip to Coombul twice a week to be with Andy. Her pregnancy

Coolibah Creek

gave her the will to go on, to continue to live out her shared dream with Andy of passing Coolibah Creek on to their child. She felt her vigour returning as each day passed and began to see again the splendorous plains filled with waving Mitchell grass and the glassy waterholes in the creeks reflecting the towering gums. She saw the miraculous change in the cattle as they became sleek and fat. Everywhere she looked she saw Andy and she could almost hear his voice, his comments about the bountiful season and the cattle. She could visualise his broad white smile and twinkling dark eyes. Andy might not be with her but his spirit was close.

As she drove back to the homestead after completing a bore run Bec's hand rested on her belly. She was beginning to show and had felt the feathery fluttering of movement. She had never cherished anything so much and her unborn child was like an energising force in her centre. Katherine was outside shifting the sprinkler when Bec pulled up at the homestead gate. Bounce flew out to meet her. 'Kettle's on,' Katherine said as the pair went inside. They had to do a stores' stocktake and prepare a shopping list for their trip to Coombul the next day where Bec had a meeting with the bank manager.

*

Bec was infuriated when she learnt that the bank had transferred yet another branch manager.

'You just get to know your manager and go through all of your business details trying to explain the cattle industry and how our business operates out here and they change them again. In comes another boy from the city, wet behind the ears and with absolutely no idea about your situation, and so we have to start with the basics all over again. It's so frustrating!' fumed Bec to her mum.

'Are you sure you don't want me to come with you?' asked Katherine.

'No, Mum. I'll be fine. You get yourself off to the hairdressers,' said Rebecca as she dropped her mother off at their family home. 'I'll meet you for lunch at one o'clock at the café.'

Why is it that everything is grey inside bank buildings? Bec wondered idly as she waited to see the manager. The walls, the furniture, the filing cabinets, the office equipment; everything was grey and cold and sterile.

The manager opened his door and came towards her dressed in his grey suit and tie, smiling an artificial smile. Even his eyes were grey.

'Mrs Roberts. Trevor Gibson. Nice to meet you,' he said, extending a cold, soft hand.

Bec shuddered involuntarily with a sense of foreboding. 'Hello, Trevor. Please call me Bec,' she replied and followed him through to the office.

'We have received all the necessary documents from your solicitor regarding the will and so forth, Mrs Roberts.'

Why do they always speak like undertakers? Bec thought as the manager continued.

'The bank has taken the liberty of having a property valuation update on Coolibah Creek as well. We have made an assessment of the current liabilities and forecast cash flow for your business for the next five years. I'm afraid that these figures are not looking at all promising. Unfortunately the extended drought and subsequent increase in loan facilities has seriously eroded your equity levels. Without any further capital available to you, stock purchases are out of the question and you will be unable to return your breeding herd numbers to sufficient levels to demonstrate a sustainable capacity to service your existing loan. Our calculations show that it will be two years before you have sufficient cash flow to fully service the loan facility and operating costs. It could mean the forced sale of breeders in order to continue to operate. Unfortunately, once your breeder numbers fall below that critical level there is simply no way out.' He paused. 'It is the bank's view, Mrs Roberts, that the best option for you at this time would be the sale of Coolibah Creek.'

Bec felt her face flush with anger. 'STOP! Stop right there, Mr Gibson. That is not and will not ever be an option. I want to be very clear about that.' Rebecca leant forward in her seat and looked straight into his emotionless eyes.

'And I would like to make it equally clear to you, Mrs Roberts, that you have no choice. The bank has determined not to extend the loan facility to you.'

'You what! That can't be right. The Roberts' family have been customers of this bank for over fifty years. We may be extended now but we have always negotiated our terms and paid on time.' The colour had drained from Bec's face and there was a tremor in her voice.

'The loan facilities were extended to your husband, Mrs Roberts, not to you. Mr Roberts is the owner of the land asset. The bank has determined that you do not have the necessary experience or financial skills to operate a business of this magnitude. You have no personal history with the bank other than a savings account. Prices for land at the moment –'

'No! No! No! Mr Gibson,' Bec interrupted him. 'You don't understand. You will never understand. But let me tell you that you will not be selling Coolibah Creek while ever I can draw breath.' Bec was on her feet now, leaning over the desk, pointing her finger and speaking through clenched teeth.

Trevor Gibson tilted back in his swivel chair and laced his fingers together in his lap. He stared back up at her, silent and unperturbed by her anger.

Rebecca wanted to hit him. She resisted the urge to knock the supercilious look off his face and up-end him off his chair. She gathered up her bag and documents folder and left, slamming the door behind her.

In the car park, she fumbled for her keys and opened the door with shaking fingers. She had never before felt such outrage. *How dare they!*

Bec gripped the steering wheel with both hands until her knuckles were white; white like the white-hot anger in her belly. Her mind raced. There was only one solution. She had to pay the loan instalments. She had to get the money from somewhere. If she sold every beast she owned it would only cover half of the total debt. Their breeding herd had been decimated by years and years of drought.

She could take on agistment cattle, but the payments came in instalments and agistment properties were everywhere at the moment as people had grass but no stock and no money to buy stock. She'd go to another bank. She'd . . .

A huge sob shook her and she slumped over the steering wheel. The sobbing was uncontrollable and it racked her body. Hot tears dripped onto the wheel as her mind frantically searched for a solution. She would not allow them to sell Coolibah. Pulling herself together she phoned Katherine and arranged to meet her at the house instead of the café.

Katherine came rushing through the front door when Bec turned into the driveway. 'What's happened?' she said breathlessly, seeing her daughter's red eyes and obvious distress.

Bec told her the story and tried to hold herself together.

'We'll sell this house!' Katherine said without hesitation. 'It's got to be worth five hundred thousand.'

'Oh Mum, that is so generous of you to even think about that, but it would take time. What if it didn't sell quick enough? There's only a certain amount of people willing to live in Coombul, let alone pay five hundred thousand for a house,' Bec explained.

Katherine frowned. 'Yes, you're right, but it's worth a try. Lord knows we don't need this huge house anymore. Dad could become your guarantor for the loan. His solicitors' business is worth a bit.' Katherine searched for solutions.

Bec covered her face with both hands but there was nowhere to hide. She flopped onto a dining chair and stared out the window. 'There has to be a way, and I'll find it,' she said with fierce determination.

The phone rang, interrupting their thoughts. Katherine answered it.

'Oh hello, Davo. Yes, Bec's here somewhere. Just hold on. I'll see if I can find her,' said Katherine, raising her eyebrows in question and pointing to the phone.

Bec nodded and got up out of the chair.

'Davo. How are you?'

'I'm good. Yeah, real good, Bec. I was wonderin' if you'd have time to go to the vet for me while you're up there. Ol' Boof's gone and got tangled up with a boar pig somewhere down the creek. He's tore up pretty bad. I've talked to 'em so you'd just have to pick up a parcel for me, love,' said Davo.

'No worries. I'll be home tomorrow,' said Bec.

'Goodo. I'll come over and pick it up t'morrow evenin'. You alright, Bec? How'd you go at the bank?' asked Davo.

'I'll tell you tomorrow, Davo. See you then, hey,' said Bec.

Out at Balmacarra, Davo pushed back his battered old hat and scratched his head. Didn't sound too good. Maybe Bec was having trouble with the bank. It'd be too much for her to cope with.

Davo frowned and reached down to rub the ears of the dog curled up by his side. 'Don't worry, little mate. Ol' Davo'll look after you.'

༂

The following evening at Coolibah, Bec poured out her story to Davo. He sat quietly, smoking and scratching and shaking his head.

'Fancy 'em havin' the hide to say you couldn't run the joint. Crikey, Bec, you're one of the best men I know . . . If you know what I mean, mate,' he said, rolling another smoke. 'So how much do you need? If it's not a rude question?'

'Over three million dollars. To pay it all out,' said Bec.

'Three million, hey. Oh well, yeeaaah, that's a lot o' money alright.' He lit the smoke and drew heavily on it. 'Anyhow, luvvy. Don't you worry too much about it. I'm sure it'll all come good in the end. Somethin'll come up.' He patted her on the shoulder and rose out of his chair.

'Better get going, if I want to get home before dark. Get this medicine into me ole mate and fix 'im up. Thanks for that, Bec.' Davo strode away down the verandah and out to his old ute.

Rebecca stayed put and reached over the table to where the mailman had left the mailbag the day before. She sighed as she opened it and tipped the contents out. Flicking through the mail she came to an official-looking envelope marked 'State Government'. *What now?* she thought, tearing open the letter and unfolding the pages. Her eyes widened and her mouth hung agape as she read the letter.

> Surveying and studies of the region have determined that an area of the Coolibah Creek Channels is suitable for listing as 'significant' as part of the Significant Wetlands Project. The State has legislative commitment to protecting these significant areas and maintaining their ecological integrity in order to preserve the natural values of the river catchment and its associated flora and fauna. Please refer to the attached map for the parcel of land that the State has identified for resumption. As the leaseholder, you will be fully compensated for the resumption at market price or above. We will be in contact with you over the coming weeks to explain the government's requirements for land management practices prior to the processing of the resumption.

Bec ripped off the front page of the letter and stared at the map underneath. A huge parcel of the Coolibah Creek lease was marked on the map; an area covering about one-third of the property and encompassing all the prime channel country. She sat staring at the map, bewildered. 'Andy. Andy. What am I going to do?' she muttered to herself.

The sun had set when the rattle of the Toyota disturbed Bec from her thoughts. George and Nudding had come home from around the run. She stood up abruptly. They'd all want some dinner soon. *Better get moving.* She really couldn't deal with the wetlands resumption at the moment while she searched for a way to take on the bank.

She busied herself in the kitchen, grateful for the distraction of having to prepare the meal. It was going to be a long night.

Chapter 22

Sitting in the office, where she'd been all morning, Rebecca ran her hands through her hair. She had been over and over the cash flow figures and five-year budgets. They were sound. Coolibah would be able to recover, she just needed time; something the bank would not give her. She was hoping to use the government's wetlands resumption as a stalling tactic. The uncertainty of tenure would limit the immediate options for the sale of Coolibah Creek, but that uncertainty would also make it impossible for her to transfer to another bank for refinancing. As soon as they checked the lease they would discover that it was earmarked for partial resumption. If the department took all of the channel country out of the Coolibah lease its productivity for grazing would be halved in the low rainfall area of Telford. Bec felt like a cornered animal. She could surrender or she could fight her way out.

As there was a better, more diverse, wetlands site through her boundary at Lennodvale, Rebecca felt she had a strong case to object to the proposed wetland resumption. She imagined that the departmental staff thought it would be easier to wrest the land from her than from Doug O'Donnell. She needed help but she didn't know where to turn.

Katherine did. She had been trying to contact Stephen in Brisbane. Now was the time to act. Their daughter's life was being stripped away from her, yet again. Stephen must help her out. Rebecca was so stubborn and independent but this was not the time to be proud.

The first glimmer of hope for Bec came from a most unlikely quarter. Doug O'Donnell phoned when he heard about the wetland listing.

'Just bloody ridiculous, Beccy. Everyone knows that the biggest area of wetlands and bluebush swamps is on Lennodvale. The channels all branch out here. It's kilometres across them and then they all run into the bluebush swamp, the lowest part that fills before the water goes on and back into the main channels. I reckon that swamp must be connected to the underground aquifer. It's a permanent hole and there're always birds there, even in the drought. No, mate, seems like someone has just got it in for you. Probably something to do with your father; you know, political. I'll ring 'em up. I want to sell this joint anyhow. Can't bear to be here now that Maggie's gone, and it's hard for the boys.' Doug's phone calls were always one way. He talked and Bec listened.

'Course Lennod's a lot bigger place than Coolibah, too. I could let 'em have that corner and I'd still have a lot of country. You gotta go over their head, Beccy. Get your ol' man onto it. Look, I'll let you know when I've talked to 'em.' Doug hung up. He wasn't one for pleasantries.

Bec was elated. Doug was right, of course, but she had been wary about approaching him. Surely the department could be swayed into an agreed resumption, rather than a hostile one. At least Doug's thoughts gave her something to cling to.

She was clearing off the table and stacking up the papers when she heard the dogs barking. Someone had driven into the yard. Bec smiled when she heard the familiar raspy voice of Davo chiding the dogs for barking at him.

'Hey, you cut out that racket, you silly ol' dog. You know it's me,' he said as he stooped to ruffle the blue dog's ears.

'Davo. G'day. Come in, I'll put the kettle on,' said Bec, surprised to see him.

'That'd be good, love,' said Davo.

Rebecca noticed that he seemed to be striding very purposefully and with a spring in his step.

'You look chirpy. Did you have a win on the horses in Coombul?' she asked as Davo pulled off his boots at the door.

'You could say that I've got some good news, yeah,' he said.

Bec made the tea and got out Davo's old tin pint that he left at Coolibah for when he visited. He reckoned ordinary cups were too small.

Davo's face suddenly turned serious when Bec sat down across the kitchen table from him.

'You know how close I was to Andy's father and mother and to Andy. Can't believe we lost 'em both.' Davo's eyes filled with tears. 'Matt Roberts was my best mate. He was always very good to me. Looked after me. All the time. And Andy, well, when Matt and Joycie were killed, I sort of looked on him as my boy, the one I never had, sorta thing. Anyway, I know you're in a bit a strife with the bank and I'm going to help you out.' Davo pulled an old bag out from under his shirt.

'There's two hundred and fifty thousand in there. I want you to take it. Go and pay the bank. Might hold 'em off for a while.' He pushed the bag across the table. 'Now don't try to talk me out of it. It's what Andy and Matt would expect me to do, and it's what I want to do and what I'm going to do. I won't stand by and watch them take Coolibah off you, love.' Davo was adamant.

Rebecca was dumbfounded. 'Where did you get this sort of money, Davo?'

'Oh well, I already had around a hundred in the bank. See, I don't spend much. I live pretty simple, so over the good years at Balmacarra I put a bit aside. I went and borrowed the rest. Never done that before, but they nearly fell over themselves givin' it to me. So now I'm givin' it to you.

'Don't care when you pay me back, or if you pay me back, Balmacarra stock will cover the whole one-fifty if I have to sell all of 'em to settle with the bank.' Davo had thought it through. 'If we do no good with this, I'll sell the whole joint and we'll just keep Coolibah and you'll have to build a humpy out on the boundary for me an' me dogs,' he chuckled. 'Now, are you gonna pour a man a cuppa?' Davo said, indicating that that was the end of the discussion.

Bec's eyes filled with grateful tears and she placed her

Coolibah Creek

hand over Davo's. 'Thank you. Thank you, Davo. Andy would have . . .' She began to cry.

'Don't cry, luvvy. No more cryin' now. You gotta get on with runnin' this place for when young Andy junior comes along, hey? Now how about that tea?'

※

The next day, Rebecca drove to Coombul with her bag of cash. She had made an appointment with Manager Gibson for eleven o'clock. The money would be enough to make the loan repayments for the year. That meant that Bec wouldn't have to sell weaners and would be able to allow her young cattle to grow out into double the value animals later on. She could also retain her aged breeders due for sale and get another calf out of them, increasing her herd numbers. With the proposed wetlands land resumption now stalling any immediate forced sale by the banks, Davo's money would mean that in twelve months' time Bec would be able to demonstrate a more sustainable and rapid return to profit.

Gibson's manner was crisp and serious when he ushered Bec into his office.

'How can I help you, Mrs Roberts?' he asked.

'Funny. I thought that helping me was one of the last things you wanted to do, Mr Gibson, but I'd like to know whether or not you have commenced foreclosure procedures,' said Rebecca with a sweet smile that didn't match the anger in her eyes.

'The paperwork is on my desk at this very moment, in fact,' Gibson said, lifting a folder out of his in-tray.

'What is the minimum amount of debt reduction required to delay the foreclosure?' asked Bec.

'Oh, that would be approximately two hundred thousand dollars immediately, and a further two hundred thousand in six months,' said Gibson.

'Check the account balance, Mr Gibson, and file your paperwork for now,' said Bec before storming out of his office. She'd deposited the money Davo had lent her before the meeting.

Outside in the car, Bec sat with the keys in the ignition and started to giggle. Then she started to laugh. She hadn't laughed for so long and once she started it seemed she couldn't stop. People passing by stared at her but she didn't care. She touched her hand to her little baby bump. 'Round one to us, bub!' she said as she started the car.

Bec met her parents at the RSL club for lunch. She got so much pleasure from relating the story to them that she couldn't keep the smile from her face.

Stephen and Katherine were pleased to see her laugh. It had been so very long since they'd heard her laughter. They ordered lunch and Stephen told her how he had just that morning organised the processing of a two hundred thousand dollar loan through his bank.

'It will be there whenever you need to draw on it,' he said. 'So I don't want you to worry about the bank and Mr Gibson at all, okay? You need to get on with looking after yourself and your baby. Nothing else matters,' he said.

'Your father's right,' said Katherine. 'Now let's enjoy our lunch.'

Bec reached across the table and grasped her parents' hands.

'Thank you,' she said simply. 'We'll pay you back. Every cent.'

Later, at the hospital, Bec told Andy all about the day's happenings. He lay motionless in his deep coma. His face was pale and gaunt. She lovingly rubbed his hands and feet with oil, brushed his hair and kissed his face. She lifted his hand and placed it on her tummy.

'Soon, when you wake up, I have the most exciting news of all. You will be so excited when I tell you,' she said. 'I miss you so much, my love. Please come back to me.' But there was no response, not even the slightest movement.

Dr Anderson came in later in the afternoon. 'Physically he's doing as well as can be expected. His leg has healed beautifully and his circulation is good. Unfortunately, his brain injury is another matter. We know so little about his particular situation. I'm sorry I can't give you anything more definite. He may come out of the coma, or he may not.'

'Thank you, Doctor,' said Bec. She had asked all the probing questions many times over and the answers were still the same. She stayed with Andy for a while longer, massaging his arms and legs again, talking continually about what was happening at Coolibah. All too soon, she had to leave. It was a long drive home and she didn't want to do it in the dark. Still, she hated leaving him.

༄

Bec was so proud of her baby bump. All the men on Coolibah treated her as if she were made of glass. She found that a bit hard to cope with. She felt strong and healthy and she focused on getting Coolibah back on track after the decimation of the drought.

Stephen was pushing her to get the artesian water project concept down on paper. 'Now is the time, Rebecca.

We have a once in a decade opportunity to try to get this off the ground. You're the one who can draft the project concept and the partnership proposal. I'd like to take it to the party and to an election, I'm that confident. The Save Our World First sustainability summit in Cape Town is the perfect venue to present your project internationally, which is where we need to go with this. Always be bold and think big. Think big and believe,' he urged.

Bec tried to dodge taking on the enormous task. 'Everything you say is right, Dad, but I just have so much on my plate at the moment.'

'I understand all that, believe me I do. But others can take care of the running of Coolibah. Nobody else can write up this project like you can, and there'll never be a better time to do it. Just think about it?' he asked.

'Okay, I'll think about it. Promise,' said Bec.

'The Cape Town summit is in September, so you have a couple of months to polish it up. You can do this, Rebecca. And I want to present it to the summit with you. I believe in you and the project, so let's get into it, hey.'

Stephen made it sound like a walk in the park, and his enthusiasm was contagious. When Bec put down the phone, she did think about it. She thought about how Andy would want her to 'have a go'. The artesian water was their shared dream of a utopian future where drought was something never to be feared again; it guaranteed a more secure and prosperous future for Coolibah, the region and their unborn child.

It was almost nine-thirty at night when she sat down at the computer to pour onto the screen a description of their vision and the pathways to achieving it. As the dawn broke, she had a rough draft outline and a name for the project:

Telford Gold. She clicked send and emailed it to Stephen before crawling into bed, emotionally drained and physically exhausted.

She'd barely got to sleep before the phone rang. It was Stephen.

'Brilliant, girl. Real big-picture thinking but with a depth of knowledge and strong solutions. It's good, really good.' Stephen was positive, as usual. 'I'll have Justine Rand go over it, with your permission, and advise on the right way to go about getting support from the environmental lobby to ensure there're no angles we're missing with regard to people getting in the way of the project development.'

'I don't like that woman, Dad, but I guess she knows her job and that's the most important thing. Time to get it out there and have a go,' said Bec.

'If we can pull this deal off – creating a partnership between three levels of government, an international environment preservation group, a local co-op of landholders and an international hotel group – it will be a world first,' said Stephen, his voice full of excitement.

'It sounds good, Dad. How realistic it is, we'll find out I guess. Getting the money to drill so far down for the water will be a big hurdle,' Bec said.

Chapter 23

Justine lay naked on the back deck of her unit, warmed by the autumn sun. Her lover rubbed coconut oil on her back. His strong hands felt wonderful on her skin after the cold, clammy touch of Angus Dalgliesh. It had all been worth it, though. Justine knew that she had power over him now and her position at Phosec was secure. Just the thought that she might agree to another rendezvous at some time in the future was enough to keep Dalgliesh on a string.

Her mobile rang. She reached out a long, lazy arm to answer it.

'Justine Rand,' she said sleepily.

'Hello, Justine,' replied Stephen.

Justine rolled over and sat bolt upright, flicking the hair from her face. The sound of his voice was having the same effect on her that it always did and she was troubled by her body's reaction.

'Stephen. How are you? How can I help you?' Justine heard herself prattling.

'I wondered if I could arrange a meeting. I have a project concept that my daughter Rebecca has drafted and I'd like to employ your skills to work through it with us. When would be a good time?' asked Stephen.

'I'm busy all of this week with Phosec. But early next week should be fine. How about Monday ten am at your offices?'

'That's good. See you then,' said Stephen before ending the call.

Justine lay back and felt the warm sun caressing her skin. *That was easy*, she thought. *The mouse came to the cat.*

A fine prickle of goose bumps rose on her body as she anticipated the encounter with Stephen. She reached for the young massager's hands and placed them over her breasts.

~

The following Monday, Bec and Stephen met with Justine at his office in Coombul. Bec was pleased to discover that Justine Rand was more than a pretty face. She grasped the Telford Gold project concept immediately and the three of them brainstormed enthusiastically for over two hours before Stephen suggested they take a lunch break.

At the café, Justine smiled and waved to Brendan, who was sitting at an outside table with his partner. *Well, well, why am I not surprised*, he thought, seeing his friend in company with Stephen Hogan. Justine winked at him as she passed.

Lunch was no distraction for the trio, who sat at a booth in the rear of the café and continued developing their ideas. 'We will be pushing for time, but there may be a great opportunity to put our concept forward on a national platform if I can convince the Feds to convene the National Drought summit. There has been some rain this year but it will be some time before graziers get any cash flow. Droughts are part of Australia's climate and we need to be better prepared for the next one. There is a lot of uneasiness among the backbenchers about the lack of support for drought-affected farmers and they are looking for new ideas,' Stephen explained. 'I should have an answer this week about whether or not they are going ahead with it.'

༄

Over the next six weeks, Stephen, Rebecca and Justine met often. They worked hard on developing and detailing the Telford Gold project.

'We need to have a trial run on our presentation before we take this to the Cape Town summit,' said Stephen. 'You can have the best product in the world but if you cannot sell it, you've lost.'

'That's your area, Dad,' said Bec. 'You're the one with the gift of the gab.'

'I agree,' said Justine, looking at him.

'I want to pull together a dinner in Canberra. Get the right bums on seats down there. We're going to need high-level support from the government and the media if we're to get Telford Gold up.

'Bec, I need you to get a good beast processed, the best you have, as well as a collection of any other produce already produced here in the Telford Shire. I have a mate, Anton – he's the head chef working at the Hyatt. I could give him the product and have him create a menu for a gala dinner. Nothing like a good wine and an excellent meal to make your audience more amenable.'

'How are we going to fund it?' said Bec. 'I don't reckon it'll be cheap.'

'Say, seventy people at two hundred a head, that's fourteen grand for the dinner, another ten for the production, printing, design etc. Twenty-five grand tops. I'll look after that,' said Stephen.

As Justine got further into the development of the Telford Gold project, it became difficult to stick to the confidentiality condition she had signed in her contract with Phosec. Telford Gold depended on getting water to the surface. Phosec intended to do just that, but Stephen and Bec had no idea that was being discussed. Justine was playing both fields. She could see how she could position herself to be the hero for both parties, but she hadn't quite worked out how to manage that at this stage. She hadn't mentioned the hatching of the Telford Gold project to Phosec, but the time was fast approaching when she would have to give Angus Dalgliesh that inside information, even though professionally she had an obligation to Stephen and Bec to keep it under wraps until the soft launch of Telford Gold to politicians and journos in Canberra.

She had successfully evaded Stephen and Bec's questioning about Phosec and their intentions for Coolibah Creek, but it was getting increasingly difficult. She would have to put her mind to working out her next move.

'See you in Canberra.' Justine gathered up her papers and left as the meeting closed.

'Have you spoken to Louise?' Stephen asked Bec.

'Yes. I have actually. Took a bit of working up to, for me to be civil to her. I'm afraid I don't have your gift, Dad,' said Bec.

'So, how did you go?'

'Oh, she came straight in. I explained to her that I had held off the bank foreclosure for now with the loan payments made and the uncertainty over the lease due to the wetlands resumption. I also told her that the value of Coolibah could increase tenfold along with the annual income if the Telford Gold project got up. The green monster took her over in a flash,' said Bec. 'But I think she was even more interested in being part of the project. I could hear her mind ticking over, thinking about how she could boast to her high society friends, and it would be good if we could get some of them to the Canberra dinner.'

'Well,' said Stephen, putting his arm around her as they left his office, 'sometimes you have to swallow your pride to get the result you want.'

෴

Stephen Hogan, Member for Telford, was in Canberra. National media coverage of the plight of outback Australians and their battle with drought had significantly raised his profile within the nation's capital cities. As a result of Stephen's campaigning, the National Drought summit had been called. The federal and state governments knew they had to develop policy around drought preparedness and future drought management as well as work out the most effective way to deal with the immediate problem of farm debt. The summit included a session on alternative and innovative industries in arid Australia. This was the ideal platform for Stephen to present Bec's Telford Gold proposal.

It was mid-morning on the first day of the summit when Stephen strode purposefully onto the stage and the resonant tones of his voice captured the audience's attention. The Federal Ministers for Agriculture, Industry, Tourism, Trade and Environment, and their advisers, had dropped their initial condescending demeanour and were really listening. Stephen was engaging and charismatic and when he invited Rebecca Roberts to speak, her sincerity and passion had shaken the attending journalists out of their disdainful slouches. This was something new.

'As Rebecca has demonstrated,' said Stephen, 'the added advantage and one of the most significant features of the aquifer is its recharge capabilities. Even though Telford is in a low rainfall area, when the rains do come, recharge is rapid and substantial due to the porous nature of the overlaying rocks and the extensive catchment area, which results in extended flow times for rivers and creeks over the recharge area. Almost all the areas of land around the world that are not developed and are still in a natural state remain that way due to the lack of water. Our vast underground water resource will make this project unique and will pioneer a land use system that is fully integrated, highly productive and does not compromise the integrity of the natural land values but in fact enhances them.

'A world first, the Telford Gold project will be leading the way and forging a path forward to where we produce food in harmony with the natural environment, as opposed to the now widespread use of chemicals to force the land to yield beyond its natural capacity. The possibilities for development and expansion are endless. Add to this the bonus of clean geothermal power availability through the "hot rocks" resource, with zero emissions, and you really wonder what we are waiting for.

'As complementary industries become established, Telford will become a vibrant and unique place to live and work, attracting the necessary personnel to carry it on to bigger and better things. Ladies and gentlemen, it's simple. When water, land and power are clean, natural, bountiful and cheap, profits come easily. The Telford Gold project will no doubt attract accolades from environmental groups and governments worldwide, and I am here today to offer you the opportunity to be part of it and take it forward.'

Stephen knew he had them. He could tell they had sniffed the sweet smell of success and they wanted to join in. They were beginning to realise that he was presenting them with something that could give them a high profile, not only in Australia but around the globe, and politicians loved the limelight. Like a school of mullet, the attendees flicked their tails and turned in unison to a new direction.

'All the scientific data, infrastructure models and costings are with the department offices. Rebecca and I look forward to your company at dinner this evening, where the chef will be serving some samples of the Telford Gold produce,' said Stephen as he closed the presentation.

Together Stephen and Rebecca were a formidable team, and by the time the meeting ended they had turned the mood of the summit attendees from one of scepticism to eager optimism. They had sold the Telford Gold ideas, and the government representatives were scrambling to jump on the bandwagon. For them it was a way out, a project that could deflect public concerns that the government was doing very little to help drought-affected farmers. Louise had come good with her pledge to get some celebrity names on the invitation list and Stephen, Rebecca and Justine were looking forward to the next step forward on the Telford Gold journey.

Chapter 24

In the cab with Stephen on the way to the hotel after the presentation, Justine had never felt so alive. Rebecca and Louise had stayed behind to finalise seating arrangements for the dinner. The last six weeks had been a blur of frenetic activity for Justine as she was caught up and whisked into the whirlwind that was Stephen Hogan's life. His determination and drive were contagious, and he pulled those around him along in his wake as he forged ahead strong and confident, like an all-conquering captain at the helm of his ship.

She glanced at him now as he stared out the window. He looked relaxed but Justine knew that his mind was racing, scanning the future, looking for minefields or ambushes, anticipating any issues that might get in the way of his plans and thinking of ways that he could avoid or obliterate such

Coolibah Creek

obstacles. Magnetism radiated from him, prickling her skin and blurring her thoughts.

She didn't speak. She'd come to know when he was thinking. She'd come to know a lot about him and everything she knew, she liked. She had been puzzled by his professional manner when he was with her. He'd kept her strictly at arm's length. She hadn't detected a hint of attraction from him. She was well aware of his reputation with women and felt put out that he hadn't made a move on her. They all did eventually. She had surprised herself, too, when she'd become so totally absorbed in the Telford Gold project. She'd worked hard on it and, as she reflected now, she realised it was probably the first worthwhile thing she'd ever done. Still, her attraction to him was so strong she was reaching the end of her rope in playing the 'untouchable, aloof, hard to get' game with Stephen. But she was enjoying the build-up, savouring the lingering, because she was certain that she would get the prize. Even so, she knew that this evening it would be difficult to stay away from room 309. Katherine had not made the trip to Canberra and they would be together with Rebecca and Louise at dinner.

The attendees at the launch had received a folder full of beautiful photographs and explanatory diagrams and maps as well as a gold-embossed invitation to dinner at the Hyatt. There were seventy people invited to the dinner. Stephen's uncanny knack of knowing just the right people, at the right time, in the right place had come good for him again. He had selected the right media and departmental heads and advisers to ensure the most positive outcomes from the dinner, and Louise's invitees added to the mix of the occasion. Anton, the head chef at the Hyatt, had backpacked through Europe with Stephen when they were in their twenties. They'd spent a couple of wild months together. Stephen knew that Anton's culinary skills were astounding, and they'd talked at length about the dinner, the menu and what Stephen was trying to achieve.

Every head in the function room turned as Rebecca, Justine, Louise and Stephen walked in. Rebecca, suntanned and glowing in her pregnancy, was elegantly dressed in a lace-overlain sage gown, clasped under the bosom, that fell full and softly to her silver shoes. Louise was sophisticated and immaculate in black sequins. Stephen, tall, imposing and confident, swaggered in his beautifully tailored tuxedo and black tie. Justine looked stunning in a long-sleeve red sheath that clung to her body and left her shoulders bare, exposing her flawless, golden skin. Stephen knew that she was the trump card in the game he was playing tonight. He knew she would captivate everyone over the sumptuous dinner he had organised.

He couldn't recall any woman he'd known being more beautiful. He'd resisted the temptation of courting her because she was doing such a good job on the project. He wouldn't risk igniting her emotions while they were working so well as a team. Doing so might compromise the very good progression of the proposal. He could wait. He was so close to helping Rebecca realise her dream and to cementing his image as a visionary and a leader, an image he wished to cultivate to further his political ambitions.

The last of the guests arrived at the sumptuous Hyatt, and Stephen kept the conversation light and humorous over pre-dinner drinks. A quartet played soothing music in the corner of the room and two enormous screens on the stage displayed images of running water and outback vistas. As each course was served, the screens showed footage and explained about the food and its production.

The entrée was tempura golden perch strips served on rocket and shredded beetroot and dressed with fresh bush lemon juice and olive oil.

'One hundred per cent native organic, the flesh of the golden perch is soft and moist and similar to the highly regarded barramundi.' The words rolled out underneath an image of the dish on the screen.

Stephen entertained his guests with comical stories of his adventures in far-flung places around the world. He didn't ask for opinions or compliments on the fare; he just waited for them to come. And they did.

'Telford Gold organic beef has an entirely different texture and flavour to the grain-fed product that most restaurants use,' the diners read as the main course was served. The description continued. 'So much so, that the chef has heralded it as an entirely new type of beef, a distinctly different cuisine. There's a delightful texture in the steak that releases the richest, most fabulous flavours of the outback. The accompanying sauce is whole crayfish tails, sautéed with garlic and chilli, blended with full cream. The dish is accompanied by a selection of organically grown steamed vegetables and topped with crisp shaved sweet potato.'

The diners' banter was subdued while they ate. They all agreed that the meat was indeed full of flavour and the red claw crayfish was similar to lobster. By the time the dessert was served, Stephen's guests were bubbling with enthusiasm for the organic products they'd sampled.

Justine was charming throughout the dinner, smiling sweetly, and speaking softly, listening and agreeing, all the while noting how the men around her became less guarded in concealing their stares as the wine took effect.

'I would like you all to raise your glasses in a toast to the time when we will be enjoying the fine wines from the Telford Gold district,' spruiked the Minister for the Environment, Minister Matthews already claiming ownership of the brand. Journalists' cameras flashed, the Telford Gold proponents were fantastic photographic subjects and the images would sit well with the news copy they were typing into their devices already.

As the dining part of the evening ended there was an air of jovial celebration in the room. The screens showed images of exotic waterbirds silhouetted against a vibrant red sunset and then faded to star-studded skies as Bec stepped onto the podium to close the evening.

'I thank you, honourable ministers, ladies and gentlemen, for your attendance this evening. It has been our very great pleasure to host this function and to present to you for your enjoyment a small sample of the unique and excellent food products that are produced at Telford. We believe that the entirely natural manner in which we aim to use the incredible natural resources at Telford will bring the whole world to our table, and we have been pleased that you could share with us the "first sitting".'

Applause erupted around the room, and journalists rushed off to write their articles as the room buzzed with compliments. The evening couldn't have been a greater success. Stephen, Rebecca, Louise and Justine bid their guests goodnight and moved to the plush lounge chairs in the cocktail bar. Louise left with her friends to go on to another party.

Stephen reached across and clinked his port glass with Justine's and Rebecca's coffee cups and looked up at them from under his brow, a mannerism of his that Justine found so appealing.

'To us,' he toasted. 'And to Telford Gold.'

'To us,' said Justine, holding his gaze, looking into his bright eyes, struggling to keep the yearning from her voice.

'To Telford Gold,' said Bec. The road to this moment, making this presentation, had been difficult. So many times, while worrying about Andy and praying for his recovery, and grieving for her lost friend, Maggie, she had wanted to give up the dream and retreat to Coolibah. She was elated at the response they had received and how the evening had gone off, but now that it was over she felt a wave of exhaustion crashing down on her.

'I think I'll head off to bed,' she said wearily. 'It's been a big day. I think it's all catching up with me.'

Stephen stood up, concerned at the way his daughter's face had suddenly paled and the tiredness in her eyes. 'I'll walk up with you,' he said, moving to take her arm.

'No. I'm okay. Truly, Dad, I'm just super tired. You stay and enjoy your nightcap. God knows you've earned it. Goodnight,' she said, kissing her father on the cheek. 'Goodnight, Justine.'

Stephen sat down and turned the conversation to business, discussing the excellent job the chef had done with the food and the dinner guests' reactions.

'Your work on this project has been invaluable, Justine. I want you to know that I value the part you're playing,' said Stephen as he finished the last sweet drops of his port and pushed himself out of the soft chair. 'I have to go. I have a few phone calls to make.'

Justine was sorry he was leaving so soon but she didn't let on. 'Of course, I do too,' she said, rising and straightening her dress.

They parted in the lift. Her room was on the floor below his. She slid her card into the lock and stomped into the luxurious room, tossing her evening bag on the bed.

'That man!' she said out loud. She caught sight of herself in the full-length mirror. She'd never looked better. She plucked the clasp from her hair and it fell to her shoulders, soft and glossy. 'That's it. Time's up. I can't stand this any longer,' she told her reflection.

She went into the marble bathroom and rummaged through her beauty case for floss. She did her teeth, reapplied her lipstick and some more perfume, slipped her card into her bag and marched out of the room again. Destination: 309.

Justine quivered as the lift glided up to the next floor. What was her excuse for coming to his room? Her mind raced to catch up with where her body was taking her. Excuses and reasons, lies and fabrications usually came so easily to her.

'Damn him. He's driving me crazy!' she cursed.

Suddenly she was at the door, the gold number 309 squarely in her face. She was knocking. She still had no excuse. It would come to her. It would just pop into her head in an instant, like it always did when she was caught out. She knocked again, a little harder. Her heart was hammering as she shifted nervously from foot to foot.

There was no answer. He was gone.

'You bastard!' she swore. 'Phone calls, my arse!'

Justine spun on her heel and bashed the lift button, frustrated and fuming.

Coolibah Creek

Outside the Hyatt, Stephen got in the cab. 'It's been a long day for me, Fiona. All day in the same room with you. Such pleasure and pain,' he said.

The ministerial adviser took Stephen's hand and looked at him with adoring eyes as they sped away into the myriad of city lights.

Chapter 25

The morning after the Telford Gold dinner, Rebecca had an appointment with a neurosurgeon. He was purportedly one of the best in the nation and Dr Anderson had forwarded the details of Andy's case through to the specialist's surgery.

'Nothing is certain in these cases, Mrs Roberts. However, if you are willing to transfer Andy into my care here in Canberra, I do believe that we may be able to progress a couple of options with the aim to return him to consciousness. Until that happens, we will not know if there's been any permanent damage to the brain which may cause dysfunction,' Dr Suko said.

Bec's thoughts tumbled around in her head. She wanted to give Andy every chance of waking but she didn't want to send him so far away from Coolibah. At least while he was at Coombul she could visit him regularly. The thought of using experimental drugs and electric stimulation of the brain was abhorrent to her, but she knew she had to do something. How long would these procedures take? What were the chances of success? These were the questions for which there were no answers. She knew Andy would want to try every avenue. She had to be brave, as brave as he would be. The specialists had advised that even though there had been no response from Andy in the past, over time there could be undetected changes in the brain's condition.

'The complexity of the brain is something that medicine is a long way from fully understanding, Mrs Roberts. My advice to my patients is that it's not unreasonable to hope for a miracle. The treatments will give Andy a chance. We will repeat the functional MRI tests as there may have been improvements. The electrical impulses of the brain will show us if Andy can in fact hear us. We will be able to monitor the changes in his brain activity. Comatose patients may have complete loss of movement and feeling and yet still have hearing and cognitive function,' the doctor explained.

Bec's heart missed a beat. 'Is that really possible?' She was thinking about the hours she had spent telling Andy all about everything that was happening.

'Yes, it is. I have to say that it's not common but there is a chance,' said Dr Suko.

'In that case I would be very pleased if you would accept Andy as your patient.'

Bec tried to quell the rising phoenix of hope that welled up inside her.

༄

At Parliament House, Stephen was meeting with Joseph Matthews, Federal Minister for the Environment.

'Great function last night, Stephen. You're to be commended for your efforts,' he said as his secretary brought in two cups of coffee.

'Thanks,' said Stephen, taking a sip. 'I'm interested in your opinion on how far you think we can go with it.'

The minister was blunt: 'A big bucket of money is required to get the water up to the surface, especially given the untested nature of the development and the state of the government coffers. Could be hard to make it stack up against other priorities.'

'The elephant in the room is the building of the storage dam for the water, if you can manage to get it to the surface. It's going to have to be a very sizeable structure, and I reckon the enviro groups and the Greens would be all over you. There have been no major water storage projects get up in over a decade, anywhere in the nation,' the minister said.

'Yes. I agree,' said Stephen. 'They are the two big obstacles. If we can manage those issues, where will the Feds stand on supporting Telford Gold using some of the infrastructure budget?' said Stephen, glad he could speak frankly with Matthews.

'Provided there aren't any huge and sustained objections from any of the big players in the green movement, I think the Feds are looking for something positive and some alternative solutions for drought management. I can see real potential for dipping into the research and development buckets across a number of departments as well,' he said.

The meeting lasted half an hour and Stephen felt buoyed by the minister's support. He picked up his messages and dialled Rebecca as he was driven to the airport.

'How did you go with Dr Suko?' he asked her.

'I'm not game to hope, really, Dad, but he told me Andy might be able to hear everything we say even though he can't move or feel,' said Bec, her voice choking.

'Sweetheart. Look, it's a possibility. At least you've been offered a chance. See you soon.' Stephen disconnected and flicked through his contacts for Fiona's number.

'Hi,' she said, answering straight away. 'Do you absolutely have to go home today?'

'Yes I do, my lovely. But I'll be back soon. And when I come back, I hope I can count on you to get my stuff through to the minister.'

'You know you can,' replied Fiona.

꿈

In the airport lounge while they waited for their flight, Rebecca talked with Stephen about Dr Suko's treatment for Andy. Justine was quiet and aloof, still angry with Stephen for not being available when she wanted him to be. The fact she couldn't yet have him only fuelled her desire.

Eventually the conversation turned to the SOWF Cape Town summit. 'It's not far off,' said Stephen. 'We need to be ready. We've had a good trial run with this presentation but Cape Town will be a whole new ballgame.'

'We'll need some solid solutions to the problems around getting the finance to bring the water to the surface and build the dam,' said Bec. 'And then there's the opposition from the Greens about building a storage of that size.'

'I can help you with both of those problems,' said Justine, looking at Stephen. 'I'm bound by a confidentiality agreement with Phosec, but very soon there'll be a development to do with the mine that will be very advantageous to the

Telford Gold project. Further, I have a strong connection with SWOF and I know that they have the power to either ignite or put out fires with regards to media reporting on particular projects. A story is only as good or as bad as it is portrayed in the media. Reality and truth are quite frankly irrelevant. You'd be aware of that in your profession, Stephen. There may be options open in this regard.'

Their conversation was interrupted by an announcement on the public address system. 'Calling all passengers for flight QF1562 from Canberra to Brisbane, your flight is now boarding at gate 24.'

The trio gathered up their hand luggage and walked towards the boarding area.

Bec couldn't wait to get home. She was too preoccupied with Dr Suko's information about Andy to dwell on Justine's comments, but she could see that they were fully engrossed in conversation as they walked through the crowded airport.

༄

It was dark by the time their connecting flight touched down in Coombul. Rebecca was tired, it had been a very busy and emotional month. Even so, she was eager to get up to the hospital to be with Andy.

It was eight-thirty when Stephen dropped her off at the hospital and continued on with Justine in the car. 'Make sure you pick up something decent from the café,' he said. 'You've got to eat properly.'

'I know, Dad, and I will. Goodnight,' she said.

Instead of going straight to the ward Bec stopped at the café and bought a chicken and salad wrap and a flat white. After she'd finished eating she went and sat in the armchair at Andy's bedside and told him all about her trip to Canberra, her visit with Dr Suko and the Telford Gold presentation dinner. At midnight she climbed up on the bed beside her husband and lay there with him.

Bec slept soundly until dawn, oblivious to nurses coming in and out of the room. She awoke with a start, took a moment to realise where she was and then got up quietly and went to the bathroom.

Walking back to Andy's bedside, she lifted his hand and placed it on her swollen belly. The baby was kicking furiously. 'I'm sure it's a boy, my darling. I've gotta go now, but I'll be back soon.' She kissed him goodbye.

∽

A week later, after travelling eight hundred kilometres to inspect then buy some bulls, Bec arrived back at Coolibah on a sunny day.

'You look fantastic. How's my grandchild?' said Katherine, hugging her daughter then patting her belly.

'Bub's being good to me. No more morning sickness. I'm a bit busted though to tell you the truth, Mum, but it's good to be home.'

Her little terrier, Bounce, ran out and started dancing around her legs, jumping up for attention. Old Jess sauntered out as well, her tail wagging.

'How've things been here? You have the garden looking good.'

'With lots of help from dear old Sam. He's just wonderful,' said Katherine.

Over a sandwich and a cup of tea, Rebecca filled Katherine in on Andy and the Telford Gold project.

Katherine worried about the stress Bec was under and how it would affect her pregnancy.

Bec smiled wearily. 'I'm convinced it's a boy, and I swear he's doing somersaults in there. The baby's the most important thing, everything else is crowding in around me, but our baby . . . I know I need to take care of myself.'

'Good. Why don't you go and put your feet up for an hour?' said Katherine, rising and collecting the dishes.

'I might just do that. The bulls won't be here till the morning and the men are away at Balmacarra,' said Bec, yawning as she walked down the hall. She liked being home. Andy's presence was all around her, and she could still detect a faint scent of him in their bedroom.

Chapter 26

Rebecca was sitting by Andy's side inside the Flying Doctor aircraft. They were on their way to Canberra for Dr Suko's treatment. The twin engines sounded loud and an acrid hospital smell coated the back of Bec's throat. A nurse with a serious, pinched face fussed over and constantly monitored Andy. The baby suddenly lurched and turned in Bec's abdomen and she felt the bile rise in her throat as a wave of nausea broke over her.

'Are you okay, Mrs Roberts?' asked the nurse.

Bec nodded, though she felt anxious about the flight and about what the next few days might bring. 'The baby's just done a swan dive. I'll be fine in a minute.'

'Here's a sick bag, just in case,' said the nurse, plucking a plastic bag from a compartment above them.

'Thanks,' said Bec, clutching the bag and trying not

to think about what would happen if Andy's treatment didn't work. What would the future hold if Andy stayed in the coma? She so desperately wanted to share their baby with him.

She'd been working on the Telford Gold project with renewed passion and belief since receiving a letter and seeing a notice in the local paper about Phosec Mining's intention to dewater an aquifer to gain access to whatever they were after. Justine had hinted that the mine's activities would be advantageous but this development was monumental with regard to advancing the Telford Gold project.

Rebecca remembered their recent meeting.

'I'm excited about the opportunity to bring Phosec into the partnership for Telford Gold development but what will the downside be? What are they mining and what will the impact be on the rivers, the land and our organic status?' she'd said.

'Good points, Rebecca,' Stephen had said looking at Justine, realising she had inside information she wasn't sharing.

'I can't tell you,' said Justine. 'It's more than my job is worth, and my reputation as a consultant would be shot if I compromised the company's information. All I can say is that everything will be revealed pretty soon.'

She'd been right. Less than a week later Justine reported that the Phosec directors wanted to meet with Stephen and Bec and they'd flown out to Coolibah Creek in the company's light aircraft. The plane levelled out and stabilised and Bec felt her nausea abating as she remembered Angus Dalgliesh, brash and bombastic, waddling down the dusty Coolibah airstrip in his smooth Italian suit and shiny shoes. Almost alien-like, he'd looked so out of place. *At least he didn't try the moleskins and hat*, Bec had thought.

The information the directors had provided over afternoon tea that day had been mind-numbing.

'High-quality diamonds. That's what our information is telling us,' said Dalgliesh. He explained how, after they'd been revealed underneath the water, the diamonds would be extracted underground and only the gems would be brought to the surface. 'The Coolibah Creek diamond mine will be listed automatically as a project of state and national significance. The listing cuts red tape and opens doors, gets the fiddly things out of the way,' he explained. 'The water and the deposit are in a structure like a bath tub with a plug hole. By removing the water, we will have adequate space to mine and process underground,' he'd said. 'We'll be shipping our product out by air, which is the most secure way to transport the diamonds. This will necessitate the construction of an airport and terminal. We may be interested in partnering with a hotel group to construct an airport capable of receiving international flights.

'There's also the opportunity for other Telford Gold products to be airlifted out to anywhere in the world once the runway has been constructed.'

Bec had felt her heart racing in her chest. What had seemed like a long shot, a distant dream, an unrealistic utopia, suddenly loomed tantalisingly close. It was amazing.

'Miss Rand is assisting Phosec with the environmental impact studies and also with our community consultation process. We would be very happy to include yourself and Stephen to assist with the community consultation phase.' He paused and looked at Justine. 'People trust locals.'

'The area of most concern for both Phosec and Telford Gold is where the water goes,' said Justine. 'Prior to finding out about the Telford Gold proposal, Phosec's option was to pump the water into existing waterways.'

'But surely that option would be even more contentious and unpopular than the construction of a dam? People hate seeing water wasted. And there are serious implications for flora and fauna if the water composition is changed so dramatically,' said Bec.

'Our whole Telford Gold concept is reliant on natural organic production. What chemicals will be used in the extraction process?' Bec asked.

'This is the best part, Mrs Roberts,' said the geologist the directors had brought along with them to the meeting. 'Mostly we will be using water only. The primary lode is, we believe, located in sand and soft sandstone. Hydraulic water jets will dissolve the surrounding material but diamonds are so hard and water resistant that there is no damage to the gems. A process called cone screening, where the heavy diamonds fall to the bottom, will be used to extract them.'

'It sounds too good to be true,' said Bec.

'We believe the Coolibah Creek deposits will be one of the richest, most valuable diamond discoveries in Australia's history, Mrs Roberts. So you can understand we're keen to progress as soon as possible,' said Dalgliesh.

'We are happy to be generous in finalising your land access agreement terms if there's any detrimental effect on your grazing business. We'll also be immediately offering you access to our power supply,' he said and smiled broadly again. Justine had told him there was no grid power in the area and residents had to rely on generators and solar power.

Stephen and Justine spoke at length with the visiting party about government regulations and response as well as legal matters. Bec remembered that, at the time, all she could think about was how she wished Andy was with her at the table to hear the momentous news. Could she dare to hope that their future would be so exciting and secure?

Her stomach lurched again as the plane began its descent. Had she been daydreaming that long? Thankfully the landing was smooth and they were met at the airport by an ambulance that transported them to the Canberra Private Hospital.

After Andy had been admitted, Dr Suko advised her that it would be better if she didn't stay for the treatment.

'We will have to attach electrodes and various other unsightly things before he goes through the treatment process. I've found in the past that loved ones tend to find this particularly stressful and there's nothing you can do to help. It's best that you get on back to living your life and looking after yourself and your baby. I'll be in touch regularly and you can phone me at any time,' he said.

Rebecca hated leaving Andy so far from home, but she steeled herself to go. Placing both hands either side of her husband's face, she kissed him tenderly. 'Good luck, my darling. I'll be back soon. I love you,' she said and reluctantly left the room.

She was pleased that she would be flying back to Brisbane and Coombul with her father. She would be glad for the company and much happier about flying in the jet than the smaller Flying Doctor aircraft. She fell into Stephen's embrace at the airport when they met and he held and comforted her. She always felt safe in his arms. Once on board, despite her fear of flying, she fell asleep before the stewards served the meal.

When she arrived at Coombul, Bec drove to Coolibah immediately, where the mustering was in full swing. The cows were fat and strong after months of feeding on good grass and those that had calves needed them to be weaned. The new bulls had to be put into the herd as well.

Clarry, Nudding, Sean and George were all good stockmen and, due to her pregnancy, Rebecca was not allowed on a horse or a bike. Driving slowly behind the backsides of the fat, shiny cattle waddling knee deep in an ocean of grass, her thoughts of course turned to Andy. She remembered when she'd first met him.

Bec had just graduated from university as a primary school teacher. Thrilled to get a position teaching with the School of the Air in her home town of Coombul in her first year, she had become friends with Maggie O'Donnell from Lennodvale. She'd always loved and ridden horses and her calling to the bush was strong. She had been excited to accept Maggie's invitation to join them for the mustering during the school holidays and was helping out tendering on the neighbouring Coolibah Creek muster. The O'Donnell boys had been young then and their father yelled and barked at all three of them all day.

Bec had a little mob of cows and calves trotting along the edge of a steep river channel when they came to the next cattle pad crossing. The leaders turned sharply and plunged down the precipitous track they knew so well. The passage of their feet crunched in the deep sand as they porpoised across the bottom of the river. A baby calf, only a few days old, struggling through the tall, dense grass, missed the right-angle turn and kept trotting forward, past the crossing. Suddenly his mother had disappeared and he bawled loudly, scampering forward, panicking, further away from the mob.

The cow, down in the channel, called to the calf and he halted his flight, looking left and right, confused and lost. Bec kept her distance, knowing that the calf would only run away blindly if she approached. She had to wait for it to get a bearing on where its mother was. After repeated calling from his mother the calf stumbled back through the tall grass towards the sound of her bellows. He struggled through the growth on the very edge of the bank, unaware of the five-metre drop beside him. Blinded by the vegetation, he weaved his way through it, till suddenly he slipped and fell over the edge. About halfway down, his back legs caught in the exposed roots of a tree that protruded from the riverbank and he hung there, calling out as if he were being eaten. The cow called frantically to him before trotting back up the pad and along the top of the bank, then she ran back down into the river, her drooping, heavy udder swinging to and fro as she went.

When the cow was at a safe distance, Bec quickly took the opportunity to jump off her horse and scramble down the slippery bank to try to reach the calf and release it. She turned to face the bank wall and slid over legs first, clutching the wiry grass and trying to find a foothold and ease herself down. Feeling with her feet, she found a tree root and gingerly placed her weight on it. She bounced on it to test it and when it didn't break she released the grass. Just as she did, the root snapped. It sounded like a gunshot in the quietness of the bush and it echoed up and down the river channel.

Bec slid down the side of the wall. Her hands snatched desperately at the grass tussocks. She hit her head and lost her hat. Her face was scratched and covered in thick mud that stuck in her hair and made it stand straight up on one side of her head in a sort of punk style. She came to rest on the same exposed root as the calf and clutched fiercely to the final clump of grass. Three metres below her was a cool clear pool of water where the river had cut away the bank. The sand would be soft and the calf was newborn and pliable. He wouldn't be hurt by the fall if she could get into a position to lift him up and free his legs.

She was contemplating how best to do this when she was startled by the sound of a deep voice. 'Can I help you there?'

Rebecca looked up sharply, still clinging to the grass with both hands. There, above her, a man drew rein on a big dancing chestnut. The blue cotton of his rolled-up work shirt pulled tautly across the bunching muscle in his arm as he sat loosely and comfortably in the saddle. His face was chiselled and tanned and, although he didn't smile, his brown eyes danced with amusement as his mount pranced impatiently on the spot.

Suddenly very conscious of how she looked, Bec let go of the grass with one hand to touch the muddy side of her face. She felt her hair sticking up and her embarrassment rose to colour her cheeks as she had tried to think of something to say. The shift in her weight was sufficient to find the flaw in the root. With a loud crack it broke and sent Bec and the calf screaming downwards, where they both crashed into the pool below. In the creek bed, not far from where they landed, the cow rushed up to the fallen pair, threateningly lowering and shaking her head. The calf sprang to its wobbly feet in the shallow water and in an ungainly gallop ran to his mother's side, and the pair turned and hurried up and out to the other side of the river. Bec, though, was firmly planted in quicksand.

She had landed feet first and been plunged thigh deep into the cold, clinging sand. Try as she may, she couldn't move. Struggling to free herself, she looked up to see where the stranger was and saw that he was scrambling down the steep bank with tremendous balance and agility. Rebecca felt so foolish and struggled furiously to release her legs from the cold vice-like grip of the sand but the more she wriggled the further in she went. She felt the sucking sand enclosing her buttocks and the icy water seeped between her legs.

'Keep still,' the man commanded. Bec didn't like his tone but she froze and looked at him, angry and embarrassed at the same time. Their eyes locked and Rebecca could see the amusement in his expression. He was gorgeous and he tried to keep the smile from his face as he instructed, 'You just stay put. I'll get a branch that you can latch on to and I'll pull you out okay.' Bec just nodded. *How did she get into this ridiculous situation?*

The stranger walked away and soon came back with a long, thin piece of wood perfect for the task. As he poked one end of it towards her he said, 'I'm Andy Roberts. I own this joint. Grab the branch and pull it past you so that you have half each side,' he said. Bec obeyed silently. 'Okay, now what you have to do is push down on the branch and try to pull yourself up. Once you can release the seal of the sand, push the branch back to me and I'll try to pull you out.' *Sounds reasonable*, Bec thought. She pushed down hard on the branch and was relieved when she felt her body move upward. 'Righto. That's good. Now pass the end back to me,' Andy instructed. 'Hold on tight,' he said, and gave an almighty heave. Rebecca came free of the sand and stumbled forward, gathering momentum in her urgency to escape. Suddenly she found herself clinging breathlessly to her rescuer. She blushed as she became aware of the hardness of his muscles and the strength in his arms around her. Shuddering with relief, she lay against his chest trying to regain her composure, dismayed by the way her body reacted to the smell and feel of him.

Extricating herself from his embrace as best she could, she leaned back and said, 'Thank you. Thank you very much. I . . . I . . .'

She was infuriated to see that he still had that cheeky, amused look twinkling in his eyes. 'You must be Rebecca. Pleased to meet you,' he said offering his hand.

Then he smiled and as Bec placed her hand in his and looked into his face she felt a shiver of delight tingle down her spine. She had never felt like that before.

'Thank you,' she said simply, continuing with the task of brushing away the cloying sand in order to avoid meeting his eyes.

'No worries. You okay?' Andy asked placing his hand on her arm.

'Sure, sure. Yes. I'm fine. Bec Hogan from Coombul,' she said and looked up. The merriment in Andy's eyes was irresistible and suddenly she started to smile and then laugh out loud. Andy had never heard a more beautiful sound. The air between them crackled with a physical attraction so strong that they both felt it like a hand clutching at their collars and pulling them together, a compelling force. Their laughter simultaneously stopped and they both looked away, startled by the strength of the emotion.

'I'll go and find your horse,' Andy said quickly. 'See if you can climb up the bank without falling back down,' he teased before scampering back up to the top of the vertical ascent and disappearing.

'We'll be right now, Bec,' Clarry's voice crackled on the two-way radio, jerking Rebecca out of her reverie and fond remembrance of her first meeting with the man she'd married and back to the muster at hand. The cattle were almost at the yards.

'All okay, Clarry. I'll head back then,' Bec said and turned the Toyota for home. She needed to get to work on setting out her conditions for the land access agreement with Phosec, and she was still working with Doug and the department to have the wetlands resumption area moved to Lennodvale.

Hours later, after Bec had everyone fed and clear of the kitchen, she phoned Stephen.

'I'm going to go for power for all of our neighbours, not just for Coolibah. Having access to twenty-four hour power would save thousands of dollars annually in fuel for generators. Do you think that's pushing things too far?' she asked her father.

'No. I don't, especially if Phosec tap into the hot rocks. It will be expensive to establish but then the energy is free. They'd have a good chance of getting some subsidisation from government to tap into it because it's emissions-free too,' replied Stephen. 'We have an opportunity to develop a really comprehensive list of resources for the future as we see it and how Phosec can be involved.'

'It will be an opportunity for Phosec and mining to enhance their public profile and social licence,' said Bec.

'Yeah, I agree; though they may think there's virtually no political pull out here because of the low population. It's a long way from city media, too,' said Stephen.

'But if the mine is as lucrative as they believe it is, the things that seem unattainable to us now might be a drop in the ocean for them, especially if we look at a staged progression of infrastructure establishment. I've made some points for the draft conditions,' said Bec and she proceeded to read out the list. I've asked for power to all within one hundred and fifty kilometres, unlimited access to a specific bore head from which the water will be sourced to go to a storage to be determined and regular independent testing of the water at nominated sites.

I've stated that Phosec should construct the necessary storage infrastructure to contain the water, and I also want annual compensation for the loss of grazing land and impact of roads and traffic on our herd.'

'You could add something about the local shire council to build, own and operate the airstrip in partnership with Phosec and the State government Royalties to the Regions bucket of money. Fees and charges to go to Telford Shire.

And of course Phosec would fund sealed roads from the Coolibah Creek mine site to the airport,' Stephen said.

'It's a good idea to try to get the local council in on the project. The construction of an airstrip of that size and specifications would create a lot of jobs. If they can get some good steady revenue from it in the future, that's got to be a positive as well. What about putting something in there regarding access to the mine by tourists for further down the track?'

'Good point,' said Bec, adding it to the wish list. 'A lot of this stuff goes way outside what I'm legally able to claim for Coolibah Creek. But perhaps we have a leg to stand on with regards to the mine's impact on Telford Gold, given it'll primarily be on our land. What do you think?'

'I don't think we'll know until it's tested. The best thing we can do now is ask for everything and be prepared to negotiate back through the legals,' said Stephen. 'But listen, it's late. Shoot those points through to me and I'll have them written up into an agreement with all the right jargon and we'll go from there.'

'Okay, Dad,' said Bec, yawning.

After hanging up, Bec picked up her empty coffee cup from the desk, took it back to the kitchen and walked outside into her garden. It was cold and still, and the moon was silver and bright. It reminded Bec of the night Andy had taken her to the special bauhinia tree for their anniversary. She remembered their laughter and lovemaking.

'Please come back to me, Andy,' she murmured, tears falling on her cheek.

Chapter 27

'I really don't think I can go, Dad,' Rebecca said on the phone from Canberra. 'It's a long flight and I can't take the risk if anything goes wrong with the baby.

'You're right, of course. The timing is a bit off, and the most important thing for you to do at the moment is get that baby baked,' said Stephen. 'Justine and I can do the presentation and I'll get you to record your message. Nobody can speak with the same sincerity as you can. Would that work for you?'

'Yeah, sure. That would be fine. I could do that.' Bec was very excited by the latest development in Andy's condition. Dr Suko had called to say that he was certain Andy could hear and possibly smell. They had monitored his brain activity while asking a series of questions, one of which was asking him to imagine he was watching a tennis match.

There had been a distinct measureable increase in activity immediately afterwards. Dr Suko had invited her to witness the procedure and she was waiting to be called through.

'We're running out of time to get your spiel produced properly for the summit; it's only a fortnight now until we fly out for Cape Town. I could organise with my PR advisor to get it filmed while you're down there. We can put the background in digitally.' Stephen was thinking on the go. 'I can't wait to hear from you later. Your mother is waiting for your call.'

'I know, Dad. I'll call straight away. The doctor is coming now. Bye,' she said, rising from her seat and extending her hand to Dr Suko.

Stephen called his Federal parliamentarian friend for a contact who could organise to record Rebecca's speech for the presentation. Then he called Justine.

'Rebecca has decided that she cannot come to Cape Town. The baby is too close and she wants to be with Andy as his treatment progresses. So it will just be you and me.'

'Okay. Right,' said Justine, sure that she had heard a suggestive inflection in Stephen's voice. Or had she imagined it? 'That's a shame, she's so genuine and real. She's a significant asset to the cause.'

'Yes, I know,' said Stephen. 'I'm having her record a piece that we can use over there.'

'That will be good,' said Justine. 'I have some good news, too. I've spoken with Doug O'Donnell and with the department and they are willing to transfer the land resumption for wetlands from Coolibah to Lennodvale. They weren't keen about it to start with but I was able to swing them in the end.'

'Well done, Justine. It's not often that common sense prevails and bureaucrats change their minds. How did you manage it?'

'Oh, there are some things that you don't need to know,' said Justine. 'See you next week.'

She hung up, her mind racing. She would finally have Stephen all to herself – and in another country!

※

'Mum, he can hear me. Andy can hear me!' said Bec. 'Dr Suko says he's more than likely been able to hear me all the time.'

'That's wonderful, Rebecca!' said Katherine, choking up with emotion.

'So he knows about the baby, Mum. He knows about everything, he just can't answer.' Bec was trying not to cry. 'Dr Suko says the fact he can hear is a really positive sign for a possible recovery because it will give him the will to fight on.'

'I'm so thrilled and relieved for you, darling,' said Katherine.

'I can't leave him now, Mum. I want to stay here and have the baby. I want him to hold our child as soon as it's born,' Bec said.

'That's a good idea. The men are fine at Coolibah and your father can handle the Telford Gold stuff. Why don't you try to get a unit somewhere close to Andy? You still have a couple of months to go.' Katherine didn't like the idea of Rebecca being so far away at this time but she knew not to argue with her.

'I'll think about that. Got to go now, Mum. They're

taking Andy back to the ward,' said Bec, walking down the grey corridor beside the hospital trolley.

※

In Africa, the sand was surprisingly cool and firm under Justine's bare feet and her stride made a plop, plop sound as she jogged on long coppery legs along Llandudno beach. The early morning breeze that drifted softly in across the cold Atlantic brought momentary relief from the oppressive steamy heat of Africa. Sweat from her exertion beaded and trickled down from her hairline to pool between her breasts before cascading down her bare belly.

Justine ignored the sweat. She was enjoying the run. There was nothing like a good workout to bring a flushed freshness to her skin and a healthy brightness to her eyes, and she was determined to be looking her absolute best today. She felt strong, as if she could run all day. The sense of anticipation and nervous energy that consumed her at the thought of finally seducing Stephen was fuelling her body and pushing her into overdrive.

She needed to run the edge off some of the pent-up emotions she'd been storing, to temper the raw sexual desires flooding her body over which she seemed to be powerless to control. She needed her mind to function with the necessary clarity to make the seduction everything she had dreamed it would be or, more to the point, like nothing Stephen had even been able to dream up. The last thing she wanted was to rush at him like some teenage nymphomaniac.

No, Stephen was a man of class, of experience and charm. That's what made their developing relationship so exciting.

He was unlike any man she'd ever met. He appeared to be totally immune to her wiles, but sometimes he allowed her a tiny appreciative glance, a suggestive twinkle in his eye, the hint of hoarseness in the timbre of his voice when he spoke her name.

He was tantalising, challenging and just out of reach. His presence put every one of her senses on full alert. She wanted to be sure she didn't mess up this golden opportunity to get a whole lot closer to him.

The Save Our World First sustainability summit ran for a week, so Justine would have time. Her wide full mouth curved into a smile and she pushed harder, lengthening her stride and pumping her arms.

In the lap pool of the luxurious Arabella Sheraton Grand Hotel, Stephen hauled his muscular bulk through the water with strong strokes. He was a good swimmer and his action was smooth as he cruised through the salty coolness like some sort of predatory marine animal. He was on the last of fifty laps and he allowed his thoughts to wander from his delegation's Telford Gold project to the incredible length of Justine's legs, her wanton emerald eyes and glorious auburn mane. Quite a woman. She had surprised him with her work ethic and her dedication to the task of bringing the Telford Gold dream to fruition.

Beauty and intelligence, a rare coupling, he thought. Stephen was fully aware of her desire for him, just as he was sure she would make him an offer he couldn't refuse while they were at the convention. He heaved himself out of the pool and looked out over the ocean. Daylight was just breaking over Table Mountain and the view of the Atlantic was magnificent through the four metre tall plate glass walls that stretched along the length of the room. A lopsided smile creased Stephen's face as he vigorously towelled his dripping body. The waiting always made the prize so much sweeter.

The Save Our World First summit was a new concept. It brought together all the powerful global environmental groups. They had combined their substantial resources to provide not only funding but, more importantly, and far more valuable, their stamp of approval to projects worldwide judged to be worthy by the SOWF conglomerate. Globally, the environment-based organisations' bottom lines were suffering as people tired of their calls for donations while the world environmental problems just seemed to be getting worse, rather than better. High-level secret meetings of the environmental super powers had been called to bring the major organisations together to look at ways of bringing the 'sympathy' dollar back into their dwindling coffers. September 11 in the States, the Indian Ocean tsunami, the Japan earthquake and tsunami, and massive aid efforts in Africa and Syria had given a compassionate public a much more humanitarian focus and the outpouring of funds to these causes was draining the empathetic dollars away from the environmental groups.

A group of influential leaders had been able to persuade a number of entities that a show of unity was required, a pooling of resources and political strength to achieve physical, high profile results. Publicity, of course, was paramount. 'It's not what you're doing, it's what you're perceived to be doing' was the philosophy of some campaigners. Impregnating a deep sense of personal responsibility and guilt in the hearts and minds of the good and then offering absolution by encouraging them to donate to a cause and become one of the righteous was a proven strategy that had been honed over the years.

So there were calls for a world summit – the beating of drums and calling to the world to take up the cause – and it was to be staged in South Africa for maximum exposure. Beautiful, wild, exotic, endangered animals; human suffering, the triumphs of Mandela; the savage, untamed, untouched and seemingly uninhabited rolling savannahs. A place that the world perceived could be 'saved'. The perfect setting. And so they had assembled at the luxurious Arabella Sheraton Grand Hotel in Cape Town. Delegations from all over the world brought with them their country's projects with the hope of being selected by SOWF for endorsement and dollars.

In a bid to ensure adequate media attention for the event, SOWF added to the agenda a top ten Hollywood A-list of worthy recipients of the SOWF Green Tree Oscars for services to the environment of the world. Normally the environmentalist hierarchy kept the Hollywood crowd at arm's length to appease their fundamentalist, equality-seeking supporters. The stars' overt flaunting of wealth, materialism and hedonism were traits the pious comrades, the masses of followers of the movement, couldn't really align themselves with. But now, embracing the Hollywood famous and that clique's new-found environmental consciousness was a move designed to recapture the spotlight for the cause. How could Hollywood resist the invitation to the inaugural summit? Dinner and a show in the company of the most influential and high-profile environmental and human rights campaigners, ex-US presidents and other world leaders, a global television audience in the hundreds of millions as they accepted their award with humble grace and teary words that sincerely said how much more important this recognition was than the Hollywood Oscars on their shelves. A mutually beneficial arrangement, and for such a worthy cause.

※

Lounging in her suite, Justine was on the phone. 'Hello. My darling, Justine. I haven't heard from you for ages. You're back down under. Is that right?' Hugh Dibbon's distinctive voice answered her call. He claimed to be from English aristocratic blood and was the personal assistant to the SOWF president.

'Hello, Hugh. It's been ages I know, but I'm in Cape Town for your big do and I thought we might be able to catch up,' said Justine.

Justine liked Hugh. They saw the world through the same eyes and regarded everyone and everything as either a stepping stone or a barrier to achieving their personal goals. They had worked together with a member organisation of SOWF on coal seam gas in the States and most recently on assisting investigations into a proposed new gold mine in Tanzania.

'In Cape Town? Justine, why didn't you tell me earlier? I'm completely tied up right through the summit. Not a moment to spare. You know what the boss is like; I've barely slept for the last three months. I'll be pleased when it's all over,' said Hugh, sounding tired.

Hugh and Justine had slept together almost immediately after they'd met many years ago while studying at university in California. Their physical compatibility was low but their intellectual connection was strong.

'That's okay, honey. I'm here with a bid from outback Australia. Telford Gold.'

'Oh yes. I've seen that one in the mix,' he said. 'Look, now that I know you're here, I'll try to get a few minutes to at least say hello. Are you at the Arabella?'

'Yes, I am. Call me,' said Justine.

Chapter 28

It was the second day of the summit. Organisers had been careful to wine and dine the buzzards of the media on the previous day, painfully attentive to their every request, and so it was that the paparazzi were clambering up against the barriers outside the hotel, jostling for positions in their traditional crumpled, black garb, cameras clicking and flashing, yelling questions and comments, so that they formed what looked like two great black, wriggling caterpillars on either side of the red carpet rolled out for the celebrities' arrival. The setting sun washed a line of shining limos with gold as the movie stars alighted with painted smiles, outrageous designer garments and pinched, bony toes squashed into impossible shoes. Squeals of hysteria and sighs of wonder gushed from the sea of locals gathered to catch a glimpse of the Hollywood legends.

On the top floor, the ballroom was crowded with dignitaries and delegates from all over the world. The glittering stage for the presentation of the Save Our World First Awards was set. Everything was in readiness and three hundred beautifully dressed men and women awaited the arrival of the last of the celebrity guests. French champagne flowed into tall slim glasses. The room buzzed with excited chatter. Men lounged in tuxedos, pretending to be unaffected by the arrival of the stars. Women in magnificent gowns raised their manicured hands to the jewellery around their necks or touched their coiffed hair and tried not to wriggle in their seats when they imagined the superstars entering through the gilded doors and passing within touching distant of their tables.

The atmosphere was crackling in what was surely one of the most original and beautiful ballrooms in the world. Its unique feature was the glass wall and ceiling, which allowed guests to look out over the lights of the city and see the fat golden orb of a yellow summer moon rising above the clouds that covered Table Mountain. Once standing on the marble mosaic of the dance floor, surrounded by exquisitely sculpted marble columns, the night stars could be seen overhead through the intricately bordered glass ceiling. The opulence and splendour of the room was spellbinding. Soft pre-dinner music drifted melodically and soothingly across the room from the orchestra.

Justine was in the powder room staring at her reflection in the mirror. She needed to be sure that her makeup and hair were perfect, and she knew that when she returned to the table, Stephen's chair would be facing her. The gown would do the rest. She had searched for just the right one in Sydney before they left Australia. With her coppery tan

Coolibah Creek

and red hair, she decided that it had to be cream. Justine had known this particular dress was perfect the moment she felt the slippery softness of the material slither down the length of her body and touch her firmly in all the right places.

As she walked through the ballroom she turned heads. It was moments like these that made all the hard gym work worth it, Justine thought, gleefully soaking up all the stares. The swathe of soft fabric fell in gentle folds from a scarf-like collar around her neck accentuating the confident carriage of her head. Her auburn locks were pulled severely back off her face, leaving her hair to cascade down the centre of her bare back in a mass of soft curls. From the collar around her neck, the material left Justine's sculpted brown shoulders bare and draped in marvellous simplicity to another band of the same delicate cream folds that hugged her narrow hips then lay flat across her taut belly before encircling her and tying in a soft knot just above the swell of her buttocks. The split skirt fell from the hips to the floor and clung to the length of her thigh as she floated towards the table, revealing a tantalising glimpse of her impossibly long legs with each step. She knew her preparations had not been wasted when, as she approached the table, smiling at Minister Matthews who was accompanying them, she caught Stephen's hungry eyes on her, then sat down gracefully on the chair that he had drawn out for her.

The eagerly awaited entrance by the A-list celebrities through a side entrance near the stage brought the crowd to their feet with applause. They craned their necks and shifted position to get the best view as the magnificently dressed stars flashed broad white smiles and acknowledged their admirers before being seated.

People at the table resumed their conversations and Justine delicately raised the thin fluted glass to her full red lips and savoured the tingling tartness of the very good wine. She glanced up at Stephen over the rim of the glass and her fiery green eyes flashed a look of mischief his way.

What a man! Justine thought. *So debonair and yet so incredibly masculine.*

They were seated side by side at their round table with its starched white cloth and sparkling silverware. Also at their table were the Australian government's Minister for the Environment, Joseph Matthews, and his boring wife, Susan; New Zealand's representative to the conference, George Manatu, a heavy-set Maori, and his charming wife, Maree; as well as Levi Rumsfold, a slightly scruffy, dread-locked professional environmentalist from England whose crumpled tuxedo failed to bring any semblance of style. Levi's boyfriend was stoned and his half-closed eyes and cynical smirk seemed to be pasted on his face.

Maree Manatu was telling an animated tale of her younger days fishing on the pristine beaches of the North Island of her homeland and how she and her brothers used to sneak into the strawberry fields and gorge themselves on the soft sweet fruit. Her tale drew appreciative laughter. Stephen leant towards Justine and, while maintaining the flashing broad smile of amusement at the story, he whispered into her ear in a voice so low and so deep that it sent a shiver of pleasure down the left side of Justine's body.

'You look stunning,' he said.

It was the first time he'd ever said anything remotely flirtatious to Justine since she'd started working with him. She kept the smile on her face and her eyes on Maree, pretending to be engrossed in the moment. Justine had seen Stephen flirting outrageously on numerous occasions with almost anything female, and it had been a source of great annoyance and intrigue to her that she'd been unable to extract any sort of a reaction from him.

Take it easy, she scolded herself. *You don't want to mess this up.*

She picked up her glass and raised it. 'A toast,' she said. 'To the land of the long white cloud, her wondrous beauty and warm people.'

With everyone preoccupied with the toast Justine leant into Stephen and purred, 'Would you judge a book by its cover?' before turning back to Minister Matthews and immediately capturing his undivided attention.

At that moment the exquisite entrées arrived, a choice of filo-encased langoustine or the renowned Cape Town sushi. 'The Atlantic Ocean seafood is amazing but not as good as the Pacific. Australian reef fish are my favourite,' Joseph Matthews proffered as he bit into the crunchy filo and tasted the delicately flavoured fusion within.

'I think the fish from our own Bay of Islands at home in New Zealand can compete with the best,' George added proudly.

'We'll be growing crayfish at Coolibah Creek as part of Telford Gold,' Stephen said. 'Technology is accelerating rapidly with regard to natural water filtration and recycling, using sand and native sedges. It is quite incredible to think that we will have the capacity to produce thousands of tonnes of crayfish in remote arid Australia and fly them out to markets around the world. The most lucrative trade will be in live cray into Asia.'

'The Telford Gold project is going to set benchmarks for the world in food production that maximises output using minimal resources. It's the sort of thing agriculture is definitely going to have to look at now if we are going to be able to double food production by 2050. That's what forecasters are predicting we will need to do to feed the world,' Justine added.

The diners enjoyed their fare and conversation as the mood in the room became more jovial. A main course of ostrich fillet with mushroom and black pepper sauce or baby kingklip with chilli ginger beurre blanc brought more traditional South African dishes to the table. George Manatu chose the kingklip eel. 'You know that they almost fished these out over here. New Zealand exports tonnes of our eels into South Africa. They are closely related and marketed here as kingklip.'

'The ostrich is good. Tastes a little like beef,' Susan Matthews commented.

'Mmmm, and that sauce is delicious,' Justine said.

Levi Rumsfold and his partner's vegan meals arrived: a kwaai braai pie, a South African dish with silverbeet, onions and an assortment of fried vegetables encased in pastry. 'We simply cannot continue to use land and water to produce meat. It takes almost ten kilos of grain to produce a kilo of beef, not to mention fifty times as much water when compared to crops, and a more negative greenhouse gas emission than cars. Over a billion beef cattle on earth are eating grain that could feed poorer nations,' Levi said, more like a well-rehearsed statement than part of the banter.

'Using US feedlot production figures and applying them across the globe to all beef production is simplistic in the extreme and inaccurate. But it suits the sensationalist agenda of the vegan movement,' Stephen said bluntly. 'Then there is the opposing argument of food calorie value. The nutritional equivalent of one kilo of beef is seven kilos of broccoli,' he said. 'The meat–plant diet antagonists must detach themselves from their cemented positions at either end of the argument and open their minds to finding balanced solutions to providing protein-based foods. Much of the land around the world that supports grazing animals is not suitable for cropping, is watered naturally and is minimally disturbed. Cropping clear-fell land releases carbon and natural ecosystems are lost. We have to look at the whole picture. Integrated food production systems that have the soil's sustained health and fertility at their core and are supported by optimal water usage efficiencies and minimal emissions will be able to produce protein with negligible environmental impacts. Natural ecosystems are designed to support animals and we need to be respectful of plant–animal associations.'

A lively discussion ensued throughout the main course and was still flowing when the desserts of syrup-soaked koeksisters and guava icecream were served. As the clink of cutlery subsided and the last of the sweet morsels was consumed, the host of the ceremony announced the beginning of the awards presentation.

'We are here to honour those wonderful human beings who are willing to use their fame and sometimes their fortune to make our planet a better place; those who put their renown to good use, who look outwardly from themselves to say, "What can I do for the world?" not, "What more can the world do for me?"

'These not so ordinary people, the stars of our galaxy, can do more for any given cause in a single photo shoot or by putting their name to a project than thousands of ordinary volunteers can do over a year. It is my very great pleasure to introduce to the stage to present the inaugural Save Our World First Green Tree Oscar Awards the president of our organisation, Mr Mujahid Govender.'

The applause was thunderous and vibrated through the ballroom as chairs were pushed back and the crowd came to their feet. The imposing figure of Mujahid Govender, with his cap of tight white curls and interesting crinkled brown face, moved towards the stage, and all eyes were on him. As he adjusted the microphone his gold Rolex watch caught the spotlights and flashed momentarily.

Justine and Stephen stood close together applauding and smiling. Justine had never felt like this before, so euphoric, so spirited, so . . . happy?

The awards continued with star after star gracing the stage as the cameras rolled and beamed the event to countries all over the world, capturing unprecedented global publicity for the environmentalist elite and recharging the coffers with very healthy broadcasting fees.

Having set the bait, Justine asked to swap places with Stephen so that she was seated beside Mrs Manatu. She then proceeded to practically ignore him for the remainder of the evening pretending to be totally engrossed in the procession of glamorous people and the New Zealander's amusing stories. Beneath her calm exterior, she was quivering with excitement and found it hard to concentrate on the ceremony.

She had not been paying attention, obviously, as the formalities had apparently ended and the orchestra was playing a beautiful Strauss waltz when Stephen asked, 'Would you do me the honour of sharing this dance with me?'

He was suddenly very close, bending so near to her face that she could smell his cologne. Justine's composure momentarily lapsed and she looked back at him with a startled expression, interrupted from her dreaming.

'That would be my pleasure,' she replied, regaining her senses and bowing her head graciously before unfolding her slender length from the chair, which Stephen drew back for her.

They walked to the dance floor and, even in this illustrious company, made a striking couple. Justine's thoughts took her back to when she'd seen Stephen at the ball at home. She'd wanted him from that moment, wanted him to take her in his arms and dance with her then.

He was a little taller than Justine so that if he'd wanted to he could have touched his lips to her forehead. As he took her into the waltz, the big hand that held hers was warm and dry and the other was firm in the small of her bare back. When he touched her and swept her effortlessly into the dance, her mouth went dry and her tongue seemed numb when she tried to reply to his question.

'You are the belle of the ball, Justine. Do you like the Strauss waltzes?' he asked.

'Ballroom dancing is not one of my strong points, I'm afraid. Not that I'm completely devoid of talents,' she answered as Stephen led her masterfully in the waltz, holding her close, cheek to cheek and steering her through the twirling crowd with such consummate skill that she felt like she'd been able to waltz all of her life. The floor soon became too congested and noisy for any further conversation but their bodies were communicating very well.

Stephen took Justine's hand and eased her across to the edge of the room. Walking quickly, he led her through the exit. Outside the ballroom, the hallway was deserted. Stephen pulled Justine close to him and kissed her. Through the thin fabric of her dress she could feel that he was an impressive man in every way. She returned his embrace and pushed her body into his, looking straight into his eyes, full of self-confidence and sass.

Breaking from their embrace, Stephen once again took her hand and strode away from the ballroom. Justine simply followed until Stephen opened the fire escape door and pulled her through.

'Where are we going?' she said.

'I'm going to take you to the top,' said Stephen, his voice thick with desire. 'The view is amazing from the roof.'

Justine really didn't think this was the time for sightseeing, she was thinking more along the lines of the king-size bed in his suite or the jacuzzi, but she followed without comment, desperate to be alone with him.

They stepped out on top of the building into the inky black night. The wind blowing in off the sea was bringing galloping low clouds to blot out the moon and stars. The helipad lights created only a faint yellow glow around the perimeter of the rooftop. But down below, sparkling like a pirate's treasure, glittered the colourful lights of the city.

The couple could barely see each other in the darkness but their sense of touch was only heightened by the night. The wind whipped and tugged at Justine's dress, fluttering it deliciously across her erect nipples. Moving her to the railing at the edge of the building Stephen enfolded her in his arms and, in the blackness, found her mouth and covered it with his in a hot and crushing kiss the force of which Justine matched and returned with equal fervour. Stephen's searching hand slid under the filmy material of her gown to find the swell of her breast and roll the hard nipple in his fingers. With his other hand he hoisted her up onto the railing. Justine immediately threw her legs around his waist and clung to him, conscious, even in her sexually intoxicated state, that there was a drop of over three hundred feet behind her.

'I've got you. Trust me,' said Stephen, undoing the clip at the back of her neck.

Justine moaned with pleasure as his mouth covered her nipple and she fumbled urgently with the buttons of his shirt, wanting to feel his skin against hers. Stephen caressed her thighs, which were wound tightly around him. Sliding his hand up under her skirt, he hooked his fingers through the band of her flimsy G-string and tore it away. Then, suddenly, savagely, he was inside her.

Justine arched her body and threw her head back, working her hips feverishly. Her hair streamed down in the wind, her bare breasts silhouetted against the lights below. Adrenalin coursed through her as she let go of Stephen's neck and threw both her arms back over her head as his rhythmic thrusting brought her to a soaring climax. Still shuddering from its intensity, Justine pulled herself back onto Stephen's chest, dazed and shaky.

Holding her, Stephen stepped back from the railing and slowly lifted her down, savouring their union.

'You can take me sightseeing any time,' Justine murmured into his ear.

'The view was exceptional from where I was standing,' Stephen replied, caressing her bare back. They remained locked in a feverish embrace, hands roving, lips touching, relishing the lingering delicious sensation of their lovemaking.

Silently, like two children with a naughty secret, they straightened their clothing and left the top of the building. As they emerged through the fire escape door at the ballroom level, Justine said, 'You go back in to the dining room. I think I need to ah . . . powder my nose.' Her green eyes dancing with mischief, she whispered, 'My room number is 351.'

༄

The powder room was almost deserted. As Justine tried to gain control of her emotions, a floating feeling of elation drenched her and she giggled out loud. Far from feeling satisfied, their raunchy first encounter had merely whet her appetite for Stephen. She snapped the clasp of her evening bag closed and looked in the mirror. She had fixed her hair and makeup but her face positively glowed back at her. She giggled as she thought about where her knickers might be after Stephen had torn them from her. Then a thought hit her and she frowned as she realised she'd totally lost control. It was supposed to be *her* tune Stephen danced to, not vice versa.

Outside, she was surprised to see that Stephen was no longer in his seat. As Justine sat back down, Susan Matthews came stumbling back to their table, dragging her huffing and sweaty husband behind her. Wiping strands of hair from her reddened face, Susan leant across and yelled above the music, 'Stephen asked to pass on his apologies but he had some urgent business to attend to. He said he'd see you tomorrow for the presentation,' she said. Then, turning towards her husband she said, 'Why don't you dance with Justine, Joseph? A beautiful girl shouldn't be sitting down on a night like this.'

'I'd love to,' said Justine, smiling at both of them, 'but I have to finalise a few things for the presentation and I want it to be just perfect. If you'll excuse me, I'll see you all in the morning.' And with that, she rose from the table and left the ballroom.

※

In his room Stephen had showered and was speaking with Katherine on the phone. 'How're my girls?' he asked.

'I'm fine and Bec is going well,' said Katherine. 'Dr Suko has recommended that Bec bring Andy home to Coolibah. He thinks the familiar surroundings, sounds and smells could trigger something.' Katherine had been relieved that the pair were coming home and not staying in Canberra.

'That's great news, but do you think Rebecca's up to nursing Andy at this stage?' asked Stephen.

'No, we'd have to employ a nurse. Bec has learned to do all of the physio herself though and the visiting physiotherapist has agreed to travel out to Coolibah from Telford when they do the clinic there every three months. He's young and very interested in Andy's case. We might have to help out with the costs because, with no grid power at Coolibah, they are going to have to run the generator 24/7 for Andy's monitoring equipment. Bec says it would be good to purchase a smaller unit specifically for that task. We need to take every opportunity to help Andy wake up,' said Katherine. 'How's everything going there?'

'Couldn't be going better. It's a shame you and Bec missed the ball tonight. You would have loved seeing all the celebs. I've got a bit of work to finish off before tomorrow's big announcement, so I'll give you a call first thing in the morning,' said Stephen.

'Okay, and give Bec a ring in the morning too. She's already in bed asleep,' said Katherine.

Stephen stretched out on the king-size bed and turned off the lights. He'd waited a long time and put so much of himself into the Telford Gold presentation. The recognition and acknowledgement he would receive if they were successful tomorrow would be crucial for taking him where he wanted to go. He lay in the dark and went over the presentation in his mind one more time.

Chapter 29

The day dawned clear and bright. Justine toyed with the sweet fresh fruit on her breakfast plate and tried not to pout. She'd been so certain Stephen had made an excuse to leave last night so that he might come to her room. His tone was entirely cool and professional this morning, as if nothing had happened. She searched his eyes for any hint of connection but there was none. Justine was nonplussed by the apparent lack of effect their tempestuous encounter had had on him.

What did you expect? she thought to herself as she sipped the delicious black coffee. *Roses?*

She chided herself for inviting him to her room and made a firm decision to match his cool demeanour. Justine had worked hard for Telford Gold. Damn hard. She'd never worked that hard before, and was accustomed to getting whatever she wanted without much effort. She'd been swept up in Stephen and Rebecca's enthusiasm and belief in the project and she was proud of what they'd put together. She'd carefully chosen her outfit for the day and dressed elegantly in a basic black suit, black stockings and shoes with a stiletto heel to accentuate her long legs.

'It's time,' Stephen said simply.

There was no more to be done but to present their project.

The room they'd been invited to speak in was an amphitheatre with a small stage surrounded by semicircular rows of velvet seats in which were seated members of the powerful environmental hierarchy of the world. The lights dimmed and a wide screen behind the stage came to life. Deep and evocative, the narrator's voice began . . .

'In the 1800s people came from all over the world to the barren outback plains of Australia to dig for gold. Fortunes were made and lost. In the twenty-first century, technology has allowed us to delve far deeper than the gold diggers could ever have imagined and what we've found is a substance far more valuable to our earth and the human race than gold. In remote outback Australia, the driest continent on earth, we have discovered beneath the dry red dirt . . . water. Precious, pure and priceless water . . . Telford Gold.'

The screen burst into life with the image of water being pumped up to the surface and gushing from an outlet, cleverly filmed in front of the setting sun so that the water looked like liquid gold, plentiful and spectacularly beautiful. Bec's face came up on the screen with the caption 'Rebecca Roberts, Coolibah Creek, Australia'.

Coolibah Creek

'The magnitude and significance of this resource is difficult to describe or imagine,' Bec began. 'A reserve the size of Sydney Harbour lying beneath millions of hectares of untilled, virgin soil. Fresh, clean soil and water, free of any trace of chemicals.' The shot cut to the open plains waving with silver-topped summer grasses.

'Incredibly, the resource is renewable. Approximately every twenty years the aquifer is recharged when the monsoons bring an extended wet season and water lies on the flat land for months, seeping through the permeable earth and then captured by the huge aquifer. At this unique location, three kilometres below the surface, underneath the aquifer, there lies a giant field of hot rocks, super-heated granite that holds an immeasurable cache of energy that can be tapped into by pumping water down and recapturing the steam as it returns to the surface. It is estimated these hot rocks could provide geothermal energy for four hundred and fifty years.'

'Here, in the same location, there is one of the most significant diamond deposits ever discovered. As if some greater power has gifted this treasure to the project in order to allow us to find a better way, the recovery of the diamond lode will finance much of the establishment infrastructure.'

Bec's voice was clear and strong. 'At Coolibah Creek, we have the opportunity to start afresh as food producers. We have the chance to begin with a clean slate. This pristine area has not yet been sullied by civilisation. Here, there is none of the effects of the disastrous mistakes made by past generations. The soils are pristine and the water is entirely pure. Here, we can demonstrate to the world how food and fibre can be produced in an entirely natural and integrated way, where one production area benefits another so that the perfect circle of nature is maintained.'

The image on the screen swirled the water into a golden circle to form the Telford Gold logo.

'Telford Gold will be the label to grace the cleanest, greenest high-quality products available anywhere in the world. From beef to bean sprouts, from olive oil to barramundi, the sky is the limit. The production methods that fit within the Telford Gold circle of nature do not affect ecosystems, biodiversity or the natural values of the region.

'We have the available technology to carefully monitor the usage and recharging of the Coolibah Creek aquifer, and the scale of all developments would be tied to the sustainable draw-down of the resource. World's best-practice water use efficiency and recycling methods will be used in all areas and further researched as the project moves forward. The opportunities for research are endless.

'The Telford Gold project will revolutionise food production methods in the expansive natural landscape of Australia and indeed worldwide, turning away from converting huge tracts of land into single industry-specific areas, like wheat or sugar cane, and changing to a totally integrated food production system that will be developed at Coolibah. Telford Gold will provide demonstrated, measurable beneficial outcomes of keeping the land biologically balanced and healthy. It will achieve higher production rates and encourage the uptake of similar systems to produce sustainable food and fibre production worldwide.'

A close-up of Bec's earnest face filled the screen. She looked straight at the camera and said, 'We are asking you to become part of a partnership the like of which has never before assembled. We are asking you to think not only about this generation but also about the next and the ones after that. We are challenging you to have the courage and vision to support something that is truly innovative and which will be a catalyst for sustainable fully integrated food production systems leading to improved environmental outcomes around the world. We are inviting you to be part of Telford Gold.'

Bec turned her head and the shot panned over the open spaces at Coolibah Creek. A series of images depicting animals grazing, cropping, forests of native trees, and orchards of native fruit-bearing trees covered the screen. They became larger and larger and swirled at random until finally they all came together like a perfect jigsaw to create a beautiful image of what the Telford Gold project would look like. Gilded water raced across the bottom of the screen and pushed up the right-hand side of the images, tearing around and across the top before plunging back down to the bottom to form the Telford Gold circular logo around the utopian picture. The sound of the rushing water roared in the ears of the audience as the curtains closed and the lights came up.

There was a momentary silence in the room. Stephen and Justine stood at the podium and gazed out across the luxurious amphitheatre, searching people's faces for their reaction. The applause began and steadily grew to become thunderous, filling the presenters with tingling satisfaction and relief as they understood they were on a winner. Stephen's handsome face broke into an irresistible smile and he squeezed Justine's hand tightly behind her back. Justine felt her nails digging into his hand and was shocked to find that her eyes had filled with tears.

'Thank you. Thank you,' said Stephen as the applause died away. 'Telford Gold would like to thank Mujahid Govender and the board of Save Our World First for the invitation to present today. I would ask that delegates please take the opportunity to look through the more detailed information in the brochures that are available at the door. Miss Rand and I will be available to answer any questions that you may have and we hope that you will be able to visit us in Australia in the near future. Thank you,' Stephen concluded and they both smiled and walked briskly to the door to meet and speak with the delegates.

Stephen was beaming. He felt such a great sense of achievement and excitement. His family's dream of Telford Gold, which had on so many occasions seemed to be just that, a dream, was gathering momentum – maybe enough momentum to make it unstoppable.

After almost an hour, the last of the delegates melted away. The following presentation was scheduled for within half an hour. Stephen and Justine gathered up the few remaining brochures and walked to the lifts. Once inside, they were alone and Stephen suddenly grabbed Justine around the waist and swung her up into the air, twirling her around and around. Setting her down again, he leant back against the lift's door and crushed her to him, kissing her hungrily.

He felt he couldn't contain his euphoric feelings. He wanted to yell out.

'We've got them, Justine. I can feel it!' he said breathlessly. 'Telford Gold is on its way! Once we get this thing rolling, it'll be like a freight train. And by coming here we have all the right people on board to open all the cross switches.' He looked down into her face with his piercing, fiery eyes. 'You've been brilliant. Thank you,' he said squeezing her arms so tightly that she winced.

The lift came to a halt and the doors opened. Another couple stepped in. Justine's legs were still shaking from Stephen's kiss and she hoped her lipstick wasn't smeared all over her face. She didn't know it was possible to feel this good, and she struggled to keep her mind off a way she knew to feel even better.

Stephen and Justine went their separate ways for the afternoon and Justine treated herself to a two-hour pampering at the exclusive hotel spa. Savouring the firm, long strokes of the masseur's hands on her back, she thought about how the evening should unfold. Stephen had organised a special dinner for carefully selected guests.

I won't be letting him get away from me tonight, Justine promised herself, as she let herself into her hotel room. She remembered well the frustration she'd felt when she'd gone to his room that night in Canberra and he'd already left.

She dressed carefully. The dinner called for very elegant formal. Justine chose a green gown that was quite demure and straight and refined in its simplicity. The cut of the dress accentuated the classical features of her face and brought out the colour in her eyes. She pulled her hair up and captured it with a pearl-studded clasp and added drop earrings and a string of pearls to her throat. 'Mirror, mirror on the wall, who's the fairest of them all?' she said to her reflection.

Poor dowdy old Katherine. How sad that you're not here, thought Justine.

The dinner was a huge success. All the guests marvelled at the scale of the natural resources available in such a remote location, and all expressed a desire to travel to Australia to see Telford Gold when the project came to fruition.

After the dinner, Stephen and Justine sat in the lounge bar with a couple of stayers. Justine nodded in all the right places during the conversation, though she was finding it hard to concentrate on the politicians and conservationists. Stephen was giving them his full attention and doing an incredible job of appearing to be enthralled by their stories. Justine was continually amazed by his people skills.

After a while she excused herself from the group and went to the bar to instruct the bartender to have room service send up a bottle of Pierre Boullmer to Stephen's room. Stephen was aware of the signals Justine was sending him, but he was enjoying keeping her waiting.

At last all their guests departed and there was nobody else left in the bar. Stephen placed a hefty tip in his empty glass before making his way out of the room with Justine. He didn't touch her or speak and they rode the lift in silence. When the doors opened at their floor, Stephen took her hand and led her to his suite. Inside, sitting on the table, was the bottle of cognac and two large snifters.

Undoing his tie and the top button of his shirt, Stephen smiled at Justine.

'Anticipation, thinking ahead. I've learnt a lot from you, Stephen Hogan,' said Justine, walking towards him.

'I've been wondering what I might learn from you,' he said, taking off his jacket, pouring them both a drink, and gesturing for her to sit opposite him.

'Oh, I'm sure there are a few lessons I could give you,'

said Justine, touching his fingers with hers as she took the glass of cognac from him.

'Here's to Telford Gold,' said Stephen. 'And to you for helping us put it on the world stage.'

'To Telford Gold and to Stephen Hogan, a man with a taste for the finer things in life and who stubbornly refuses to settle for anything less. May this be the finest day of your life,' said Justine, before getting up to dim the lights.

Kicking off her shoes she walked across the room, knelt on the floor at Stephen's feet and began to undo his shirt buttons, feathering his chest and belly with kisses, trailing down to his belt. She undid his belt and trousers slowly, all the while titillating his torso with her tongue. Teasing him, she stood up, unzipped her dress, let it fall to her feet, and said, 'I'm going to the spa, if you'd care to join me.'

Stephen watched as she turned and walked away from him, taking in her toned and strong back, her firm thighs and perfectly rounded buttocks.

In the spa, he remained submissive as she washed him. Snowy froth floated on and off Justine's body as she massaged him with the slippery soap, all the while conscious of displaying her nakedness to its best advantage. When their bodies were pink from the hot tub they moved to the bed, where Justine made Stephen lie on his back as she towelled him dry.

She went into the kitchen and returned with a glass filled with ice cubes, which she scooped up in each hand. She flung a leg across his body and sat on his belly and proceeded to rub the ice in tiny circles on his temples, then his neck, followed by his nipples. Leaving a cube in his navel and sitting up straight, she pushed her breasts forward and circled her own rosy brown nipples with the ice, making them pucker and stand erect.

Justine reached into the ice bucket and placed another ice cube in her mouth. She bent down and sucked the ice cube from his belly before wiggling her cold tongue downwards. The feeling of Justine's cold mouth around him was excruciatingly intense. When the ice had melted, Justine swallowed and sat up, straddling him immediately.

Plunging into the heat of Justine's body, the sensitivity of Stephen's ice-cooled skin was deliciously increased. Her body felt as if it were on fire as she writhed and thrashed on top of him, driving herself to her own orgasm.

Afterwards, Stephen lay back, sated. Justine looked down at him, her eyes bright with pleasure and she smiled. She felt the control coming back to her side.

Stephen could tell what she was thinking and with one deft movement he flicked her over onto her back and with smooth, rhythmic movements he started making love to her again. He was masterful, discarding all Justine's defences as if they were layers of clothes and she was lost in his lovemaking. Long tendrils of her hair stuck to her neck and her face as Stephen brought ecstasy to her body. She clung to him unashamedly, desperate to hold him, never wanting to let him go.

॰ॐ॰

Justine woke with a start and sat up. She was alone in Stephen's suite. A glance at the bedside clock revealed it was 5am. Her head thumped viciously from the alcohol the night before. She had to get up, get back to her own room before the hallways filled with people. She scrambled around in the half-light, gathering her things and closing the door quietly.

Breathlessly she rushed down the empty hallway to her room, her shoes and bag in hand. Once inside, she couldn't stop smiling as she dragged the expensive dress up over her head and tossed it aside. Turning the cold shower tap on full, she stepped underneath the stream of icy water.

After her shower, Justine made herself a cup of coffee, then walked out on the balcony in her robe and sat watching the sun rise over the ocean. It felt like this sunrise was the beginning of something fateful in her life. She felt different, strange.

Looking down she saw television crews arriving outside the hotel and got up to dress for the last session of the summit.

൞

Stephen was consumed with anticipation for what would happen at the presentation luncheon. Although he was confident that Telford Gold would be successful in its bid to secure substantial monetary investment from the SOWF alliance, it was never over until the fat lady sang. The level of bribery and corruption within the lobbying process could not be underestimated. As a further incentive to the fund's investment in Telford Gold, Minister Matthews made very clear that the Federal government would surrender large tracts of northern Australia's savannah rangelands and rainforests, currently listed as National Parks and managed by the National Parks and Wildlife Service, for proposed World Heritage Listing. It was a good hook.

SOWF would make the announcement about the winning projects at around midday. The timing was carefully arranged to coincide with the morning news bulletins in the United States. His thoughts drifted to Justine, his 'red Ferrari'. *Whew! Hot! Very, very hot*, he recalled and felt his body respond to the memory.

The headlines in the morning paper heralded the final day of the conference and the much anticipated announcement of the projects that would be judged worthy of the SOWF group's endorsement and financial support.

Stephen looked up over the pages to see Justine coming through the door of the breakfast lounge.

'Good morning,' he said as she took a seat at his table. 'Are you hungry?' His eyes flashed and one corner of his mouth tipped upwards.

'Starving,' said Justine.

They talked about the various media reports as the suspense built around today's announcement. After the hearty hot breakfast, they had separate plans.

'I promised the minister I would give him directions to get to the Constantia Winelands before we leave this afternoon. He and Susan are staying on for another week. See you inside,' said Justine, flashing her brilliant smile.

She walked briskly to the foyer of the hotel. Hugh Dibbon was waiting there, pacing and talking on his phone. He quickly disconnected when he saw Justine.

'Oh, you look as gorgeous as ever,' he said, holding her at arm's length. 'No. You are even more gorgeous.'

'And you are just as smooth as ever, my darling Hugh,' said Justine. 'You know I never seem to realise how much I've missed you until I see you again.'

They had only a few minutes to speak to each other but their bond was instantly restored.

'How are you feeling about your Telford Gold bid?' Hugh asked.

'Confident. Very. Only thing I see as being a problem is having mining in the partnership. No matter how this new mine is operated, it's hard to break away from mining's negative image,' Justine said.

'You can never be too confident in this game, Justine. You know what it's like; hard to push past those with the biggest wallets,' Hugh said, glancing around to see who was in earshot.

'Yes. I know,' Justine said. 'So, do you have any inside information on the winners?' she asked.

'I may have seen the list, but they would have my guts for garters if I told you anything,' he said.

'Pleeease. Come on Hugh. It's me,' Justine begged.

'You'd better get in there. It's almost time,' Hugh deflected. 'Call me,' he said and scurried off.

✼

A hush fell over the huge reception hall where five hundred people were seated. The MC had just introduced Mujahid Govender, who was about to announce the winning projects. His speech was passionate and delivered with aplomb. He knew that the eyes of the world were upon him.

'So, having brought together an unprecedented number of environmental groups from all over the planet, we now have an alliance committed enough and strong enough to bring about real change, to find real answers to the environmental challenges faced by our natural world and its people. It is my very great privilege to be able to announce the outstanding winning projects of our inaugural Save

Our World First awards, the winners of which will not only receive the commendation and whole-hearted endorsement of the Save Our World First alliance, but will also receive substantial funding support, support that is made possible because people, everywhere, still care.'

The winners were duly announced and celebrated. Expeditions to hamper the Japanese whalers, studies on effects of global warming, projects to begin to rehabilitate Asian rivers and, finally, much to the joy of the Australian delegation, 'The Telford Gold project, Australia!'

The Australian group erupted with uninhibited, exuberant joy. Photographers clicked furiously to capture the images of their success, and Telford Gold and Australia were headline news around the globe. The photo that was in the local newspaper at Coombul showed Stephen's broad white smile, with Justine looking adoringly at him, mouth open, laughing. The Minister for the Environment was standing behind them, with both arms thrust into the air in triumph.

Chapter 30

Stephen and Justine returned to a lot of media attention in Australia. The cameras loved the handsome pair. It took them three days to get out of Sydney and back to Coombul after a series of interviews with morning television shows and presentations to government departments and environmental groups.

Bec was busy at Coolibah Creek. The price of cattle had skyrocketed as a result of the widespread rains and severely depleted stock numbers. She was redoing her cash flow projections. Her circumstances had changed dramatically since the breaking of the drought. There was a long way to go but things were looking positive for Coolibah. Immersed in the Telford Gold project as well as her pregnancy and Andy, life for Rebecca was insanely busy.

As Telford Gold became a juggernaut, Stephen had only been able to service a select few of his biggest clients in his legal practice and had employed extra staff to handle the rest. His parliamentary duties were pressing, with an election less than twelve months away. Powerbrokers from conservative politics were flooding him with offers and propositions for more involvement in the federal arena. The minders and spin doctors would have been blind not to recognise his potential: smart, a gifted orator, strong and progressive, irresistible charm and charisma. Add to that the strong environmental tones of the Telford Gold project, his very clever and marketable daughter and his gracious wife and Stephen Hogan was a guaranteed vote-winner. The race was on to get him into federal cabinet.

While there was no denying that Telford Gold would be a renaissance for the outback, it was not civic duty that drove Stephen; he wanted recognition and the glory of success.

Katherine was spending a lot of time out at Coolibah Creek with Bec's due date getting closer, so it was easy for Stephen and Justine to continue their affair. Justine was swept up in the whirlwind rise and rise of Telford Gold and Stephen Hogan. She was working fourteen hours a day, researching scientific methodology and tracking down world experts with the relevant knowledge to establish best practice strategies for the development of the project. The early stages included the vital trialling and monitoring of suitable industries and then making judgements on the ability of those industries to mesh together to complete the 'circle of nature' upon which the project was designed. Then there was her work with Phosec involving pulling together community consultation and engagement and liaising with SOWF.

It was an enormous undertaking but she was tackling it head on. She was continually inspired and encouraged by

Stephen and Rebecca's passion and belief in the project and excited to see it all coming together so quickly. Rebecca was as clever as her father and could so clearly portray her vision for the future. Unlike Bec, who tried to avoid the limelight, Justine absolutely loved all the constant media attention. They didn't seem to be able to get enough of the Telford Gold team. As Stephen had predicted, now that they had the SOWF stamp of approval, red tape was being slashed and doors were opening in every direction.

Less than two weeks later, Stephen was due to leave for a series of meetings in Sydney. Justine was sulking because she couldn't go with him and Stephen had told her he would be flying down a few days before to put in the groundwork. He'd made it clear that he would need her to stay behind to continue their local work on the project. Justine didn't like being left behind and they had not been able to get together in the last few days, even in Stephen's office. Justine was aching to be with him.

Late one evening, on her way home from a trip out to the Coolibah Creek Phosec mine site, she saw that the lights were on in his office. She pulled into the car park and got out, slamming the door of her four-wheel drive and stomping up the back stairs of the building. It was late but she'd forgotten some documents that she needed to go over for Stephen's Sydney trip. She was tired and hungry and getting frustrated with the fact that she couldn't have Stephen to herself.

She felt for the key in her pocket and let herself in. The bright security lights on the exterior of the building were sufficient for her to find her way down the corridor and to the office. As she turned the corner she noticed that the lights were on in the front desk rooms.

'That dopey bitch is too stupid to even turn the lights off!' Justine swore under her breath, referring to Sharon, the office girl. *Unless she's still here finishing off those six cream donuts that she has in the fridge. Fat pig*, she thought viciously.

Marching down the hall, full of indignation, she burst through the door, eyes ablaze, ready to hurl an insult at the unsuspecting Sharon if she were in there.

Sharon's huge white thighs looked like enormous loaves of unbaked bread wrapped around Stephen's bouncing bare buttocks. Her trademark bright red glossy painted nails dug into the fabric of his white shirt, which was stretched across the muscles in his back. She made little grunting sounds as her plump body rocked and jiggled back and forth on top of the desk.

Justine froze in the doorway, her mouth open in utter disbelief. Stephen heard the door but wasn't quick enough to avoid the stamp of Justine's boot on his posterior. She kicked him hard as all her fury was released into the assault.

Stephen was hobbled by his trousers as he spun around to face her and defend himself, catching Justine's flailing fists with both hands. Sharon began to scream and Justine screeched a torrent of foul language, stomping on Stephen's feet before trying to bring her knee up into his groin. Stephen managed to get his feet free and in one movement threw Justine into a wrestling halt to control her.

'Be quiet, Sharon!' he said through clenched teeth as Justine kicked and swore and tried to bite his arm. 'Go home *now*!' he yelled at the receptionist.

Sharon quickly gathered up her things and made a hasty exit.

Justine was strong and the extent of her anger added to her strength. She fought hard, but was no match for Stephen. He held her and waited for her to calm down. Eventually she quietened down because she knew she couldn't win. Not at the moment. But all her anger turned inwards and she relished bottling it up. She would need to draw on it when the odds were in her favour.

'How could you choose that fat cow over me?' Justine asked. 'You bastard! You fobbed me off tonight to be with *her*! Let me go. I'm leaving. I hope you enjoy many more evenings with Miss Krispy Kreme.'

Justine hated sharing Stephen with Katherine but at least she was a worthy adversary. That wasn't the case with Sharon, of all people.

Stephen gradually released his grip. Justine turned to face him and let go with a long tirade of abuse until Stephen took her by the arm again and shook her to make her be quiet.

'I won't cop this from you, Justine. You have no claims on me. You can be the best, sweetheart, but you can never be younger and you can never be someone else,' said Stephen, determined to put her back in her place. 'We'll talk about this when you cool down. Now go home.'

Chapter 31

Katherine fussed around with pillows and blankets as the paramedics transferred Andy to the special bed they'd purchased for him. Bec held on to Andy's hand and talked to him throughout.

'You're home at last, Andy,' she said, trying to keep from crying. 'It won't be long before you're up and about around the run. The boys are missing you. The place is a picture, Andy, and you will have to get out and check the new bulls I bought. I hope they're alright. It's getting hot; summer's almost here again.'

Bec was determined to continue to talk to Andy while ever she was with him. She knew now he could hear her.

'You've got an absolutely gorgeous nurse. Not sure I'm too happy about that.' Bec winked at Denise, the middle-aged carer. 'I'll get the kettle on and we can have some lunch.'

Katherine spoke to the helpers in the room. 'You will stay for lunch, won't you?' she asked the ambulance driver. They followed her out of the room, leaving Andy and Bec alone.

'So I have you to myself now, my love. It's so good to have you home. We've got so much to talk about and do. I can't wait to lie down beside you tonight. I'm going to open the windows. You need to get the sounds and smells of home back into you,' Rebecca said as she opened the bedroom windows wide. The sweet perfume of the flowers in the garden wafted in on a gentle breeze, and Bec could hear Bounce barking excitedly out the back, no doubt trying to encourage Jess to play with him. The bedroom was dominated by the king-size bed they had purchased in their first year of marriage. Bec had pushed the bed up against the wall, under the windows, in order to make room for Andy's cot and the equipment that he was connected to.

Sitting on the edge of her bed, she leant over and kissed Andy's lips, gently stroking his forehead and curling his hair in her fingers. As she did so, she noticed that she could see herself and Andy in the dresser mirror against the opposite wall. Despite the physical glow of her pregnancy and her excitement about getting Andy home, there was a sadness in the eyes that she was now staring into. Determined not to allow that sorrow to distract her or to be sensed by her husband, she turned back to Andy and said. 'We need to work towards getting you awake in time to see our baby born.' She placed his hand on her swollen tummy and sat with him for a while longer before joining the others for lunch.

Outside, the wind changed direction, swinging to the north and bringing the hint of moisture. Across the plains, the front line of a bank of clouds peeped over the western horizon.

After lunch Denise went to tend to Andy, and Rebecca and Katherine walked down the front steps with the ambulance driver. 'Looks like I'd better get moving,' he said.

'It is looking a bit threatening all of a sudden,' Rebecca said, amazed to see the black clouds rising into the sky. 'Funny, the bureau said little or no rain on the forecast this morning.'

The ambulance left and Katherine and Bec wandered through the garden, talking about what plants were flowering and what was struggling.

'I felt like putting you in that ambulance too, when I saw those clouds,' Katherine confessed.

'Oh, Mum. I'm fine. No more than a few millimetres they are saying. I can always call Clarry to come and pick me up in the chopper.'

'Due dates can be very wrong and there can be complications,' Katherine chided her.

'Well, Mum, if something happens, we have a nurse here,' said Bec, and Katherine laughed with her.

Later in the afternoon, Bec could see that the weather system rolling in from the west wasn't storm clouds; it was dust clouds. High cloud cast shadows and blackened the palls of risen red dust, making them look like thunderheads lined up and pushed to the ground. Everyone at Coolibah swung into action, tying things down, as they knew the wind would be cyclonic and might blow for days. 'Nudding, start the pump, we want to make sure the tanks are full for the blow. Make sure Andy's generator is full too,' Bec instructed. 'I'll go and bring the horses up to the yard,' she said striding out to the Toyota. 'Mum, can you make sure that the quarters are all closed up and get the clothes off the line,' Bec yelled over her shoulder as she was getting into the car.

As she drove out of the house yard and into the horse paddock she could see Sam gathering up his gardening gear and stacking it in the shed. Bouncing along over the rough ground to the back of the horse paddock, Bec could see that the rolling barrage of dust being driven in by cold lifting winds from the desert had grown and boiled angrily up into the sky, blocking out the sun. It hung like an orange orb reflecting an eerie rusty light. The evening was strangely still but the wind was coming at a racing pace, ripping across the ridges and tearing over the plains, bearing down on Coolibah. Bec found the horses and they immediately set off at a gallop for the yards. They could sense the oncoming storm. Sam had the gates open through to the stalls at the back of the yards. The horses trotted straight in and he shut the gates behind them.

'Jump in, Sam,' Bec called. 'It's almost here!' Sam hobbled as quickly as he could to the car and Bec drove back to drop him off at the quarters.

'Send Nudding over to the house and we'll give you something for dinner. Looks like this will be an all-nighter,' Bec said. As she drove towards the homestead the first erratic gusts of wind and some spiralling whirly winds slapped into the car.

Katherine had the house locked up. She had pulled the roast from the oven and they quickly made sandwiches for the men and wrapped them in alfoil.

'They've got tea and coffee over there,' Bec said.

Nudding came in. 'Is that tank full?' Bec asked.

'Yep, it was almost full already so I didn't have to start the pump,' he said.

'Okay. Good. You better get hunkered down. I don't think we've got much longer before it hits,' Bec said, walking to the door of the homestead with Nudding and looking out.

'I've checked Andy's generator. It's full,' he said, jogging away across the yard.

⁂

Later, as the driving wind and dust blasted the homestead, Rebecca lay in the room with Andy, her bed pushed up against his. Coloured lights blinked on and off on the monitors but otherwise it was pitch black.

'Listen to that, Andy. A proper Bedourie dust storm. Wonder how long it will blow for. Keep us all busy cleaning up after it that's for sure,' Bec whispered.

She kept talking in the dark. Despite the battering dust storm, she felt a contentment that had been missing from her life for many months. Having Andy at home just felt right. She dozed off, one arm across Andy's chest with her bed pushed up beside.

Bec awoke with a start, clutching at her swollen belly. A vice-like contraction gripped her and held on. Her eyes shot open and she curled up trying to ease the discomfort. As she did, her waters broke and a warm, sticky flood escaped between her thighs.

She groped for the bedside table lamp and turned it on. The contraction was beginning to ease. Bec stood up, scooping the sheet between her legs as she did so, and padded down the hall to Katherine's room. She went in, her voice shaky.

'Mum. Mum,' she called. All the bravado of her afternoon conversation about having the baby had vanished.

'What is it?' Katherine sat bolt upright in bed.

'I'm in labour.'

Katherine leapt up and turned on the light. She could immediately see that Bec's waters had broken. Rebecca leant forward and held her stomach as another contraction began. 'Lie down here,' Katherine instructed. 'I'll get Denise.'

'No, Mum. I'll go back to my room,' said Bec. 'I want to be with Andy.'

'Okay. But just lie here until this contraction passes. Then we'll go back to your room.' Katherine went out the door to get the nurse.

Rebecca started her practised breathing, and it helped with managing the contraction. Katherine was back in a flash with Denise.

'Well, girls,' said Bec, 'we're going to have to do this here at Coolibah. There's no way we'll get out or anyone will get in. Even a chopper wouldn't get through this dust. Visibility would be less than a metre. You wouldn't be able to see your hand in front of your face in this.'

'How many weeks are you?' asked Denise.

'Close to thirty-seven.'

'Okay. That's good. Sometimes the dates can be a little bit out but baby should be well developed. I'm not a midwife but I've been involved with enough deliveries in remote clinics in the Top End. Did you say your doctor was Dr Morris in Coombul?'

'Yes, that's right,' Katherine answered for Bec.

'I'll go and call him now,' said Denise. It was 2.30am.

Bec rose with some difficulty from the bed. 'I need a shower, Mum,' she said, as she waddled down the hallway.

Katherine hovered behind her daughter. She recognised the inflection in Bec's voice, one of focus and determination to get a job done no matter what. There were so many things that could go wrong. Katherine began to pray silently.

'That's fine, Bec. We just have to do things between the contractions, so how about we have a little walk around and after the next one you can go straight into the shower?'

As the night went by and Rebecca's labour continued, the dust completely enclosed them and seeped through every tiny space into the homestead. When the grey dawn broke, Bec lay in her bed drenched with sweat, her dark hair clinging to her face and neck. She felt as though she was anchored to the bed with lead weights, such was the force of her contractions.

'You are ready to deliver, Rebecca,' Denise told her in her calm, professional voice. 'You can push with the next contraction.'

Bec squeezed Katherine's hand with such strength that Katherine feared her bones would break. Overpowered by the dust, the sun rose more like a yellow moon and shone a feeble orange glow through the windows. With one final exertion and all of her strength and will, Bec brought her son into the world.

He was squawking immediately as Denise checked and cleared his airway and placed him on Bec's bare belly. He was pink and plump and squirmy, and Rebecca had never seen anything so beautiful in all her life. She reached out to touch him as Denise invited Katherine to cut the umbilical cord.

'Andy. Look. A son. A son, Andy. Our son.' Bec was crying as Katherine placed the baby in her arms and said a prayer of thanks.

'Hello, little man. Hello,' she cooed, and her life changed forever.

Chapter 32

Brendan tutted and pursed his lips as Justine fell to pieces before him. She had come to see him at the gym and he was appalled that she had allowed herself to be so totally consumed by a man. She wanted revenge for the pain Stephen had caused her, and Brendan was willing to help. The worry vanished from his smooth face and a wicked smile turned up the edges of his mouth.

'Don't you worry about a thing, darling,' he said. 'I'm going to give you Mr Stephen Hogan's balls on a plate. Come on now, do stop crying, your makeup's all over the place.' He handed her a box of tissues from his desk.

Justine wiped her eyes, pushed back her dishevelled hair and stared at Brendan, waiting for him to proceed. She was still staring blankly into space. She'd never experienced anything like the pain and confusion she was going through right now. She kept waiting for it to end but it just kept getting worse.

'I have a little umm . . . business, other than the paper and the gym. It's a very lucrative business and all cash money. It's helping with my plan to sell the paper and the gym and go to the States next year. I'm just totally bored with this hick town. Now, Justine, I'm going to let you in on my secret business. I'll be shutting it all down soon anyway. Come on,' he said, taking her by both hands and hauling her out of her chair. 'I'm going to show you something that will bring Stephen to his knees.'

It was about 6pm and the gym was full of people. Brendan led Justine to the storeroom at the back of the building. The little room was hot and dusty with a jumbled assortment of weights and broken equipment, filing cabinets and cardboard boxes. Behind a line of tall shelves along one side of the room was another door, which he opened to reveal a set of stairs. Brendan stepped into the dim stairwell and signalled for Justine to follow. It was dark inside the ceiling of the building but there was a vast space dimly lit by the skylights in the roof. Brendan moved to step around her to lock the door behind them and he accidently stood on her toes.

'Shit, Brendan. What the hell are you doing, you idiot!' Justine swore.

'You'll see, darling. Come on, hold my hand.'

He was pleased to hear her swear. At least she was showing an emotion of some kind. As they edged forward past some old filing cupboards, Justine was astounded by what she saw in front of her. They were standing inside what looked like a production room in a television studio.

On specially constructed shelves along the far wall, ten screens winked and blinked in the darkness.

'What the . . .?' said Justine. The monitors displayed, in full colour, from a vantage point above the shower heads, the interior of all the shower cubicles. Two of them were trained on the workout areas.

'What's the matter? Cat got your tongue?' Brendan was squirming with delight as he saw the shock on Justine's face. 'You see, darling, people are sick and tired of the same old manufactured porn. Reality is the keyword these days. I'm selling these recordings into Asia for huge dollars, American dollars, in cash, posted to me with equipment purchases.'

'How long have you been doing this?' Justine had found her voice.

'Oh, a couple of years. I set it up myself. The camera lenses are so small now. It was easy. You know I've always had a flair for electronics.

'Oh look. There's old Mrs Johnstone and that's that little blonde from the bank. If we look across at eight, there's Gary and Ishaan. Of course, the thing is, people get very warmed up by a workout at the gym, if you know what I mean.' Brendan winked. 'You'd be amazed. You know I've even seen –'

'How many hours have you got of me?' Justine interrupted him.

'Oh now, I'm crushed that you think I would sell any of those pictures.'

Justine had drawn herself up to her considerable height and she towered over him. 'You better not have. You're a very sick puppy, Brendan. If I find out that you've sent –'

'Wait, wait. Shhhh. No, listen to me. I've got a lot of footage of our Stephen. But it's nothing compared to the movie I'm going to get next time he comes in. Here's the plan.'

Brendan rushed ahead to skim over the issue of images of Justine in the showers.

'You know how Gerard drools over Stephen and has been infatuated with him for years?'

Justine nodded.

'Well, if he were to get a note inviting him into the showers with Stephen, what do you think he'd do?'

Justine's face was still beautiful even as she frowned and twisted her mouth to one side considering the plan.

'Imagine the power a couple of photos would give you over our stalwart federal member, macho Stephen Hogan, in a very compromising position in the shower with another man. The threat of a front page story: "Member for Telford has Gay Affair" in the locals and "Rising Political Star Caught in the Act" or something better in the nationals. It'd be an absolute disaster. There's no way he could deny the story; the evidence would be there. Two naked men together in the shower. The macho Stephen Hogan: gay.'

Brendan started to giggle.

'You're such a deviant,' said Justine, though her mind was racing.

Without Stephen, Bec would have trouble carrying the Telford Gold project through to fruition. Without his expanding political clout, the project would stall. She would make sure that Rebecca had a lot of trouble keeping the momentum going as a way of crushing Stephen Hogan.

'Of course the police would investigate, but I'd be long gone by then and all the evidence would be gone. We could disassemble the gear and have it all out in one evening. Only you and I will know. You could come with me, darling. You're far too good for this backblock, one-horse town.'

'No. No. I want to stay,' said Justine. 'I want to smile at that bastard in the street knowing I've finished him.'

'You'll have to sit on the photos until I'm gone and the new people have taken over the newspaper,' Brendan suggested.

Their plan was taking shape rapidly. Brendan would carefully attend to the finer details. Justine knew that he was meticulous and wouldn't leave a trace of evidence. She had regained her focus and Stephen Hogan was doomed.

The plotters' opportunity came quite suddenly. Stephen returned from Canberra where he'd had a series of meetings with the ministers of the various departments and their advisers, the real decision-makers, and an in-depth discussion with the heads of a political party to construct a pathway to ease him into the ministry. After several days locked in offices, he was keen to clear the cobwebs and refresh with a good hard workout at the gym. Brendan phoned Justine immediately and she hurried to join him and put their plan into action.

Gerard was instructing an aerobics class so it was easy to slip the note under his towel in his gear bag. Stephen was working out hard, oblivious to what was about to happen. Justine and Brendan made a show of leaving the building and quickly re-entered through the back door and took up their positions in front of the monitors.

They watched intently as Gerard finished his class and walked over to his gear. As planned, the folded white note fell to his feet and he bent to pick it up. His mouth fell open when he read the words: 'Time I got to know you. Meet me in the showers. Stephen Hogan.'

Gerard stuffed the note in his pocket and looked around before sauntering out past Stephen, who was pushing weights. Gerard gave him the eye and patted the note in his pocket.

Stephen ignored Gerard. He was thinking about Justine. She'd surprised him. He didn't think that she would be so hurt by his infidelities. He was sure that she knew the score; she was a player after all. He counted their dalliance as a feather in his cap, nothing more.

He looked at his watch and noticed that time was up. He warmed down, grabbed his bag and headed for the showers.

'Here he comes!' Brendan whispered in anticipation.

Justine leant forward, watching intently.

Gerard was already in the shower room and was loitering around waiting for Stephen to show up. He would wait for him to go to the shower and then follow him in. Justine and Brendan could barely contain their excitement as the suspense built.

Stephen stripped off in the shower and was obviously relishing the stinging burst of water. Just as he raised his muscular arms to wash the sweat from his hair, Gerard appeared at the door, dropped his towel and with a look of pure ecstasy embraced Stephen from behind. Stephen's reaction was unequivocal. The blow from his elbow sent Gerard flying backwards, hitting the door of the cubicle and sliding down to the floor. Stephen grabbed him by the throat, hauled him up, opened the door and threw him out in a sprawling heap.

Brendan and Justine were snorting with laughter trying to keep the noise down in their hiding place. Brendan hit the rewind button and paused the frames at the moment of the embrace. The freeze was much better than they could have hoped for. The expression on Stephen's face as he enjoyed the cooling water and the lovesick look on Gerard's face made the picture absolutely perfect for their cause. They clapped their hands together in a high five salute.

Later that night, Brendan helped Gerard ice his bruises and listened to his tale of woe. The following afternoon he was suitably shocked when Gerard showed him the anonymous letter he'd received in the post.

'This was in your letterbox?' Brendan handed back to Gerard the sheet that he himself had printed with the words 'TIME TO LEAVE TOWN, POOF'.

Brendan advised Gerard that he thought it was the only thing that he could and should do.

'You'll have to leave as soon as possible. It's obvious that Stephen Hogan is a homophobic psycho! Lord only knows what he's capable of. He must have left that note to you in the gym purely to set you up for this. He's obviously a very disturbed man. We're going to the States soon anyway, so you'll just have to go on ahead of me. I'll give you the cash. You get yourself out of town and out of the country.'

The plan was all coming together wonderfully.

Chapter 33

Stephen was unsure what had happened to change Justine's attitude but she was definitely much more amenable and cheerful. She was keeping him firmly at arm's length and obviously had no intentions of resuming their affair despite the fact that he had terminated Sharon's employment and recruited an older woman, but it seemed she was getting over the incident with the receptionist. He was handing more and more of the Telford Gold negotiations and dealings over to her as he felt more comfortable with her loyalty.

For the next couple of months, at least until the election, he would really need to lean on her to keep Telford Gold bubbling along and handle the PR. Rebecca was absorbed with her new baby. So, for this week, Justine was carrying the project. He phoned her.

'Rebecca and I won't be able to make it to the Phosec meeting scheduled for next week. Can you handle that, Justine? I have forwarded the Telford Gold project planning documents and the Coolibah Creek land access agreement terms,' he said.

'Not a problem.' Justine was cool and professional. 'Pretty straightforward.'

'Good. I have to go. I'm in a meeting,' Stephen hung up.

Brendan and Justine were sitting at the outside table of their favourite café. They had just shared a coffee with the purchasers of Brendan's newspaper and gymnasium businesses.

'So, what do you think of the buyers?' he said, lolling back on his chair in his suit and shades. 'Hard to believe that they would want to move to the backblocks of Australia from New York, isn't it? They're so excited about it. I don't think they'll last twelve months myself, but anyway it's not my problem. The money's in the bank and very soon I'll be winging away to the States.' Brendan waved his cigarette in the air with a flourish. 'Will you miss me, darling?'

Justine turned her cold eyes to him. 'Of course I'll miss you, Brendan,' she said absently. She had been longing for her friend to finalise the sale of his business and move on so that she could post the photos. Her hatred for Stephen was consuming her with the same intensity her attraction to him had done.

'Oh, I give up on you today, Justine. You're just not here. I've got to get down to the travel agent now.' Brendan crushed the butt of his cigarette in the ashtray and adjusted his sunglasses before leaving.

Justine glanced at her watch. She'd better get home, shower and change. She had a rendezvous to deliver some afternoon delight to Angus Dalgliesh. She shivered slightly with disgust at the prospect, but her feelings of revulsion were overpowered by the rush of delight she felt in knowing what it would mean to crush Stephen and Rebecca's dreams.

Two o'clock that afternoon she stood in the carpeted hallway outside Dalgliesh's hotel room. 'Angus,' she purred as the director opened the door and she stepped inside, slipping out of her jacket as she brushed past him.

'I wanted to speak with you about the Telford Gold project.' Justine got down to business first. 'I know I've been a supporter of it in the past, but I've had some negative signals coming through my networks about the proposed dam and other things. I have to inform you that I no longer believe it would be the preferable option to dewatering into the existing waterways.'

Justine got straight to the point. 'I understand that the majority of your board are very enthusiastic about the Telford Gold partnership and the social licence benefits for Phosec, but I recognise you, Angus, to be the man with the greater intelligence and the most clout. That's what makes you so attractive,' she said suggestively, lowering her eyelids.

'I'm actually very pleased to hear your views, Justine, because I've never liked the idea of being tangled up with the leafy lefties and the yokels from the sticks. Way, way too messy for my liking. Always take the clearest path and see if people can stop you. That's my tenet.' Dalgliesh's eyes clouded with desire. 'I'm sure I'd be able to convince the board to have a change of heart, Miss Rand. Why don't you convince me that I can?' he said and began to unbuckle his belt.

Rebecca stood in the kitchen at Coolibah talking on the phone. She had been desperately trying to contact Stephen. 'Dad, thank goodness. I've been trying to reach you all day.'

'Sorry, love. I've been in conference and meetings all day. What's the matter?' asked Stephen, worried.

'It's Phosec. I had a call from the general manager and they're not happy with the land access conditions. He said they'd be responding formally but they have serious concerns about an extremely negative public reaction to the construction of a dam. He said he considered all the other conditions other than compensation for loss of grazing area to be outside the mine's lawful requirements for compliance.' Bec drew breath.

'The final straw is he said that he couldn't accept the land access agreement document because I'm not the legal owner of the lease.' She'd been dismayed by the Phosec executive's curt manner and tone.

'Right,' said Stephen. 'That's an abrupt about face. Something's happened. Just hold off on talking with anyone. I'll be home tonight. Your mother and I will slip out to Coolibah tomorrow. She wants to see little Drew anyway. How is the little fella?'

'He's great. Feeding like a bull calf, getting chubbier and stronger every day,' said Bec. 'I have to take him into town for his three-month check-up tomorrow, so that will save you the trip. The call was very strange, Dad. Anyway, I won't do anything further until we can get together.'

༄

Justine was on the phone to Hugh Dibbon. He owed her a favour.

'I took a call yesterday from Govender. It seems there are people on the executive who are getting cold feet about Phosec's involvement in the Telford Gold project. They are not happy about SOWF getting into bed with mining, albeit for a good cause,' she said.

'Ha. Is that what he said? What a joke!' Hugh's laughter was heavy with contempt. 'There's not much use talking to me about it, Justine. As of yesterday I'm no longer in his employ.'

'Oh,' said Justine. That really didn't suit her. 'What happened?' she asked.

'The bastard got wind of a little inside information I had used; all to do with a big advertising production contract that the board awarded to my family's company. Govender has big chunks of shares in another marketing company – not in his name, of course . . . It's a long story. But I can tell you this, he will be sorry to see me go. Very sorry,' Hugh said with malice.

'How so?' Justine was now intrigued.

'I know all about a racket he has going. He's hauling in big dollars from developers all over the place in order to use his influence to minimise protestor action and keep any protestor activity out of the media. The board of SOWF has incredible influence globally over the media.'

'Hugh, do you have evidence?' Justine asked eagerly.

'Enough to put the smell of it on him,' said Hugh.

'Good. Give me the info. I want him to pull SOWF support for Telford Gold. If Phosec remains as supportive as they are of the Telford Gold project, and given that they claim the mine's production will have minimal environmental impact, it could be a global first partnership in a positive way for both organisations. I don't want that to happen. If we have the goods on Govender we can give him a simple little task like having SOWF withdraw support for Telford Gold for a start. If that works, then good, we can ramp it up from here. Could be a profitable piece of information, something you could retire on.' Justine fed the ideas for Hugh to contemplate.

'Justine, Justine. We are so alike. I like your plan,' he said. 'Govender is powerful on the board. Stopping or delaying the Telford Gold project would be easy for him and he loses nothing personally, particularly now that the others are getting shaky about the mining aspect.

'Give me Govender's private mobile number and the names of a couple of the companies he's been tangled up with. I'll wait until you're clear before I call him. When will that be?' Justine asked.

'I'll be gone tomorrow,' said Hugh.

Justine put down the phone, her mind racing. She was excited. Everything was falling into her lap. She was going to crush Stephen Hogan. The smell of blood was in her nostrils and she was loving it. She rubbed her hands together with glee as she thought about the next step.

She had a mail-out to do.

Chapter 34

Stephen was brewing coffee. He and Katherine would have a number of functions to attend next week as he began his election campaign in earnest. A return to his elected position would be just another small step in his journey forward. He was supremely confident about a win.

Whistling cheerfully, he pulled his robe together and tied it to go outside and get the paper from the front lawn and collect yesterday's mail. He sauntered back inside, poured himself a cup of the aromatic black coffee and sat down at the kitchen table. Katherine came out of the bedroom. She had showered and had a towel wrapped around her wet hair.

'Coffee's made,' Stephen announced as he tore the plastic from the paper.

'Thanks,' said Katherine and poured herself a cup.

At the table, she idly flicked through the mail before turning over an unfamiliar envelope. It looked personal and felt like photos. She tore open the envelope and pulled out the contents. It was photos, two of them, of Stephen and a stranger naked in the shower together.

Bile rose in her throat and shock seemed to anchor her to the chair for a second. Suddenly she stood up with such force that her chair fell over and crashed onto the floor. She ran to the bathroom and threw up. Her legs turned to jelly and she knelt on the cold tiles, her head hanging over the toilet bowl.

Stephen leant over in his chair to pick up the photos from the floor. His face turned ashen as he stared at them. His mind raced, searching for reasons why they existed.

The election? The project? Katherine? Who? What?

He got up and went into the bathroom, where Katherine was sitting on the floor crying. He bent down and tried to help her up.

'*Get out*!' she screamed at him, her body shuddering with the force of her yelling.

Stephen retreated. He had to get to the bottom of this. Right now. He remembered the incident at the gym. But photos? How? They must have had a camera in the shower.

His mind sprinted ahead. Why would anyone do it? Who was he anyway, that queen from the gym? He filed back through his lovers for someone capable of this.

Justine.

She was friends with Brendan at the gym. Brendan and Gerard had left town. How convenient!

Stephen ran into the bedroom and pulled on a pair of jeans and a shirt, grabbed his keys from the dresser and jogged to his car.

There was no sign of Justine at her flat. Her Porsche was gone. She wasn't answering her phone. Stephen just drove. What could he do? He had to find Justine. Fast.

Katherine had gone when he got back to their house. Stephen let himself in and tried to call her. There was no answer.

'DAMN!' He swore viciously.

He rang Bec to ask if she'd heard from her mother.

'Why? Where is she?' said Bec.

Stephen hesitated and then launched into his version of the event that was unfolding. He thought he'd better start practising his explanation as Bec would find out soon enough.

He told her about what he believed to be the set-up for the photo and how the pictures must have been taken. He left out the reason why: the fact that his affair with Justine had not ended well.

'As you can understand, your mum is very upset. Please try to explain if she calls and let me know if you hear from her,' said Stephen, his guts churning.

'I'm coming to town for Drew's appointment,' said Bec. 'Send a text to her and let her know I'll be there. I'll get away from here within the hour.'

'Right. Good. Be sure to take care,' said Stephen, slamming down the phone and racing out to his car. He had to find Justine. He had nothing to go on, no evidence, no proof. And the photographs were real.

Bec was horrified at what her father had just told her. If it was all a set-up as he claimed, what was the reason? Were his political enemies so devious? She threw some clothes into an overnight bag and packed the baby's things. She went to say her goodbyes to Andy.

'I'll be home late tomorrow afternoon,' she told Denise. Just as she was walking out, the phone rang. It was Katherine. She was distraught.

'I have to come out and see you Rebecca. I can't go into what's happened on the phone.

Bec could hear the distress in her voice. 'Mum. I've spoken to Dad. He's told me all about it.' Bec heard her mother draw in a sharp breath down the line. 'It's okay, Mum. Look, you can't be driving in the state you're in. Please don't,' Bec said.

'Well I can't go home. I won't go home,' Katherine said vehemently. 'Oh God, Bec, it's so awful,' she said, the quaver in her voice suggesting she was about to cry again. 'You shouldn't be hearing all this,' Katherine said trying to get control.

'I'm on my way out the door to come to town. I have Drew's appointment with Dr Morris tomorrow. I'll get on to Dad and tell him not to go home. I'll meet you there in about three hours. Okay?' Katherine didn't reply. 'I'm sure things are not as they seem. It's been a terrible shock for everyone and we just have to stay calm and deal with it,' Bec said reasonably.

'I guess that's about all we can do at the moment,' Katherine conceded. 'If you promise to get on to your father I'll meet you at home,' she said.

'I'll do that now and call you back,' Bec said and shifted baby Drew from one hip to the other.

༄

Justine had just pulled into her driveway when Stephen's car came flying up behind her. He got out and strode towards her. The stormy look on his face made her flinch but she rejoiced inside knowing that he must have received the photos.

She sat calmly in the car and wound down the window. 'Hello, Stephen. What's up?' She smiled into his livid face.

'You know exactly what's up. Where's your friend Brendan from the gym? Katherine opened the photos this morning. Now get out of the car,' said Stephen, his voice menacing.

'What are you talking about? What photos?' said Justine, getting out of the car and staring back at Stephen calmly. 'You'll have to explain what you mean.'

Stephen's certainty about her being the perpetrator wavered. 'Can we go inside?' he asked.

'Of course,' said Justine, gesturing for him to follow her.

'I'm being blackmailed,' he said once they were inside.

'Really. How dreadful! But why? And who'd do such a thing?' said Justine.

'Give me the contact number for your gym buddy. Where did he go?'

'What's Brendan got to do with anything?' asked Justine, keeping her expression totally innocent.

'That's not something you need to know. Just give me the number now!' said Stephen.

'And what if I don't?' said Justine

Seething, Stephen thought about how Justine might be tangled up in what was happening. Realising he had nothing to go on with, he turned on his heel and left, slamming the door behind him.

Justine fell into the sofa and laughed. It was a shrill, maniacal laugh that verged on crying. Abruptly, she stopped laughing and sat up.

'This is only the beginning, Stephen Hogan, only the beginning,' she said to herself. She reached for her phone and dialled the number Hugh had given her.

※

It was late evening when Justine got the return call she had been waiting for. A motion to suspend the SOWF support for Telford Gold would be put to the board meeting next week. She was elated that everything was falling into place and she needed an adrenalin rush to let off steam. She decided to go for a drive. For Justine, other than sex there were few things like the thrill of speeding along an open road to relieve stress. The Porsche bucked and played under her as she drove dangerously fast along the road to Telford, relishing the power of the car. How deeply gratifying her revenge would be.

She'd decided to stay on in her position with Phosec now that she had buttered up Dalgliesh. He was an influential man. She had him firmly gripped between her long hard thighs. Like a tiger toying with its prey, she had him scurrying in whatever direction she wished him to go.

The Porsche hurtled down the highway at a terrifying pace. The needle on the Porsche's speedometer was just touching on 180 when Justine glanced down at her phone to see who was calling her. When she looked up, the bend was upon her. In sheer panic she gripped the wheel and over-corrected, instantly putting her on the wrong side of the road as the white line and the bitumen rushed up at her. She turned the wheel the other way and just as she did a semitrailer appeared, seemingly from nowhere, filling up her windscreen.

Justine screamed, jerked the steering wheel and closed her eyes. The Porsche had only slowed marginally. It fishtailed, throwing Justine hard into the seatbelt, before locking up into a four-wheel drift and rolling, over and over and over. The sports car rolled along the side of the road before the underside of the tumbling vehicle slammed into a tree.

Chapter 35

Justine awoke in the stark white hospital room. There was a bright fluorescent light overhead and flashing green and red lights beeped on a monitor beside her bed.

It hurt to breathe. Her chest felt like it was weighted down with a nail bed. She moved her right arm to try to scratch an itch on her head. A searing pain shot through her elbow to her shoulder and she felt as though the skin was splitting on her forearm. An involuntary groan escaped her lips. Immediately a nurse appeared at her side.

'Hello. Please don't try to move. You've been in an accident. You just lie still now and I'll go and get the doctor,' she said. She left as quickly as she had appeared.

Justine felt her pulse quicken as she remembered the bitumen rushing up into her face, the kaleidoscope of tarmac and sky as the Porsche flipped and spun. The agitation laboured her breathing and the pain in her chest increased. Fear and dread swamped her but she daren't move. Cautiously she tried to wriggle her toes and sighed with relief when she could move both of her feet. She gingerly moved the fingers on her left hand and feeling no pain raised her hand to her face. She was horrified to feel bandages. As she investigated further she found that there were bandages all over her face and head. She tried to move her mouth but she couldn't.

'Hello there,' the doctor said cheerily as he walked up to her bed. 'Good to see you awake. You're doing very well considering,' he said in a deep, comforting voice.

He could see the look of terror in her eyes as they darted about the room before focusing on him. 'You won't be able to speak for a little while, Miss Rand. We've had to wire your jaw. You've been in a serious accident and you have some pretty severe head and facial injuries. Don't be too concerned, though. I'm sure they'll be able to be repaired with time.

'You're in the Wesley hospital in Sydney, the best hospital in the country. You are a very, very lucky girl. Your father is here. He must have just ducked out. He's been constantly at your side for ten days. We're going to keep you fairly heavily sedated for the next few days in order to control the pain and restrict movement. Do you understand everything I'm saying, Justine?' he asked. 'Just blink twice if you do.'

Justine blinked.

She has the most beautiful eyes I've ever seen, thought the young doctor. He took her hand to comfort her.

Just then Jonathon Rand entered the room. 'Is she awake? Oh, thank God! Thank you, God.' He rushed to Justine's side.

The doctor stepped away. 'Remember to be careful not to touch her or move her, Mr Rand,' he warned, 'except her left hand and arm which are not damaged. She can't speak but she can hear and understand you, which is a marvellous development. I'll leave you with her for five minutes before we give her the medication. Justine can blink to communicate if you want to ask her questions,' he explained before speaking briefly with the nurse and leaving.

Mr Rand sank into the chair, holding Justine's hand in his and crying unashamedly. 'My baby. Thank the Lord you're going to be okay. Everything's going to be okay.'

Justine lifted her hand to her bandaged face and blinked furiously.

'You have some pretty nasty injuries on the right side of your face and head, but we're going to get you fixed up. Don't you worry about a thing. The main thing is that you're alive and I'll make sure that you get well again,' he said with conviction.

༄

Stephen had gone to Canberra, supposedly on Telford Gold business but, really, he'd gone to remove himself from Katherine's presence. She refused to speak with him and they communicated through Rebecca. With Justine in a critical condition in a Sydney hospital and no idea how to contact Brendan Oliver or Gerard, Stephen was stumped. He sat in his motel room drinking brandy staring at the photos. If you were unaware of the actual circumstances, the pictures were very convincing. With Justine's accident and the urgent requirement for him to try to repair relations with Phosec and SOWF and the ongoing commitments he had to his election campaign, he hadn't even had the mental space to try to figure out who was behind the photos and what they intended to do with them. Given there had been no demands forthcoming, the purpose of the photos remained a mystery. He strongly suspected Justine; she was the only one clever enough to do something like this but he had no proof. For the first time in his life, Stephen felt vulnerable. He didn't like it. He was being bombarded from every direction with seemingly insurmountable problems. 'When the going gets tough . . .' he said out loud, slammed down the half glass of brandy and got up out of his seat. At the desk, he opened his tablet and entered into the search engine 'private investigator Sydney.'

Less than a week later Stephen was still in Sydney and he took a call from the man he'd hired. 'Got your man, Mr Hogan. He's living in New York currently, but you'll be pleased to know that at this moment he's on a plane to Sydney, I presume to visit Miss Rand in the hospital there,' said the investigator, pleased at the offer of a substantial bonus if he could find Brendan quickly.

'Got him,' said Stephen. 'Great. Thank you. Do you have a flight number?' At last a breakthrough to sorting out this mess.

'Yes, I do, and I've just sent it to you via text.'

'Thank you very much. I'll take it from here. I'll transfer the cash now.' Stephen hung up.

༄

Knowing when Brendan had arrived, Stephen planned to stake out the hospital to intercept his quarry. He sat in his car, running his campaign by phone, keeping a sharp eye on the entrance. He thought about Justine. Knowing her as he did, he wondered if she would ever recover mentally from the facial and body scarring she had been reportedly left with from the accident. Then he saw him, getting out of a cab at the hospital's entrance.

Stephen stepped out of the car and quickly caught up with Brendan, walking up behind him and slapping him on the back like an old acquaintance, conscious of the multiple security cameras that would be operating and not wanting to give Brendan any excuse to charge him with assault. He smiled broadly and put his mouth close to Brendan's ear, his right thumb digging deeply into the muscle between his neck and shoulder.

'Walk with me,' he said, directing him along the corridor.

Brendan let out a little whimper and came up on his tiptoes to try to get out of Stephen's grip.

'Smile,' said Stephen, and pinched a little harder. They entered the hospital and at Stephen's direction they were seated in the noisy cafeteria. Stephen stared ominously across the table. Brendan broke out in a sweat as his eyes glanced around the room, looking for an escape route.

'You won't be going anywhere until you give me some information, you slimy little grub,' said Stephen, controlling the urge to punch him in the face. 'I had some photos sent to me in the mail. They came from your gym. How could that have happened?'

'I don't know anything about any photographs. What are you talking about?' Brendan's reply was unconvincing.

'I know you're involved. Be very sure of that. But it's not you I'm after. I want to know who and why. You tell me that and I'll leave you alone.'

Coolibah Creek

Stephen leant forward and the action made him seem bigger and more intimidating. 'Come on. I know all about you. I've had a private investigator on your tail. I know where you live, where you work, everything. There'll be no escape from me, not ever. I know all about your little racket in video sales. Best you just speak up now and you can go on your way, no more questions, no more pain.' Stephen smiled.

Brendan had no intentions of being a hero. He spilled it out. 'It was Justine's idea, the whole thing. Justine. Justine Rand. You brought it on yourself, anyway, the way you treated her.' Brendan was brave enough to take a little shot.

'Give me proof,' Stephen said ominously. 'How do I know that Justine's involved at all? Easy to put it on her; she can't defend herself,' he said.

Brendan shifted in his seat, his eyes darted about the room as he tried to think of a solution to his dilemma. He looked back at Stephen's glowering face and it terrified him.

Brendan had a light bulb moment and he began to relax a little. 'The phone. Justine's phone. It's all on there. Her messages to me, the photos – that's your proof.'

'Get it,' Stephen said simply. 'I'll wait.'

Brendan didn't move for a few seconds.

'Now,' Stephen said and Brendan sprang up and walked away quickly, glancing back over his shoulder as he went.

Everything clicked into place in Stephen's mind. Now it was all clear. He stood up and walked out of the cafeteria. Justine would keep and she wasn't going anywhere. All he needed now was possession of that phone and he could get home and start sorting out this debacle. Within half an hour, Brendan handed him the phone with trembling hands and stood in front of Stephen waiting to be dismissed. There was nothing more to say and Stephen turned on his heel and left. He needed to get home.

Chapter 36

Back at Coolibah, Bec was busy drafting a letter to Phosec regarding their abrupt change of direction on the Telford Gold project. The letter would be a precursor to a face to face meeting, which she would attend with Stephen when he came back to Coombul. Her parents' separation was horrible. Katherine was broken hearted and she spent most of her time at Coolibah with Bec.

'It's as if everybody knows,' she had told Bec. 'I just can't face anyone or keep pretending that nothing's happened. It's hard with the campaign in full swing.' Katherine had said miserably. Rebecca hoped that her father would sort it all out soon. That was what usually happened when he'd stuffed up.

It was mid-morning and a beautiful day on the property. Rebecca took baby Drew in to see Andy. 'Better give your boy a cuddle,' she said and placed Drew gently onto Andy's chest, as she had done so many times in the past. She took her husband's hand and put it on the baby's back; their gorgeous baby boy. She leant across Andy to gently sandwich baby Drew between them for a group hug.

The curtain of her hair fell across the baby's head and he started to giggle. Bec had never heard anything so delightful. She stood up and rolled Drew over on his back. He smiled a beaming smile. Bec leant down and allowed her hair to tickle his face again and, to her absolute enchantment, he giggled again, louder and even more joyful than before. Bec couldn't help but giggle too and she continued the game.

'Listen, Andy. Can you hear that? It's the most beautiful sound.'

Bec looked up at Andy. Her own laughter caught in her throat and she stopped breathing. Andy's eyelids moved. They moved.

'Andy, darling! Andy. I'm here. Come back to me. Andy. Come back to me. Please. You have to meet our son. Andy!' Rebecca pleaded as emotion made her chest constrict painfully.

There it was again! His eyelids fluttered this time.

'Andy?' she murmured hesitantly and she saw one corner of his mouth tug upward. 'Andy!' Bec squealed. 'Hello. Come back to me.'

She stroked his hair and kissed his mouth, placing baby Drew really close to Andy's face so that he reached out and tugged at his father's chin. Ever so slowly, Andy's eyes opened. Bec was speechless and motionless as she watched the miracle occur right before her. For a second their eyes met and Andy recognised her, his eyes saying hello, his mouth trying to smile.

Rebecca covered his face with kisses. 'Oh Andy, my love. I've missed you so much. Don't ever leave me again.' She stared at his face as he struggled to open his eyes again. 'Can you see him? Darling, this is Drew, your son, our son.' Bec's words caught in her throat.

'Mum! Denise! Come quick!' she called as she started laughing and crying at the same time, hugging baby Drew to her chest.

༄

Over the minutes, hours and days that followed, Bec rarely left Andy's side. She had the two-way radio moved into the bedroom so she could talk to the workers out in the paddock and had set up her computer in a corner where she could do the station's bookwork within earshot of Andy, just in case. When the physiotherapist came to Coolibah, Katherine made sure that Bec and Drew got away from the homestead and out around the property for a drive. Each day Andy did something more but he remained mostly comatose. Bec was there for every tiny improvement, sitting and sleeping beside him, feeding and playing with Drew in the room. She had little room in her life for anything else. Day by day his awareness periods and movement increased, and Bec's heart sang with every new development.

One morning, Katherine came in to bring her a cup of tea. 'Come on. Outside with you,' she commanded. 'You need to get a bit of sun on you and the spider orchids are flowering. Take your tea outside and have a stroll around. I'll stay here and play with Drew,' she said as the baby put up both his arms and smiled at her.

'Righto. Some sun would be nice,' said Bec.

Outside in the garden, the warmth of the early spring sun felt wonderful and the sweet aroma of her garden was an elixir to her. Bec wandered over to where the spider orchids with their weirdly beautiful spidery petals were open in the dozens, their pretty white and maroon colours standing out against the foliage. She put her mug down on one of the big limestone rocks that she and Andy had collected, with great struggle and laughter, for the garden, years ago. It came from near the limestone caves. She'd always wanted to explore the caves but Andy was claustrophobic and refused to go down. Out of nowhere, Bec had an idea. What if they could pump the water from the mine into the caves? She didn't think they were deep but apparently they were very long. The O'Donnell boys had been a fair way along inside them. If the caves didn't drain away and the bottom was not too fractured, the water could be stored there. It could mean there would be no evaporation, no seepage and possibly a number of different access points.

Bec felt her heart racing. Could it be possible? Her tea forgotten, she walked over to the shed to see if Sean and George were there. She found them working on a firefighter motor.

'What can you tell me about the limestone caves, Sean?' she asked him. 'How far into them have you gone?'

Sean wiped his brow with the back of an oil-stained hand. 'Daniel and I walked in, I reckon over a kilometre one day, till we got too scared and came back.'

'How wide, how deep?' quizzed Rebecca.

'Aw. Well, it varies a fair bit. In some places you could just fit a man on a horse through and in other places you could drive three double-decker cattle trucks through side by side. Then you come to these big round lake sort of things. The roof is low but the floor widens right out. You can walk around them.'

'Would you take me there?' asked Bec, excited to see for herself.

'Sure,' said Sean.

'You be careful goin' down there, Missus. That's dibble dibble place. Bad spirits. Blackfella doesn't go down there,' said George, shaking his head.

'What's the stories about the caves from your people, George?' asked Bec.

'Only Kadatchi man can go in there, and it's a two-day walk to the end. But if you get there, you never get back,' he said, hunching his shoulders with a little shiver.

'Thanks, fellas,' said Bec. She'd been away from Andy too long. She would ring Stephen and have him do some research to see if there was any scientific data or mapping available.

She spoke on the phone to Stephen, while sitting next to Andy's bed.

'I think the limestone is too permeable,' Stephen was saying. 'But gee, it's a great concept and well worth investigating. Are there any bat colonies or other rare creepy-crawlies down there?'

Bec laughed. 'Maybe. Sean has promised to take me down for a look. Andy would never allow me to go down.' She glanced at Andy fully expecting him to open his eyes and argue with her at any moment.

'I'll give the geologist at Phosec a call,' said Stephen. 'They've come around a fair bit. I've set up that meeting with them for next week. There's still a lot to work through with SOWF though, trying to bring them both together.'

'How's your mother?' Stephen asked, as he always did.

'She's fine, Dad, but she's very sad. What are you doing to sort this photos thing out? It needs fixing,' Bec chided.

'I'm close to getting some solid information that will expose the perpetrators,' Stephen said.

'How? What have you got?' Bec asked.

'Too soon to say, love,' Stephen was evasive.

'It better be soon, Dad,' Bec said.

※

The next morning when Bec woke up she decided it was time to get back in the saddle and went out and walked Mischief in out of the paddock. Sam had been looking for a new baby calf that a milker cow was hiding somewhere and he'd been unable to find it. Bec offered to saddle up and ride the paddock to see if she could pick it up.

Mischief was shiny and fat. She hadn't been ridden for months and she snorted with feigned alarm as Bec threw the saddlecloth across her wide, glossy back.

'Oh stop it, you old ratbag.' Bec was smiling. She was drinking in the familiar horsey smell of the mare and enjoying the feel of leather on her hands again. Mischief pranced about like a young colt as Rebecca tightened the girth. Bec found she was smiling with the joy of living.

She clicked to the mare and sent her out into a circle to lunge. Mischief was beautifully trained; Bec had broken her in herself. The mare obediently trotted in a circle and, when her mistress gave the command, she bounced into a canter, before pigrooting, kicking her hind legs high in the air. An explosive fart broke the silence of the morning and brought Bec to tears of laughter.

Coolibah Creek

She swung lightly onto the mare's back and as soon as she picked up the reins Mischief stepped out in a good walk, ears pricked, alert and eager to please. Bec kicked her into a rocking canter and revelled in the cool morning air in her face. She soon found the calf, picked it up and carried it over the front of the saddle back to the yard. Sam was there waiting and took his little hostage to the calf pen as the cunning old cow came galloping to the yard bellowing, her huge pink udder swinging comically side to side.

On impulse, Rebecca rode over to the homestead. The dogs barked as she took Mischief in through the gateway and rode her up to the open window of her bedroom.

'Hey, Andy!' she yelled. 'Come on. Come for a ride.' She kicked the mare forward.

'Wait for me, Bec,' she heard Andy say as plain as day.

Bec flew off the horse's back and vaulted up through the window. Still in her boots and spurs, she clambered onto the bed.

Andy raised his arm to touch her. 'What happened, Bec? Did we get the big bugger?' he asked.

Tears of joy ran down Bec's face. 'No. No, we missed him this time,' she said, her voice breaking with emotion as she remembered the accident.

Chapter 37

A constant stream of visitors came to Coolibah to see Andy and celebrate his miraculous recovery. Andy was walking unaided, albeit with a limp, and was able to sit up in the squatter's chair on the verandah for a couple of hours at a time now as his strength returned rapidly. His memory was scattered and he had periods of confusion, but other than that there was no lingering evidence of brain damage.

Andy's sister, Louise, had surprised everyone by turning up at Coolibah. Bec was always suspicious of her motives. It was morning smoko time and Stephen, Katherine and Louise were in conversation with Andy on the verandah when Bec brought out some freshly baked scones, syrup and creamy homemade butter along with a steaming pot of tea on a huge tray. After she set the tray down, Bec sat next to Andy, who was bouncing baby Drew on his lap. He clutched the infant to him in one arm and reached out with the other to hold Bec's hand as she turned to her father and said, 'Now that there's only family here, Dad, tell us what you've found on Justine's phone.'

Curiosity about its contents had been burning in everyone since Stephen had told them about it. He had been careful to edit the messages that had been retrieved from the phone. There were a number of saucy texts Justine had sent to him, which he'd deleted.

'I can't believe how vicious Justine has been and the lengths she has gone to, to try to bring down Telford Gold,' he began. 'I've got a copy of the messages that I've brought out for you to have a look at, but she has inveigled the Phosec Chairman, Angus Dalgliesh, in what's obviously a pretty hot affair and some of the lies she was feeding him about Telford Gold you will have to see to believe. But then,' Stephen went on incredulously, 'she somehow got connected to this bloke Hugh, who we have found out is Hugh Dibbon and he was the PA to Govender, the SOWF president. Through Hugh she got something on Govender and basically blackmailed him into suspending support for Telford Gold. She didn't write down any details of whatever it was she was using as leverage, so we may never know.'

'So what was the connection between Justine and your set of candid photos, Dad?' Rebecca asked.

Katherine stiffened in her seat and looked away. Stephen noticed her reaction. She was still keeping him at a distance but at least she would remain in the same room with him. He missed her so much. He hadn't been prepared for the emptiness he felt without her. The severing of their connection was something he had never imagined would happen. So much was dependent on what he was about to say.

'Well, that's a whole different story,' said Stephen. 'It seems that extortion is a common pastime of Justine's friends. Brendan Oliver, the gym owner, had secret cameras set up in all the showers. He organised for his friend to try to surprise me with a cuddle so that he could use the photos to blackmail me into not running for Telford at the next election. Apparently he has some connection to the opposition. He ran out of guts at the last minute when he sold the business and didn't follow it through.'

Stephen lied so smoothly and convincingly that nobody doubted him, not even Katherine. A lively discussion ensued about what possible motives Justine had for trying to scuttle Telford Gold.

'My theory is that she could see the opportunity to gain a position of power and influence, which would lead to some sort of very lucrative pay-off at some time in the future. She craves power and fame, so perhaps she was even planning to be the saviour of the project as well,' said Rebecca.

'The messages suggest that Dalgliesh had offered her something very desirable in order to scuttle the Telford Gold project. There's one from him saying that he's too old to wait for the "Telford Gold bullshit", as he put it. He wanted to be rich sooner rather than later and talked about the world being their oyster,' said Stephen. 'So I think that was probably the main reason,' he continued, hoping that Justine never exposed the primary reason for her vengeful acts.

'I've heard that she has gone to the States, living with Brendan Oliver, so she can get access to the best plastic surgeons. Her face has been horribly disfigured, they say. So the nurse from the Wesley told Laurie,' Louise added.

'Well. Is that karma? Let's hope she stays there,' said Bec. She was so angry about the way her mother had been hurt.

'Good news came through this morning, though, and I've been waiting for the right moment to tell you all.' Rebecca squeezed her hands together with glee. 'The geologist's report has come through on the caves. Pete from Phosec says, and I'll show you the report, that at about five hundred metres into them, the floor turns from limestone to marble.' She raised her hands as the others opened their mouths to speak.

'I know. I know. That sounds too good to be true, but evidently it's one of the miracles of nature that when limestone is heated and under pressure, it turns to marble; hard stone that very little water will seep through or dissolve. The change from limestone to marble more than likely happened during the volcanic event that brought the diamonds up from the mantle,' Bec went on enthusiastically.

'The summary of the report says that further investigative work will have to be carried out to determine the water storage capacity of the caves, but that in his opinion they would hold water and be an excellent water storage facility.'

'That's incredible,' said Stephen. 'What about protection of the wildlife and insects?'

'We'll have to get a full study done, Dad, but Pete said he saw no evidence of bat colonies, and he also said that the caves slope away and get deeper pretty rapidly. He reckons that we could pipe the water past the first five hundred metres or so of the caves through to where the marble begins, where it is completely dark and less inhabitable so there will be minimal impact,' said Bec.

'If the water can be stored in the caves and there's no need for a dam, it'll free up some capital we can swing towards locking in the geothermal power,' said Andy. 'The life of the mine is estimated at thirty years. When it shuts down, the infrastructure for pumping water up will remain and Telford Gold should be well established, so perhaps we won't need the storage then anyway, we can draw directly from the aquifer as needed,' he said.

Drew started whinging and rubbing his eyes.

'Time for your feed, mister,' Bec said as Andy handed the child to her.

Bec took Drew back inside the house and on instinct Andy followed.

Once inside, Bec took Andy aside. 'Could you make an excuse to take Louise away somewhere? I'd like to leave Mum and Dad alone.'

'Sure. How about we all go for a drive out to the caves,' he said.

'That sounds good. You get ready. I'll feed Drew,' Bec said.

Louise was keen for the trip and pretty soon they were leaving the homestead.

'Leave those dishes,' Katherine said. 'I'll do those. You go.'

'I'll give you a hand,' Stephen said as the others drove away.

'He's a beautiful grandson we have, Katherine.' Stephen tried to break the ice as they gathered up the cups and plates.

'Yes. Yes, he is.' Katherine's stomach was churning as she tried to process all of the information that had come forward in the last hour.

She carried the teapot inside and placed it on the bench. Stephen followed with the heavy tray. She was deeply affected by the nearness of him now that they were alone. 'Katherine. I've missed you so much. Can we talk?' he said as he put the tray on the bench and stood beside her. Katherine didn't trust her voice and she didn't answer but just stood there looking into the wall of the kitchen. For the first time in his life Stephen was uncertain about what to do. He didn't want to make a mistake; Katherine was so precious to him. He had only realised how precious now that he risked losing her. Both struck mute by their situation, the seconds ticked by in silence. Gradually Katherine summoned the courage to turn and face him and saw that tears were streaming down Stephen's face. He stood before her, like an open book, his eyes met hers and with words unspoken he pleaded for her to return the love he felt for her. In an instant, she was in his arms, the place she was meant to be, the only place where she felt complete. The warmth of his strong embrace miraculously healed her bruised heart and she felt her mouth curve into a secret smile. She inhaled the smell of him and turned her face up to his to taste the salty tears on his lips. 'Don't ever leave me, Katherine. I couldn't live without you,' he said and, still kissing her, scooped her up into his arms and carried her down the hallway to her bedroom.

Chapter 38

'Go faster, George!' the tiny rider urged his leader. 'Please, George, can we canter?'

Drew Roberts was almost four years old. His cowboy hat was jammed down tight on his head and loose blond curls framed his animated face. His dark eyes danced and his little legs kicked furiously into the leather of the saddle as he tried to boot the old mare into a canter.

George's face creased into a smile. He had Drew on a lead rein as they trotted out on the coolish autumn morning. It was the first round of the muster at Coolibah. Bec, Andy, Davo, Nudding and the O'Donnell boys had headed off to the back of the paddock with the horses and bikes to meet up with the chopper. They'd dropped George and Drew at the yards so they could ride out to the corner, where they would wait for the others to bring the cattle in.

'Pleeease, George, can we canter now?' Drew beseeched his leader and continued to boot the old mare furiously. The horse ignored him and trotted along obediently beside George's mount.

'Okay then, Bung Eye.' George used his pet name for Drew, which he'd labelled him with for having a swollen eye from the black fly bites. 'You ready now?' he asked.

'Yep. I'm ready now.' Drew leant forward in anticipation.

George pursed his lips and made a kissing sound. Both of the old stockhorses bounced into a slow canter. He glanced back at Drew. The child was smiling broadly, exhilarated by the floating, rocking motion of the horse and the increased speed. *He's just like his father*, George thought for the thousandth time.

༄

Davo and Bec chatted amicably as they drove along the dirt road. In the truck, loaded with horses, they slowed to go down into a river crossing and the pungent smell of eucalypts filled the cab. The season had been very kind and once again the land was bursting with growth. The river country was packed with green feed a metre high and the plains were oceans of silver Mitchell grass seed waving in the cool morning breeze.

Every time she crossed the river Bec thought of poor Maggie O'Donnell. Doug had never recovered from losing her, and his cancer and the rum had finally put him out of his misery two years ago. Sean and Daniel were young to be managing Lennodvale but Davo and Andy helped them out wherever they could. The boys had been taught well by their father and, as mean as he was, he'd left them with the skills to successfully work the property. They were like chalk and cheese, forever arguing, but nevertheless getting the job done. They constantly jousted with each other, but if anything threatened either one of them or the interests of Lennodvale, they stood shoulder to shoulder in an unbreakable bond.

Thinking about unbreakable bonds, it seemed to Bec that for the first time in his life Stephen had a true understanding of the depth of his love for Katherine and, having lost her once, he would never lose her again. With his wife back by his side, Stephen had easily won the Federal seat and was now the Minister for Agriculture. Telford Gold was surging forward with the signing of a comprehensive partnership agreement between Rebecca and Andy and a co-operative of adjoining landholders; Phosec; local, state and federal governments; Hotels International; and SOWF. Projections were that returns to cattle producers would be double what they were previously once the organic beef processing stage of Telford Gold was up and running. Extensive work was being done on a myriad of trials on native plants, animals and industries that might meet the strict criteria for fitting together to form the circle of nature that was Telford Gold.

Andy and Bec's financial situation had improved markedly and the outlook for the future was strong. Davo had refused to take repayment of his loan until the Telford Gold project was up and running. Stephen and Katherine had been the same, saying that they saw it as an investment in the project. Rebecca and Andy had taken advantage of the loans to make a significant payout to Louise, so the financial pressure was off them now with the return of a number of good seasons in succession.

Davo brought the truck to a stop when they arrived near the back of the paddock, and Rebecca unloaded the horses. Sean and Daniel rode further out on their bikes and Davo went out to meet the chopper as it came swooping down from the clear blue sky like an enormous black wasp. He and Clarry, the pilot, yelled over the noise of the machine, pointing and gesturing as Andy gave instructions on how they wanted the paddock mustered. Everyone had UHF radios so that they could communicate while they were bringing the cattle out of the steep and scrubby channels onto the plains.

Bec and Davo mounted their horses as the whacking blades of the chopper drove the air downwards to flatten and whip the grass, causing the ripe, fluffy white seeds to be flung into tumbling circles like confetti.

'Copy there, George?' Bec spoke into her mike as they trotted away.

'Gotcha, Missus,' George replied immediately.

'How's Bung Eye going?' Bec asked, smiling and imagining her precious son bobbing along on his horse. Bec trusted George implicitly and she knew that Drew was just as safe with George as he would be with her.

'We're both going along good 'ere. Nearly at that corner already.' George's voice crackled in her earpiece.

Davo and Bec rode down the steep banks of the river and into the sandy bottom. The sand was still wet and there were crystal-clear pools of water glistening in the early morning sun. Great clumps of green grass sprouted along the tops of the banks from the bases of magnificent white gums that stretched up into the blue sky. Breaking the stillness of the morning, a chorus of bird songs echoed along the riverbed.

Davo rode ahead to the next channel of the river and Bec turned north to go along adjacent to the one they had crossed. She could hear the chopper working with the bikes a few kilometres away as she kicked Mischief into a trot and scanned the bush ahead for cattle. Pretty soon she picked up a little mob and took them along. Most of the cattle had already heard the chopper and were trotting out onto the plains. She and Davo would pick up the stragglers and keep an eye out for cunning old bulls that had a habit of hiding and running back.

George and young Drew waited in the corner. Drew shadowed the old stockman and peppered him with questions as he lit a small fire and filled his quart pot with water from the bottle strapped to the front of his saddle. They would have quite a wait here until the others arrived with the mob.

George explained to the boy about how to make a good fire. He wanted to teach him all the things he knew.

'Come on, boy. You hungry? Let's go and find some bush tucker,' he said, rising from the fire and taking the youngster's hand.

'Do you think we could find a goanna?' Drew asked excitedly. He loved goanna and all the bush tucker that George could magically find and cook.

'Oh, you never know what we might find till we look, hey Bung Eye? You look for tracks. What can you see?'

George taught Drew to track and stopped to show him all the signs of the animals that had been moving overnight. There was a fascinating story of the activities of the night drawn in the loose dirt if you knew how to read it. After a little while, walking through the bush, Drew was intrigued and delighted when George extricated four big, fat, creamy witchetty grubs from their holes in the ground at the base of a tree. They were as long and thick as George's fingers, and their soft, silky feel fascinated Drew.

'Hoo-hoo. Good tucker this bloke, Bung Eye. Real good tucker,' said George.

Drew dug with his stick looking for the tell-tale tunnels that led to the captivating creature. He was excited when he unearthed the wriggling mass of another giant grub and picked it up. The grub filled his tiny hand as he offered it to George.

'Good boy, Bung Eye. Let's go and cook 'em up.'

Back at the fire, the quart pot was bubbling steadily on the coals. George and Drew sat down cross-legged beside the embers with an empty tobacco tin that George had retrieved from his saddlebag.

'You can eat 'em raw but they much better when you cook 'em up,' said George, raking out some coals with a stick. He placed the tin on the coals and then, taking one of the larvae from his pocket, pinched its head between his calloused fingers to kill it before dropping it in. The grub curled up and then straightened as it browned and cooked. George picked it up and turned it over with his fingers, as Drew watched with fascination and curiosity. When it was cooked, George blew on it to cool the delicacy before handing it to Drew.

The boy didn't hesitate as he took a bite of the insect. It was buttery and delicious, soft and gooey like scrambled egg.

'That's good tucker, George!' he said, nodding his little blond head in approval as he watched George put another grub into the tobacco tin. George giggled with delight. He so enjoyed Bung Eye's company. Drew suddenly jumped up.

'I can hear cattle, George. They're coming!' The little fellow was already trotting to his horse.

Ever patient, George rose from his squat at the fire, doused the coals and hoisted Drew up into the saddle. 'Well, we better go and give 'em a hand, hey mate?'

※

After what had been a big day in the saddle and a good muster, the cattle had been yarded. Andy and Bec drove home together with young Drew sound asleep on Bec's lap. Rebecca couldn't recall ever feeling this happy before. She reached over to touch Andy's arm and he smiled that gorgeous smile at her. They didn't need words.

Arriving at the homestead just on dark, Andy and Bec busied themselves bringing in a stack of assorted boxes from the verandah that the mailman had left in their absence. Drew was grizzling. He needed a bath, dinner and bed.

'I'll get this, love,' said Andy. 'Think our number one ringer needs a tub and a feed.'

'Yeah, I reckon you're right,' said Bec, grabbing one of the smaller boxes and scooping Drew up.

Once inside, she rushed eagerly into the bathroom and ran a shallow bath for Drew, who stopped whingeing as he began to play with his bath toys. She opened the bathroom cabinet and found a small pair of scissors. Using the blade, she slit open the packing tape on the lid of the cardboard box she'd brought in. Fumbling through the contents, she quickly found what she was looking for and opened the small container.

Coolibah Creek

In the kitchen, Andy stacked all the boxes in the pantry and took the ones marked 'cold' through to the coldroom. As he was coming back, he almost ran headlong into Bec in the hallway. She had a wet Drew in one arm and water dripped from his chubby little body to the floor. 'Oh!' she said as she bumped into her dusty husband. She thrust Drew into his arms. She was grinning widely with one arm held behind her back.

'What are doing, you crazy woman?' Andy asked, puzzled as he grinned back at her.

Rebecca leant into his arms and kissed him full on the mouth. Andy steadied himself but his bare feet slipped out from under him in the water pooling on the lino from the wet toddler. The trio crashed to the floor and they all started to laugh as they untangled themselves and sat propped against the wall.

With a flourish, Bec produced a small white stick from behind her back. 'Ringer number two, Andy,' she announced, showing him the positive test, suddenly serious and quiet but still smiling broadly. 'I'm pregnant.'